Jack growled so. ...continued. "This is unprofessional of me, but I'm going to do it anyway. Will you have dinner with me?"

"Dinner?" Beth felt like an idiot echoing him, especially since on some level she, too, had felt the attraction. But she'd assumed he was married, or that he would be put off by her problems. "I'm sorry, but…"

"Why not?" he asked bluntly.

He was big enough that she felt crowded in the booth. His knees bumped hers as he moved restlessly; his shoulders blocked her view of the front of the café.

"Surely you can see this isn't a good moment for me to be thinking about getting involved.…"

"Don't let him stop you."

She blinked. Was that it—did she fear she'd anger her ex-husband more? But she knew even without deep analysis that her reasons were more complex. "I'm flattered that you're interested, but you'll have to accept my regrets. Now, I really should be getting back to the store."

Hands flat on the table, he had gone very still. "If you change your mind…"

She made a face. "I'll call the Butte County Sheriff's Office and pass on a message."

His mouth crooked into a faint smile. "That wouldn't be a problem."

Dear Reader,

My daughter read my PATTON'S DAUGHTERS trilogy and said, "I'm not sure I like Jack." I pointed out that, like most of us, he's a work in progress, a mix of cowardice and nobility, kindness and impatience. In other words, he's as real as I could make him. Jack is a hero who doesn't believe he is, a man who has spent his life trying to make up for one moment of fear and weakness. All these years later he still hasn't convinced himself that he has in him the ability to be heroic. And our perceptions of ourselves are as important as our behavior, right?

For me, this added up to a character who demanded his own story. Perhaps I always intended him to have it. For those of you who've read PATTON'S DAUGHTERS, I hope you're waiting for this book. For the rest of you—Jack *is* a hero, and the most interesting kind: flawed, self-aware and stronger than he knows. I loved writing these books, and as always, I'm eager to hear what you think!

Sincerely,

Janice Kay Johnson

You can reach me at: www.superauthors.com

JACK MURRAY, SHERIFF
Janice
Kay
Johnson

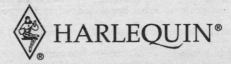

HARLEQUIN®

TORONTO • NEW YORK • LONDON
AMSTERDAM • PARIS • SYDNEY • HAMBURG
STOCKHOLM • ATHENS • TOKYO • MILAN • MADRID
PRAGUE • WARSAW • BUDAPEST • AUCKLAND

ISBN 0-373-70913-7

JACK MURRAY, SHERIFF

Visit us at www.eHarlequin.com

Printed in U.S.A.

JACK MURRAY, SHERIFF

CHAPTER ONE

BETH SOMMERS STARED blindly at the screen of her computer. She squeezed her eyes shut, drew in a long breath and tried to release tension as she exhaled. But even as she opened her eyes, her glance strayed to the wall clock.

Nine, long past time for the girls' baths and the gentle rituals of getting ready for bed. And they still weren't home.

Beth stood restlessly and went to the window, which overlooked the street. Street lamps illuminated the sidewalks and front yards, leaving pools of darkness. Headlights approached, but she could tell that they didn't belong to her ex-husband's pickup.

"Damn him," she said aloud, the intensity in her voice shocking her.

How could Ray use their children this way? He had once loved them, she knew he had. He hadn't been much for changing diapers or giving baths, but she remembered how gently he had held Stephanie when she was a baby, the look on his face when she smiled at him with wonder and delight.

And Lauren, the quiet one, the shy one, coaxed by her daddy into riding on his shoulders, so terrifyingly high up. Beth remembered her younger daughter clutching his hair, eyes saucer wide. By the end of the ride she was giggling and kicking him with her heels and shouting, "Giddyup!"

When had his anger swamped his love to the point where he could hurt his daughters just so he could hurt her?

She was turning away from the dark window when the high bright headlights of a pickup truck appeared around the corner down the block.

"Please, please," Beth whispered, frozen in place.

The pickup stopped at the curb, and her muscles unlocked. In an agony of relief, she ran out of the office and down the stairs to the front door. Wrenching it open, she hurried along the walkway to meet the girls, who tumbled out of the high cab of the pickup and raced to her.

"Oh, sweeties!" Beth swept them both into a hug so hard her muscles quivered. Tears burned in her eyes, but she lifted her head and smiled shakily. "Did you have a good visit with your dad?"

Eight-year-old Lauren had been crying, Beth could tell. Her older sister's face closed at the question, and she glanced nervously over her shoulder. "It was okay."

"You guys get your stuff and go on in," she told them, trying to sound casual, natural. "I need to talk to your dad."

Stephanie said in a low hurried voice, "I think he's mad at me 'cause I asked him when we were going home. He said that his apartment *was* home. But it's not! I was scared—" She broke off abruptly, a sixth sense seeming to tell her that her father had grabbed their bags out of the back of the pickup and was approaching.

Both girls lowered their heads and turned to meet him, taking their overnight bags from him and obediently accepting his hugs. Then they fled into the house, leaving their mother and father facing each other on the front walkway.

Despite her best effort to speak levelly, Beth's voice was trembling with suppressed anger. "You are three hours late. I've been worried."

He shrugged and smiled. "We were having a good time. What's the hurry?"

Dear God, to think she had once been attracted by that slanted, lazy grin! Now she wanted to erase it, once and for all.

But, heaven help her, he was her daughters' father. Somehow she had to convince him that they counted more than his feelings of anger.

"You scare them when you do this," she said. "Please be a father Steph and Lauren can rely on. Please."

His grin faded, all right, as his lips drew back from his teeth. Just like that, he was shouting. "I'm not the one who drove their father from them! You want to run your own damned household, run it, but don't tell me how to run mine! You got it?"

Her own anger exploded. To her eternal shame, Beth couldn't stop herself from yelling back, "You bring them home late one more time, and you won't take them again. If you can't be a decent parent, then forget you ever were one!"

A few equally nasty exchanges later, Beth retreated to the porch, but Ray followed as far as the steps. When she reached for the doorknob, a clay flowerpot smashed into the door, barely missing her. She turned around and screamed, "Go away! Just leave, or I'll call the police, I swear I will!"

"Don't push me," Ray snarled. "This was my house, too, and I haven't seen any bucks from my half!"

"The court order…"

"I don't want to hear about the goddamned court order! You know what you can do with it? You can…"

Beth darted inside, slammed and locked the front door, then with shaking hands fastened the chain. With her back to the door, she whimpered for breath. Stephanie and Lauren were huddled on the bottom step of the wide staircase, staring at her with identical looks of terror on ghost-white faces.

There was momentary silence outside. Would he go away? Seconds ticked by, then a minute. Beth straightened and bit her lip. Should she look? What if he was still standing there? He had a key, and the chain wouldn't stop him if he really wanted to come in.

At that moment something else hit the door and shattered. Beth jumped away and clapped her hand over her mouth. Behind her one of the girls screamed, and the door quivered again under the hammer of fists.

"I'm scared!" Lauren wailed.

Suddenly a siren gave one ear-splitting burst outside, and Beth saw the reflected dazzle of blue and red lights off a living room window.

Through the heavy door she heard an obscenity,

and then Ray's feet thudding down the steps. Beth wrenched open the front door and hurried out, stumbling over the shards of broken flowerpots. A big man in a dark suit, the jacket pulled back to show the butt of a gun in a shoulder holster, was coming up the front walk. Behind him the lights of the cruiser still flashed.

Ray waited at the foot of the porch stairs. "This is none of your business," he said loudly.

"Domestic disturbances are our business," the man replied, his voice carefully dispassionate. He extended a badge, his gaze flicking past Ray to where Beth stood silhouetted in the open doorway. "Are you all right, ma'am?"

"Yes, I…" she faltered, pressed her lips together. "I believe he was just leaving."

Ray turned. "I told you not to call the cops!"

"I didn't!" she flung back, before remembering the audience. How had her marriage, her life, come to this—two people arguing so violently that they had frightened the neighbors, that the police felt compelled to intervene?

"We'll talk about it later," Ray snapped, and stalked across the lawn past the police officer.

"Ma'am?" the officer repeated, a note of inquiry in his slow, deep voice. "Are you, or is anyone else, hurt?"

"No." Her knees suddenly wanted to buckle, and she grasped for the porch railing. "No, it was just…angry words."

He was beside her so quickly she hadn't seen him coming. One large hand closed firmly over her elbow and steered her into the house. He kicked a large piece of clay pot aside. "More than words," he commented.

The wide entry hall was deserted. She had a mother's moment of panic—where were the girls?—before Stephanie poked her head cautiously out of the dining room. Her frightened gaze took in the stranger before she asked, "Is Dad gone?"

"Yes. Oh, sweetie…" Both girls stumbled into her arms again. All the time Beth held them, she was conscious of the police officer waiting. After a moment, she eased her daughters back. Looking into first Stephanie's eyes, then Lauren's, she said, "Guys, your dad is angry and upset right now, but he's never hurt any of us, and I don't believe he ever would. He was just…throwing a tantrum." She actually managed a smile, and Lauren giggled weakly. "Now, you two go take baths and get ready for bed. Lay out your clothes for school tomorrow, and I'll be up in a few minutes to tuck you in. Okay?"

They both nodded, collected their bags from the floor where they had been dropped and started up the stairs.

Beth took a deep breath and turned to the officer. Only then did she become aware of how tall he was, of the breadth of his shoulders and the bulge of the gun nestled beneath his smooth-fitting suit jacket. Only then did she recognize him, from the article a few weeks ago in the local paper. The witness to her humiliation was the Butte County sheriff and former Elk Springs police chief. She had heard him speak at Rotary Club and Chamber of Commerce luncheons, although they had never met.

Only then did she realize that he had no jurisdiction here, because she lived within the Elk Springs city limits.

Elk Springs had once been a small ranching town nestled at the foot of Juanita Butte and the Sisters in eastern Oregon, while the county had been entirely rural; thanks to the new ski resort on the butte, development had sprawled far beyond city limits. Even the new high school and middle school complex was Jack Murray's problem, not the Elk Springs PD's.

So what was he doing on her doorstep in Old Town Elk Springs?

Quietly, she said, "You must have been passing. Did you see him? I...thank you."

His dark eyes were perceptive enough to make her uncomfortable. He nodded toward the porch. "You have a real mess out there. That was quite a temper tantrum."

She was gripped again by shame. How would she be able to face the neighbors after this, knowing that they had heard every word tonight, had seen the revolving lights on top of the police car in her driveway?

"I...we..." Beth stopped, tried again. "We divorced some months ago. By my choice. I'm afraid my ex-husband is still very angry."

"I live on Maple." He nodded toward the cross street half a block away. "I've heard from neighbors that this isn't the first time you and your ex-husband have had this kind of exchange."

She was already flushed; now Beth was assailed

by a wave of dizziness. "Would you mind if we sit down?" she asked.

She must have swayed, because that large, competent hand gripped her elbow again. A second later she found herself planted at the kitchen table. "Let me make you some tea or coffee," he said, already filling the kettle.

"Thank you...that cupboard... The sugar bowl's on the counter." She sounded like one of those virginal heroines in a Victorian novel, swooning whenever confronted with a crisis. Beth was disgusted with herself, which helped clear her head.

The kettle made noises; he sat at the table without waiting for an invitation and held out a hand. "I'm Jack Murray, with the Butte County Sheriff's Department."

"I recognized you." They shook hands solemnly, and she said, feeling inane, "How nice to meet you. I'm Beth Sommers. I own Sisters Office Supply."

A small pun, she had intended the name of her business to be: a reference to the triple mountains rearing jaggedly to the west, and to the fact that she, a woman, was sole owner.

"Ah." He pulled a small notebook from an inner pocket of his suit coat, then without opening it replaced it. "I can't help you officially."

"I realize that. I do appreciate you stopping."

"Would you like to tell me about it?"

Like was hardly a word she would have used. And yet she'd had nobody familiar with such situations to give her advice. Her best friends were happily married. People threw things and screamed at each other on the other side of town, where lawns were shaggy and yellowing and paint peeled, not here. Or so she had always believed. This man, she guessed, knew better.

Without having consciously made up her mind, Beth began to talk, giving him the facts: Ray had moved out nearly a year before, at her request. At first he hadn't believed she meant it. When he picked up or dropped off the girls, he alternated between charm and feigned indifference, both designed to show her what she was missing. When she went ahead and filed for divorce, he tried arguing with her, only at the last minute getting a lawyer to represent him. He hadn't disputed custody; Ray was a long-haul trucker who was gone for days on end. The visitation was to be liberal, agreed upon between the two of them. So far he had picked up the girls when they expected him, which was the only positive Beth could think of. He had paid the child support until the divorce was final, but since then he had changed, giving freer rein to the anger that was one of the principal causes of the divorce. He wanted her to beg for the support check, and she refused.

At first he had said things to her, but out of the girls' hearing; when she stayed calm, he said them in front of Stephanie and Lauren. Which upset her enough that she couldn't pretend composure she didn't feel. That it upset them, too, seemed to have no weight with him.

Once he realized he'd found the way to get to her, Ray escalated his tactics. He gave one or the other of the girls "messages" to pass on to Mom. He had little talks with them about how crazy it was that their mother had broken up the family. Tonight was the third time he had brought them home late—so late, it couldn't possibly be innocent. Maybe the first time had been; Beth was willing to give him that much credit. But by the time they showed up four hours later than she had expected them, she'd been terrified.

She might as well have handed him a weapon.

"If I didn't react, he'd probably quit doing it," she concluded with a long sigh. "Maybe I could, if it weren't for all the articles about noncustodial parents who disappear with the kids. Every time I see a picture of a missing child, I can't help imagining…" She gave an involuntary shudder. "I don't think Ray would do that. I don't think he really *wants* the kids full-time, he just enjoys these little jabs. But when they're due and an hour goes by, and then another one and another, every time I wonder…" She didn't have to finish. Instead Beth lifted the mug of tea for a sip, needing the second it gave her to regain her poise.

The sheriff listened to her bleak story without interruption or comment. Nothing she said surprised him; his expression told her that he'd heard worse, and probably seen it, too.

He wasn't a handsome man. In fact, he should have been homely with a crooked nose and features that were too crudely sculpted, yet somehow he wasn't. She might have even found him attractive, if his eyes hadn't been so cynical, his mouth so hard. Sheriff Murray had been sympathetic to her, but he wasn't a soft man.

When she set down the mug, he met her gaze squarely. "What if I hadn't shown up tonight?"

"What do you mean?"

"Your ex-husband struck me as a very angry man, Ms. Sommers. If he got some satisfaction from scaring you this time, he's going to do it again. Question is, what will he do next time? And how long will just scaring you be enough?"

"I...don't know," she admitted, feeling sick. It was ironic, when she ought to know Ray better than anyone else in the world. They had been married for twelve years, and had dated regularly for two years before that. But Ray had changed, even his anger becoming more unpredictable. She was no longer confident that she knew what he would or wouldn't do.

"Let me check on the girls," Beth said, and at his nod hurried upstairs. Stephanie was in her nightgown, bending over the tub to rinse Lauren's hair. Beth paused in the bathroom doorway to watch for a moment, unobserved.

"Too hot!" Lauren exclaimed.

Her sister adjusted the water, then dumped another cup over the eight-year-old's soapy, sodden red curls.

"Too cold."

"For Pete's sake," Stephanie muttered, but she fiddled with the knob again. The mirror and the sliding doors that turned the tub into a shower enclosure were both steamed up. Kneeling on the bathroom floor with the towel wrapped around her head, Stephanie looked like a mother in miniature. With the mild exasperation in her tone, she even sounded like one.

The normalcy of the scene was reassuring. Beth hated the weekends when her daughters went to their father's, but it helped to know that they had each other. At eleven going on twelve, Stephanie was the usual confused mixture of maturity and childishness, but Beth had confidence in her judgment—up to a point.

"How are you doing, guys?"

Stephanie turned her head. "Okay."

"Too hot!" Lauren yelled.

Stephanie rolled her eyes. "It's never perfect!"

Beth stepped forward to kiss the top of her older daughter's head—actually, to kiss a wet towel, but the gesture was understood. "Sweetheart, it was never perfect when I had to rinse your hair, either. Forget toilet training. I was *really* happy when you started taking care of your own hair."

"How come *she* isn't old enough to?"

"Lauren's doing everything but finishing up the rinsing," Beth reminded her. "Now, I'll be back to tuck you two into bed in a few minutes."

"Can we read in bed?"

She ought to say no, as late as it was, but she was afraid once they went to bed, they would lie in the dark remembering tonight's scene and worrying about the next visit to their dad's. Maybe a good book would give them pleasant thoughts instead to fall asleep with.

"Why not?" Beth said.

She'd half expected to find the sheriff waiting in the hall, eager to make his departure. But no, he was still sitting at her kitchen table, his head back and his eyes closed as if he were catnapping. When she entered the room, he became alert instantly, his eyes appraising. She was suddenly uncomfortable, perhaps only because she hated being in this situation. Or was it that, for a moment, she had been aware of him as a weary and very sexy man, not just a police officer?

If so, she must be crazy. She had every reason to feel grateful, humiliated, frightened, you name it. But attraction was ridiculous. Unless her hormones had decided that any man who came charging to her rescue was worth keeping around.

If she had imagined that *his* appraisal had been masculine rather than professional, he quickly disabused her. "Have you changed the locks on the house since your divorce?"

"No. I've been intending to..."

"Do it. You might consider a security system as well."

"The only trouble is, I *have* to let him in," she pointed out. "He has a right to see the girls."

"Yes, but at least then he couldn't surprise you."

She nodded slowly. Steph and Lauren would be well aware why Mom was having a security system installed.

"Do you have a brother or a father who could be here when Mr. Sommers picks up and drops off the children?"

"No," she said tersely. "I think that would make matters worse, anyway. Ray would get more belligerent. And I don't want anyone hurt on my behalf."

He frowned. "You need protection, Ms. Sommers. A woman alone with two children is vulnerable.''

Beth set down her mug with a click. "Exactly what is it that a man could do to protect me that I can't do myself?''

"Exert physical force, if need be." Before she could respond to that one, he switched directions. "Tell me, do you know how to handle a gun?''

"No, and I wouldn't shoot my ex-husband if I knew how!" Beth said. "That's all the girls need, to see their dad bleeding to death on our front porch.''

Jack Murray leaned back in his chair, an expression of impatience on his hard face. "Ms. Sommers, I have the feeling you're not taking this threat seriously. I know it's hard to picture a man you've lived with doing violence to you, but...''

Beth stood, pushing her chair back. "Sheriff, I'm a capable woman. I own a business. I employ six other people. I consider myself competent and reasonably intelligent. I would probably lose a fistfight with my ex-husband, but since that hardly seems like a solution to my problem, I'm afraid I don't see how I could take this threat more seriously.''

Their gazes met, before he said in that neutral tone a policeman must have to master, "I didn't mean to imply that you're incapable. The problem is, in a situation like this you have the reasonable facing the irrational. What if he'd come through that door tonight?''

"He has a key," Beth said. "He didn't use it. When I told the girls that their father was throwing

a temper tantrum, I meant it. That's all it was."
Please, God.

Jack Murray made a sound under his breath, one
in which she read disbelief and impatience. But pre-
sumably it was also a form of concession, because
he, too, stood.

"I'll talk to the people at ESPD." His patronizing
tone was enough to set her teeth on edge. "I'm sure
they'll have a patrol car come by regularly for now,
especially on weekends, if that's when Mr. Sommers
takes the girls. And you know where to call."

"Yes, I do," she said, inclining her head with
unaccustomed coolness. "I certainly hope I won't
need to."

"Ms. Sommers…" The sheriff seemed to think
better of whatever he'd intended to say. He only
shook his head. "I'd best be getting home."

He followed her to the front door. Beth held it
open and said again, "Thank you." She meant it.
Jack Murray might be patronizing, but he *had* come
to her rescue. His intentions were good.

The sheriff looked at her freshly painted front
porch, strewed with shattered clay pots, spilled dirt
and shreds of bright petunias and lobelia, and shook
his head again. "Be careful. Call if you're even a
little nervous."

Beth was stubborn, but not an idiot. She didn't
tell him that she was afraid his showing up tonight
had made things worse, not better. He thought she
was insisting on being self-sufficient to the point of
foolishness. Truth be told, she was scared. Ray
wasn't going to disappear from their lives. She had
to find a way to make him see that the girls were

what was really important. Carrying hostilities further than she already had would only get in the way of rapprochement.

She watched the police chief step carefully around the shards of pottery and down the front steps. She had forgotten that the lights on top of his cruiser were still revolving, a beacon in the midst of her quiet neighborhood. He reached inside and turned them off even before getting in. A moment later, the police car pulled away from the curb and started down the street.

Beth hugged herself against the cool night air. She made herself stand on the porch in defiance of a panicky desire to flee inside and lock up tight. The night was calm, Ray long gone. He was angry, not sly; it would never occur to him to park his car around the block and sneak back. When she saw a shadow move under the old lilac, her pulse took an uncomfortable jump, but, just to prove something to herself, Beth waited until first one cat, then a second, strolled out.

Only then did she go back into the house and lock the door behind her.

Time to kiss her daughters good-night, time to try to convince them that their world was a secure place.

THE LITTLE REDHEAD in the third row looked familiar. Jack Murray paused a moment in his presentation to the third-grade class.

Long red curls caught up in a bouncy ponytail on top of her head. Big blue eyes, freckled nose, a mouth that had no intention of smiling. She was watching him with unusual intensity, too, as though…what?

Like a slide projector, he clicked through recent pictures stored in his mind. It didn't take long. She was the one whose father had been trying to smash down his ex-wife's front door. The one huddled in the hallway with her older sister.

The one whose mom had blue eyes just as guarded, just as cool.

Aware of the concerted stare of twenty-four eight-year-olds, Jack continued, "Are any of you ever home alone?"

A scattering of hands went up.

"Do your moms or dads tell you what to do if the phone rings and you're by yourself?"

At the same moment as a little girl piped up, "Don't answer it," a boy said, "Mom checks to make sure I'm home, so I have to answer the phone."

Jack strolled toward the boy's seat by the window. "What if the caller isn't your mom?"

The boy, whose hair was crew-cut but for a tiny pigtail in back, shrugged. "It's usually a friend or something."

"Usually?"

"Mom says if they ask for Mrs. Patterson, it means they want to sell her something, so I just tell 'em we don't want to buy anything and hang up."

Jack stood just above the boy, letting his height and the uniform awe the kid just a little.

Then he raised a brow. "Do you think they ever guess that your mom isn't home?"

The boy squirmed. "Naw…"

Jack looked around. "What do the rest of you think? Should he answer the telephone when he's alone?"

All sorts of small, high voices chimed in with a variety of negatives. No way. *Their* parents said…

"But his mom wants to make sure he's home safe. So she has to call, right? And he has to answer."

It was the little redhead who said solemnly, "He could call her instead. I call my friends all the time."

"Could you do that instead?"

The kid had lost his bravado. "She doesn't really like me to call her at work."

"Would she make an exception for one call every day?"

He hung his head and shrugged again.

Jack touched the boy's shoulder and said, "Mrs. Stewart will hand out pamphlets for all of you to take home today and show your parents. Maybe that will make it easier for you to talk to them about things that scare you when you're alone."

A few minutes later, he strode out to his squad car. He so rarely wore a uniform these days, he felt conspicuous. But that was the whole point: he still liked to do some of these school talks to keep from becoming a remote political figure in Butte County, a politician quoted in the newspapers. He wanted kids to go home and talk at the dinner table about Sheriff Murray as a real guy. This was his first visit of the new school year; nights were growing cold, but leaves had already turned and the bright yellow school buses were flashing red lights on every narrow country road morning and afternoon.

Jack grunted with faint amusement, thinking what Ed Patton would have had to say about a sheriff spending an hour talking to eight-year-olds: a pansy-ass waste of time, is what the Elk Springs police chief would have said.

But then, Ed Patton had been a grade-A son of a bitch.

As he headed back to the station, Jack's mind reverted to the redhead's mother. Lord only knew how many domestic disturbance calls he'd been on. Hundreds. But he still remembered the first, when he'd been a rookie in Portland.

It was also the only time he'd ever had to shoot anyone. He and his partner had been called out to a nasty argument reported by a neighbor. Working-class neighborhood, a cluster of folks standing within earshot of a modest, neatly painted house from which crashes and vicious obscenities came. The siren brought a man in his undershirt to the door. His nose was bleeding and one eye was swelling shut. He wiped blood from his nose and told them to get the hell out of there.

Jack's partner had been walking ahead of him up the cracked cement driveway. So fast it was still a blur in Jack's memory, the man had a rifle in his hands and was shooting, just spraying bullets and screaming the whole time. The nosy neighbors dived to the ground and behind parked cars. Jack's partner went down with a bullet to the chest and this look of shock on his face. Jack shot the man, didn't even think about it, just shot. Then he had to listen to the wife calling him a murderer while he held his dying partner and listened to the faraway sound of sirens.

To this day, every time he went to a house where a husband and wife were arguing, he thought about that afternoon. He never went casually, never assumed anything. There was nothing deadlier than a man and woman who hated and loved each other at the same time.

But the faces of the women had run together in his memory. The eyes were all stricken, the bruises stark, the body language the same. In recent years, when he thought of an abused woman, he saw his high school girlfriend, Meg Patton, lying about her broken arm or the yellowing bruises.

So why hadn't Beth Sommers joined the anonymous company? Why hadn't she become another chink in the wall of guilt he'd built since he found out how badly he'd failed Meg?

Why did he keep thinking about this woman of all others? Why did her face keep coming back to him?

Okay, it was partly because she was pretty, tall and slender, with a long graceful neck, a mass of mahogany brown hair and bright blue eyes. She was the kind of woman who could wear capri pants and a tank top and still look as good as any fifteen-year-old. But that wasn't all of it.

In some ways she was typical of the women he saw in the same situation. The jackass who threw the tantrum might be her ex, but she was still defending him, still insisting he didn't really mean it. But the way she protected her children, the way she tried to let them keep some respect for their father, wasn't typical at all. Divorce, especially from an abusive man, was an ugly thing. There weren't too many women who were able to resist the temptation to use their kids as a battleground.

Beth Sommers was a gutsy woman who reminded him of Meg Patton in this way, too. Meg had put her son first, had done what was needed to protect him from her own father. Jack had learned to respect her for the hard choices she'd made, although those same choices had cheated him of seeing his son grow up.

Like Meg, Beth Sommers was determined to take care of herself and her children, too. He admired that, even if he did think it was stupid. She might be a successful businesswoman, but she was still vulnerable in a way a man wouldn't be. Damn it, she was fragile! Jack didn't like thinking about that. He didn't want to see her with a bruised face and broken bones and defiant terror in her eyes.

He'd driven by her house several times himself. He had made a point of being there Sunday afternoon, but apparently that hadn't been one of the girls' weekends with their dad, because Jack saw the older one in the bay window, just sitting on the window seat with her arms wrapped around her knees, staring out. Her head turned when she saw the police car, but he was too far away to see her expression.

Jack remembered the relief on the little girl's face when her mother said that their father was just throwing a temper tantrum. He didn't think the older one—who was maybe eleven, twelve—had been convinced. He wondered what their visits to their father were like.

And he wondered about the mother. What did *she* do weekends, when her daughters were with their father? She'd been quick to tell him she had no brother or father to be there when she needed him. It had seemed a little too pushy to ask if she had someone else, a man who for other reasons would put himself on the line for her. Did she date?

Or was Beth Sommers so soured by her ex-husband, she wasn't interested in men?

Jack hadn't gotten any further than thinking about her. He hadn't tried to find out yet. If he did, he wasn't sure what he would do about the knowledge. It would be asking for trouble, dating a pretty woman whose ex-husband didn't want to let go of her. Sommers wouldn't like any man dating his ex-wife.

Jack figured he could handle Ray Sommers. He half wished Beth lived outside the city limits so her problems were his business. The scene he'd walked in on wasn't the first between them, according to neighborhood gossip, and it wouldn't be the last. One of these days, she'd be calling the cops. Unfortunately, she wouldn't be calling him.

Irritated at himself, Jack accelerated when a street-light turned green. Instead of daydreaming about being her personal hero, he ought to be worrying about *her*. Figuring out how to get her some help even if she didn't believe she needed it.

Gut instinct told him somebody should intervene. Before the ex-husband who both hated and loved her tipped a little too far toward hate, and a hell of a lot more than a few plant pots were broken.

CHAPTER TWO

BEHIND THE BARTENDER, a mirror decorated with a beer slogan reflected a portion of the dimly lit room. Ray could see himself in it, though the reflection seemed a little fuzzy. Hell, it must be the mirror. Couldn't be him. He hadn't had that many.

He lifted his glass and downed some raw whiskey that burned his throat and brought warming anger in its wake.

"Bitch," he said clearly, continuing a monologue. "That's what she is. Don't give a damn what you think." He thumped his glass on the bar. "Gimme another one."

The bartender frowned. "Ray, I think you've had enough. Why don't you go on home now?"

Just like that, his anger spilled over. Ray picked up the heavy glass and flung it as hard as he could. It bounced off the padded wall beside the mirror and clunked out of sight onto the floor.

"You don't want to hear what a bitch she is?" he snarled.

He was vaguely aware that somebody had stopped behind him. He didn't give a damn who it was. They should all know what she was like.

A hand closed on his shoulder and turned him on the revolving stool. He wrenched himself free of the grip and blinked to bring the man's face into focus. Who the hell?

Frank Eaton. Frank owned the pizza franchise over on Lewis Street. He was a chunky guy, going a little soft, liked his beer. Well, hell, Ray liked his beer, too.

"Damned bitch," Ray said again, giving his head a shake to clear it. "Called the cops on me because I was a little late bringing the kids home. Doesn't want to remember they're my kids, too. Can you believe it?"

"Beth's a nice lady," Frank said, looking steely-eyed. "I don't like to hear you talking about her this way."

Ray squinted. "You think you know her? You don't know shit. You buy forms from her. You're a goddamned *customer*." He spit the word out. "Maybe you'd be good enough to touch her. Not me. I wasn't a *customer*." He swayed, caught himself and straightened. "Maybe you did touch her. How about it? Is that why I wasn't good enough anymore?"

Frank grabbed him and shoved him off the stool. Ray stumbled back into a table and chairs.

"Go home," Frank said with disgust. "And stay there if you're going to talk filth about Beth."

Ray was suddenly so angry he was blind. His head felt like it might burst with the fury dammed up. He launched himself at the other man. It felt so good when his fists connected that he swung again and again. Frank fell backward and Ray went after him, swinging, swinging, feeling a nose crunch under his knuckles, the soft gut give like bread dough.

His anger roared in his ears, drowning any other sounds.

Hands were yanking him off, and he fought them, still trying to make contact with his bloodied fist, needing to shatter, to hurt, to exhaust himself until that anger had dwindled like gas in his rig.

Next thing he knew, he was being sick outside in the rain, just before he was tossed in the back of a police car. Alone there he hunched in on himself, his stomach still heaving. Cops. Somebody had called the cops. If it was the same bastard...

Through the grille he couldn't see who was in front. But he didn't know either of the cops who hauled him out in the dark alley behind the public safety building. They shoved him through the door and propelled him down a hall. When he started to retch, they pushed him in a small bathroom, where he threw up again. Then they locked him in a cell.

Ray was past caring. He was drunk and angry and sick.

Bitch, he thought woozily. Thought she was too good for him. Called the cops on him. His own wife. *Ex*-wife. Had the whole damned town on her side.

Well, there was one way he could get to her, make her pay attention to him. One way he could feel strong again.

It wasn't like he'd really hurt her. He didn't have to. He just wanted to see fear in those blue eyes. Fear that told him he still had some power over her.

He passed out still thinking about her, the woman he loved.

WHEN THE PHONE rang a second time, only moments after Beth hung up the receiver, a twinge of uneasiness, even fear, made her hesitate to touch it. But she knew she had to answer.

Nothing. The response was the silence she had expected. She couldn't even hear any breathing. It was almost creepier than an obscene phone call. Beth slammed the receiver back down and closed her eyes, breathing slowly to calm herself.

"Who was it?" Steph asked from right behind her.

Beth jumped, but managed a casual mien by the time she turned. "Hm? Oh, nobody. Wrong number."

"How come there're so many wrong numbers lately?"

"Heaven knows." Beth forced a smile. "I think that's a pun. When we first moved in here, the phone company gave us a number that used to belong to the Assembly of God Church. We got ten calls a day from people wanting the church. Maybe this is something like that."

Stephanie nodded, satisfied. "What's for dinner?"

"Meat loaf. Get your sister, and both of you wash your hands."

Beth made a point of having a sit-down dinner as many evenings as possible. This was the one time they had together when nobody was distracted by the TV or homework or a friend. Working as many hours as Beth did, and with the girls' nonstop activities, dinnertime sometimes seemed like a peaceful oasis in the middle of their lives.

But tonight she had a hard time concentrating on Stephanie's complaints about the science teacher.

"Everybody's afraid to ask him questions. If you do, he just gives you this look and says you weren't paying attention. I mean, maybe you weren't, but maybe you just didn't get it the first time."

Beth made appropriate noises of sympathy even as her thoughts went back to the troubling phone calls. They'd gone on for a week now, several a day, sometimes two or three in a row like tonight. She'd hurry to answer the phone, but there was never anybody on the other end. It was dumb, petty—but also unnerving.

Should she get Caller ID? She had always thought of it as a nuisance, when ninety percent of the calls were from the girls' friends. Some of their parents undoubtedly had blocks on their phones, and it seemed so unfriendly to forbid those calls. Caller ID would certainly stop this silent stalker—but then what might he do instead?

She sighed unconsciously. What if she called the phone company and complained? Hadn't she read there was another technology that allowed calls to be traced instantly? Would they be interested enough to bother, when the caller wasn't obscene or threatening?

Beth wanted to believe some stranger was doing this to her and her family. Maybe even a teenager, who thought it was funny to scare somebody.

But underneath she couldn't help remembering what the sheriff had said. *If he got some satisfaction from scaring you...he's going to do it again.* Ray knew she didn't have Caller ID. *Had* he discovered he liked scaring her? Only, why would he choose a method so juvenile? Did he just hope to unsettle her, eroding her basic sense of security?

What if she asked him outright? Would he let himself smile when he denied making the calls, just to make sure she knew?

Damn it, she could ignore the calls, Beth thought in frustration. They weren't what really bothered her. It was the motive behind them. If the caller was older than fifteen, he had to be sick. No normal human being enjoyed scaring total strangers. And if it was Ray...

Automatically, Beth took another bite. The meat loaf was tasteless in her mouth.

Dear God, if Ray was the one calling...

Her mind wanted to balk. Not Ray. It couldn't be Ray. She had loved him once, married him! How could she not have known what he was beneath the facade?

Again she heard, as though as a faint echo, Murray's voice. *How long will just scaring you be enough?*

"Mom."

Beth tuned in to find both girls looking reproachfully at her.

"Are you listening?" Stephanie asked.

"Yes, of course," she lied. "But let's hear about Lauren's day now."

Her younger daughter wrinkled her nose. "It was boring. But I forgot to tell you...." Strangely, she hesitated, darting a glance between her sister and her mother. "Well, last Tuesday...or maybe it was the day before...anyway," she finished in a rush, "you know that man who came to our house when Daddy was so mad.''

Stephanie looked down at her plate. Beth nodded. ''He's the county sheriff.''

''Well, he came and talked to our class.''

Surprised and disturbed, Beth said, ''About anything in particular?''

''Just what to do when you're home alone. Stuff like that. He was really nice.''

Nice. If you didn't mind being treated like a helpless woman who ought to be grateful for ''protection.''

No, that wasn't fair, Beth admitted reluctantly. He *was* nice. He'd stopped when he didn't have to get involved, listened patiently, offered sound advice and never given her the feeling that he considered her to blame in any way.

''I'm glad you thought so,'' she said neutrally. She tried to make her voice casual, the new subject not an obvious extension of the last one. ''Listen, guys, have either of you talked to your dad this week?''

Out of the corner of her eye she saw Stephanie duck her head again. Stick-straight brown hair brushed her cheek, and thick dark lashes shielded her eyes. She crumbled her garlic bread without actually eating any of it.

But Lauren said, ''He called last night.''

''Did he have anything special to say?''

A small frown furrowed her brow. ''I don't think so.''

''Did he tell you what time he'll pick you up Saturday?''

"I don't remember."

Without looking up, Stephanie mumbled, "The usual time."

"Is he taking you anywhere?"

"He said maybe to a movie. Mom—" Stephanie stopped abruptly. "Never mind."

"Come on." Beth reached over and brushed her daughter's hair back from her face. "You can't start and not finish."

Stephanie shrugged, looking almost sullen for a moment. "It's not any big deal. It's just… He's always promising to do something with us, and then he doesn't. I mean, I'd *like* it if he'd take us to a movie or Art In The Park or someplace, but he never does. I wish he wouldn't promise something when he doesn't mean it."

"Oh, honey." Beth reached over to lift her daughter's chin. She struggled to hide her own sadness. "Have you talked to him about this?"

There Steph went again, hunching her shoulders and refusing to meet her mother's eyes, as she had increasingly often lately. "No," she mumbled.

"You know, he isn't a mind reader. Maybe he's just been tired, maybe having you at home with him makes your dad feel more like you're a real family. Try talking to him."

For what good it would do, Beth thought grimly. There had been a time when Ray listened. Now, it seemed as if he was too self-absorbed to think about anyone else's feelings. Or was she just being negative, projecting her own anger?

Stephanie shrugged and made an unhappy face. "But if I say something, it sounds…oh, I don't know, like I'm saying he lied! And it's not that. It's just that it's kind of boring at his apartment, and I wish he wouldn't tell us he's going to take us somewhere and get us excited and stuff, and then not do it. You know?''

"Sure I do." Beth stood long enough to give her daughter a quick hug and kiss on the cheek. "But I still say you need to talk to him. If you don't tell him differently, he may think you'd rather not go anyplace special."

Another twitch of the shoulders and an unenthusiastic "Yeah, I guess."

Lauren had been listening without comment, but now she said, "*I*'ll talk to him. I don't mind."

"No!" Stephanie said with quick alarm. "You'll tell Dad I think he breaks his promises. I don't want him to know that."

"I won't..."

"Yes, you will! Don't you dare say anything to Dad!''

Lauren stuck out her tongue. "Well, then you do it."

They were off and running with the kind of bickering calculated to fray any parent's patience. As she dealt with them, Beth reminded herself of how well they usually got along. And at least the quarrel was reassuringly normal. The day when neither wanted to talk about their father at all was the day when she really had to worry.

As if she wasn't worrying now.

BETH ADDED PAPER to the copying machine, snapped the tray back into place and smiled at the customer. "All set."

"Thanks." The woman, a volunteer at the local animal shelter, went back to copying fliers about a free spay/neuter day.

Hearing her name, Beth turned. Maria Bernal, a friend who owned a women's clothing store half a block away, was hurrying down the aisle between printer cartridges and pens. Hispanic, a little plump and very pretty, Maria took Beth's arm and steered her into the back room. "Well, did he bring the kids home on time this weekend?"

"More or less." Beth automatically gathered up the remains of an employee's sack lunch left on the one table and tossed it in the garbage. "He was only an hour late." Her dry tone didn't reveal how torturous that hour had been to Beth, who had come to dread every one of the girls' visits to their dad.

"You look tired." Never less than blunt, Maria studied her with the practical eye she'd give a new clothing line. "Why no sleep? Is he still calling and hanging up?"

Beth took a can of cola from the tiny refrigerator and, after Maria shook her head at the offering, popped the top. She needed the caffeine, although the artificial energy would do nothing for the weariness adding years to her face.

"I don't know that *he*…" she began.

Her friend waved an impatient hand. "Okay, whoever. Is it still happening?"

Beth's voice went flat. "The past two nights it's been the doorbell instead. The first couple of times, one of the girls answered and nobody was there.

God, I was scared when I realized—'' She broke off. ''What's horrible is that he must have been watching somewhere. The second time it was Steph, and she was scared to death. She had the sense to slam the door quick and lock it, but when I came running she was shaking. He must have *seen*.'' Beth searched her friend's face. ''How could he do it to her, Maria?''

''God, I don't know.'' Maria took her hand and squeezed. ''The son of a… Well, you know what I think of him. And we're not talking about 'whoever' here, are we.'' It wasn't a question.

''I don't know,'' Beth said desperately. ''It's hard to believe Ray could be so cruel.''

''A woman scorned is nothing on a man. You know, he may not let himself realize that Steph and Lauren are scared, too.''

''It's getting so I hate him.'' Until she heard herself say the words, she hadn't known her feelings were so caustic. ''And what if it wasn't him?''

The question was unanswerable. Maria made a helpless gesture. ''Have you called the police?''

''What can they do?'' Beth asked. ''I've tried hiding by the window where I can see the front door, but then no one comes. If he's able to figure out when I'm watching, do you think he's going to come striding up on the front porch with a police car in my driveway?''

''I think they can be more subtle than that.''

''Maria, I *can't*.'' All Beth's misery poured out. ''This is Stephanie and Lauren's father we're talking about. What if I'm wrong?''

Maria's dark eyes were compassionate. "You'd still have a problem. Maybe a worse one."

She hadn't thought about it that way. Was it scarier to think of a stranger persecuting them this way, or Ray?

The question wasn't one she could shake. It stayed with her long after Maria had bustled out.

Usually Beth snatched a quick lunch in the back room, but she'd been so tired this morning she'd given the girls lunch money instead of sandwiches, and now she had to go out herself. The Bluebird Café three blocks away had good daily specials and the booths offered more privacy than the tiny tables at the deli around the corner, so she chose to go there. The walk would do her good.

She'd barely taken a forkful of flaky crust from her turkey pot pie when she saw Sheriff Jack Murray enter, a big, broad man in another of those beautifully cut gray suits that hid the gun he undoubtedly carried. She should have sat with her back to the door, Beth thought belatedly, although she had no idea why she was so reluctant to face him again.

Because he'd heard her screaming at her ex-husband?

Six or seven booths were occupied, but his gaze went straight to her and he waved off the waitress, coming directly to Beth. "May I join you?"

What could she say but "Of course."

The waitress followed, but he didn't take the menu. "A cup of coffee and apple pie," he told her, before he scrutinized Beth as directly as Maria had. "Your clerk said you were here."

Surprised, she said, "You came looking for me?"

Justifiably, he ignored the question. "How are things going with your ex-husband?"

Beth opened her mouth to say a bright "Just fine!" and found she couldn't get the lie out. She closed her mouth, opened it again and finally sighed. "Well, we've had no repeat of the infamous temper tantrum. I guess I can deal with everything else."

That was a lie, too, of course; even at this moment, even when she was distracted by this blunt-featured man who knew too much about her life, her stomach churned and her chest was crowded with anxiety. What would tonight bring? A ringing telephone, with no caller on the other end? The chime of the doorbell, with no one standing on the doorstep? Or would something scarier yet happen?

She met the sheriff's eyes and had the unnerving feeling that he had read her mind. More roughly than her remark called for, he said, "You shouldn't have to deal with anything. If he's trespassing or violating his visitation rights—"

"I should have him arrested?" How she wished she could! "I don't think that would solve our problems."

"It might wake him up." He stopped when a newcomer slapped him on the back and wanted to talk about a speech he'd apparently given the night before.

Beth took the opportunity to eat, watching Murray respond with the easy geniality of a born politician. He had a reputation as a tough cop—too tough, according to his opponent in the last election. Beth had voted for him, anyway, liking the job he'd done as chief of the smaller Elk Springs city police force before he ran for sheriff.

At the same time the waitress brought his coffee and pie, the other man moved on with apologies for interrupting their lunch, and Murray's expression became grave. "Are you aware that your ex-husband was arrested for assault and battery over a week ago?"

"Assault?" Staggered, Beth shook her head dumbly. The fork dropped from nerveless fingers. "No. No, I wasn't."

"Got in a fight at the tavern. Not all his fault, apparently, but he broke the other man's nose, really worked him over. According to the bartender, the fight was over you."

"Dear God." Beth bent her head and pushed her plate away, struggling with her nausea. A fight in a tavern. For the thousandth time, she asked herself how it had come to this. She and Ray had been high school sweethearts. She had thought he was so strong, someone she could lean on forever.

When she raised her head again, she had regained control. Almost steadily, she asked, "What do you mean, over me?"

Murray surprised her by covering her clenched fist with his large hand. "It would appear that Mr. Sommers was insulting you. The other man took exception to what he was saying. They'd both had a few too many."

"Is he…is he in jail?"

"He was held overnight. My guess is he'll plea-bargain and end up with no more than probation and

a promise to attend AA or go into alcohol treatment.''

"I wouldn't have said he had a drinking problem." Beth sighed. "But then, he's doing a lot of
things I never thought he would."

"Does he drink when the girls are with him?"

"Oh, God." She'd never asked. Wouldn't Steph,
at least, have said? "I don't know. In the past when
he was mad, like the night you saw him, he didn't
seem drunk."

"No, he didn't," Murray conceded.

Neither said anything. The silence began to feel
awkward. Beth looked at her half-eaten lunch and
decided she wasn't hungry. The sheriff hadn't even
picked up his fork to start the pie the waitress had
brought.

"Ms. Sommers..." He growled something under
his breath and rubbed the back of his neck as though
the muscles were stiff. "This is probably unprofessional of me.... No, it's damned unprofessional, but
I'm going to do it anyway. Will you have dinner
with me?"

"Dinner?" She felt like an idiot echoing him, especially since on some level she, too, had felt the
attraction. But she had assumed him to be married,
or that he would be put off by her problems, or...

He looked uncomfortable. "I'd like to take you
to dinner," he said again.

Beth was shaking her head even before she had
thought any further. "Sheriff..."

"Jack."

The title had helped her think of him as a police
officer, a public official, not as a man. She needed

the safer distance that gave her. But she could hardly refuse to use his first name.

"Jack, then," Beth agreed. "I'm sorry, but…"

"Why not?" he asked bluntly, his dark gaze square on her face.

He was big enough that she felt crowded suddenly in the booth. His knees bumped hers as he moved restlessly; his shoulders blocked her view of the front of the café. Beth imagined wrapping her arms around his neck, ruffling his silky hair, feeling that hard, crooked mouth on hers, and gave a shiver of near panic.

"Surely you can see this isn't a good moment for me to be thinking about getting involved…."

"Don't let him stop you."

"I…" She blinked. Did she fear that she would anger Ray more? But she knew even without deep analysis that her reasons were more complex.

"If I'd let him stop me from doing what was right for me, we'd still be married. This is just…not the best moment." She didn't add that he wasn't the man with whom she would have chosen to start, either. "I'm flattered that you're interested, but you'll have to accept my regrets. Now, I really should be getting back to the store."

Hands flat on the table, he had gone very still. "If you change your mind…"

She made a face at him. "I'll call the Butte County Sheriff's Office and pass on a message. Right."

His mouth crooked into a faint smile. "That wouldn't be a problem."

Despite herself, she hesitated. ''Thank you,'' she said, and meant it.

Murray cleared his throat. ''Ms. Sommers…Beth. I, uh, hope I haven't made you uncomfortable. I want you to be able to call if you need me. I live close by.'' He reached inside his suit coat and took out a business card, extending it across the table to her. ''My home phone. I can be at your place in not much over a minute.''

Her sinuses burned and she gripped the card so tightly it crumpled in her fingers. ''I don't know what to say.''

He picked up his fork. ''Don't say anything. Just don't hesitate if you need me.''

For an instant their eyes met, and her pulse took an odd leap. Then she pressed her lips together, gave a jerky nod and slipped out of the booth. One more ''Thank you,'' and she fled, pausing only long enough to pay the cashier.

She could feel his gaze on her back as she waited for her receipt and hurried out the front door. Why she was compelled to hurry, Beth couldn't have said. Her heart was beating too hard; exhilaration was mixed with a need to run. She tried to convince herself that the news about Ray was the cause of her turmoil, but failed.

Not that it wasn't upsetting. During the final months of their marriage, Ray had scared her by the depth of his temper; several times he had viciously flung a chair or lamp across the room, breaking it, and during that last, memorable fight, he'd slammed his fist through the wallboard. But even then, he hadn't hurt her.

Had that changed? If Ray could break a man's nose in a tavern brawl, what might he do to her?

He had been drunk, she reminded herself, but Beth recognized the excuse for what it was. Anyway, there was no saying he wouldn't come to her house drunk some night.

The locksmith had already replaced the locks and added a few on windows and the French doors leading out to the deck in back. But she hadn't done anything about buying a security system. It seemed so ridiculous in Elk Springs, for heaven's sake!

But now she imagined Ray, drunk, pounding on the door, his fury rising because she wouldn't let him in. The locks on the French doors wouldn't stop him from breaking a pane of glass and opening the door.

She would definitely call around this afternoon and get some bids.

Beth's pace slowed as she reached the main street and turned the corner. Face it, she told herself, stopping to look in the bakery window without seeing the temptations arrayed there. It wasn't just the news about Ray that had upset her. It was Jack Murray. Why did he have to be interested in her?

And why now?

She wasn't ready. In that part of her mind reserved for vague thoughts about the future, she had imagined another man, someday. He would be nothing like Ray, nothing. He was some sort of compendium of the modern men found in television commercials. She had seen him clapping at school plays, stir-frying dinner in the wok. He was a reader, a man who would think nothing of running over to

Portland for a major museum exhibit, who never raised his voice, who listened intelligently, asked for her thoughts. He was faceless, this man, almost sexless, pleasant, thoughtful, even-tempered…unreal. A bloodless fantasy for a woman who had had too much of strong emotions, who didn't want gritty and real, who'd had enough of that.

Jack Murray was real. She could imagine him strolling the hushed galleries of the museum, but when she closed her eyes, she saw him playing one-on-one basketball at the gym, sweating, grunting, using his elbows, slamming against another man as they went up for a rebound. He had been soft-spoken with Ray and her, but he also patronized women, undoubtedly raised his voice, and probably got some kind of charge out of wearing a gun.

And he tweaked something sexual in her that hadn't been touched in a long time, and certainly not by the faceless man she tried so hard to see when she lay alone in bed at night.

Beth let out a long breath of air, blinked and realized that through the glass she was staring right at Mrs. Parker behind the counter in the bakery. The woman was smiling uncertainly, and Beth managed to pull herself together enough to return the smile.

Damn it, she thought a minute later, pushing open the door of Sisters Office Supply, a woman could make intelligent choices. Ray was all she'd ever known. The sexual part of her had been tuned to him; it was natural that she responded to the promise of brawn and dominance.

But she could change that, and would. Jack Murray's capacity for violence might be harnessed on the side of angels, but it was there, as much a part of him as it was of Ray. She'd spent enough years tiptoeing around to avoid rousing the beast that was anger and violence. Somewhere she'd found the strength to wake him and not quail, to lock him out of her house.

She would not invite him in again, not in any guise.

CHAPTER THREE

"I WISH I COULD GIVE you better news," Beth's lawyer said, shaking his head. "We could go back to court and contest your ex-husband's visitation rights, but frankly, I don't think we'd win there unless you can bring proof that he's done more than be late a few times bringing the girls back." Mr. Knightley held up one hand to forestall her protest. "I'm not telling you what I think, I'm telling you what the judge will think. I have no doubt whatsoever that Mr. Sommers is at least trying to scare you. But we need proof."

Beth let out a long breath. "Thank you, Mr. Knightley. I really didn't expect anything else. But I hoped."

The attorney was perhaps fifty, a handsome man who had gained more presence and authority with the addition of an extra thirty or so pounds that might have looked like fat on another man. He had done some legal work for her business, so she had turned to him when she decided to file for divorce.

"How do the girls feel about their father?" he asked, rolling a rosewood pen between his palms.

"I'm not sure," Beth admitted. "The divorce upset them, of course, but also..." She hesitated. "I think they were relieved. There was a lot of yelling going on. And yet, until recently they seemed happy to see their dad and looked forward to their visits. It's harder for Stephanie, because even though she only sees Ray every other week, she feels like she's missing out on things her friends are doing. But lately…'' She sought for words to define her amorphous awareness of their uneasiness. ''I know they've both been, maybe not scared, but uncomfortable when he's kept them so late. But I can't in all honesty say he's a terrible father or they're frightened of him. That's why I've hesitated about doing anything too drastic. I think it's important for them to have a relationship with their own father.''

The lawyer nodded and set the pen back in its stand. ''I wish I knew better how to advise you. Have you considered talking to a counselor? You might find somebody who's an expert on anger management, who could at least give suggestions on the best way to defuse any situations.''

''That's an idea,'' Beth agreed, picking up her purse. ''I won't take any more of your time, Mr. Knightley. I appreciate the information you've given me.''

He stood, too. ''If the police catch him redhanded pulling one of these malicious tricks, we might have the ammunition to go back to court. I think that would qualify as compelling evidence showing that Mr. Sommers is an unfit parent.''

And then what? Beth thought bleakly. How would the kids come to terms with a label like that put on their father? He was half of them; she had no desire to make them despise that part of themselves.

But what else could she do?

Nobody had any other suggestions, that was for sure. All she heard was "Call the police." Wasn't that supposed to be a last resort?

Well, one thing she could do, Beth thought, was talk to Stephanie and Lauren. It didn't seem to her that a father could succeed in disappearing with a child as old as Stephanie without some cooperation from the child. On some level Stephanie especially would have to be willing to believe that her mother didn't care, didn't mind losing her, or would be hurt in some way if she called home. Beth's job was to make sure her girls were unwilling to cooperate if Ray tried to take off with them.

So that evening she sat them down on the couch in the family room at the back of the house.

This was the time of day she had always—and still did—read bedtime stories to Lauren, who didn't yet want to give them up although she could read herself. Stephanie, who claimed to be too old to listen, usually sat in the overstuffed armchair and pretended to read herself while eavesdropping avidly. Every few pages she'd ask to see the picture, and Beth would obligingly hold it up. "Why don't you come and sit with us?" she'd ask, and Steph would curl her lip. "Little kids' books are boring. I only wanted to see the one picture, that's all."

But tonight Beth patted the sofa next to her. "Come here. I want to talk."

Her older daughter hovered in the doorway. "The phone's ringing. I'll go get it."

"Just ignore it. Half the time nobody's there anyway." Beth had abandoned the fiction of wrong numbers. The girls had answered the phone themselves and found nobody on the other end too many times now. The doorbell hadn't rung since that second night; the phone had, off and on. It hadn't ceased to unnerve Beth, but the repetition had begun to make her impatient instead of terrified.

"But it might be one of my friends." Steph was verging on a whine.

"Then she can call back," Beth told her firmly.

Eleven years old, and Steph already had a sneer down pat. She sat reluctantly where Beth had indicated. Lauren curled trustingly against Beth's left side.

She took a deep breath and began her prepared speech. "I just thought it was time we have one of those talks about safety."

She'd expected rolled eyes, but instead Stephanie sat stiffly, looking down at her hands but not saying anything.

"Mostly we parents talk, just in case, about stuff that will probably never happen. This is one of those just-in-cases. I hope nothing bad or scary ever happens to you, but you should know what to do if it does.

"Once in a while, somebody steals a child. It isn't always a stranger, either. Sometimes it's somebody the child knows, like a neighbor. Sometimes it's even a parent. Mostly with parents it's when a mother and father are divorced and they're fighting about who the kids will live with. You know your dad and I have already settled that. But I just wanted you to know that it isn't always a stranger. It might be somebody you trust."

Lauren's blue eyes were wide and dark; Stephanie

still had her head bowed. Beth could feel her tension as though it were a violin string quivering from the lightest touch.

"Now, if you took a child, not to hurt her, but because you want to pretend you're her mother or father and she doesn't have anybody else, you couldn't keep her locked in the bedroom forever, right? So what you'd do is try to convince the child that she was supposed to be with you, that whoever she was living with really didn't want her anymore."

Tiny creases formed on Lauren's smooth brow. "I would never, ever, believe anybody who said you didn't want me," she informed her mother staunchly. "'Cause I know you love us."

Momentarily Beth's eyes stung, and she had to blink hard as she bent to kiss the silky top of her younger daughter's hair. Then she reached out and gathered Stephanie's stiffer body into a hug.

"I just want to make sure you know that. That you don't believe anybody at all who tells you different. If something like that ever happened, you should get away as soon as you can. You can call home—you know the number—or you could go to the police or most adults, like a grocery checker or a librarian. You tell them over and over again where you live and what your phone number is. Will you promise me to do that?"

Lauren nodded dutifully, her eyes still saucer wide. On Beth's other side, Stephanie mumbled agreement.

"Then that's all I have to say. I love you two

more than anyone or anything in the whole world. And I always will.''

Lauren nodded, as though to say "Of course.'' "Can we read some stories now?''

"You go pick something out,'' Beth said, kissing her forehead before she released her.

The eight-year-old skipped out of the room on her way toward the bedroom bookcase. Once she was out of sight, Stephanie said, "This is about Dad, isn't it?''

Treading delicately, Beth said, "Not altogether. I really don't think your father would do something like that. This is the kind of thing we should talk about no matter what. But, yeah, it was his being late with you that brought it to mind. *After* I'd gotten over being scared that you'd been in a car accident.''

Her attempt to reassure apparently worked, because Stephanie gave her a look. "Oh, Mom.''

Beth was able to laugh. "I know, I know. I'm a worrywart. But I can't help it, okay? Humor me.''

Stephanie nodded. There was a moment of silence, and Beth waited, sensing that she had something else to say. Suddenly Stephanie burst out, "I don't want to live with Dad!''

A chill wrapped itself around Beth's chest. "Did he ask you if you wanted to?''

"No...'' She bit her lip. "Sometimes he says stuff...but mostly he talks about us all together, like he thinks you're going to change your mind. Are you?''

"No. Do you wish I would?''

Stephanie ducked her head. "Not really. I mean, sometimes I wish we were like other families, and

I didn't have to go visit my dad, but... I didn't like it back when he lived here and he always got so mad.''

"Me, either."

"He gets so mad about even little stuff."

That same chill held Beth in its grip. "At you?"

"No-o," her daughter said uncertainly. "We never do anything to make him mad. Except when I ask him if it's time to go home. But it's just—" she shrugged and made a face "—everything. He yells at the TV when he thinks some referee made a dumb call, and he yells and flips off other drivers, and I was afraid he was going to punch some guy at the gas station one time because Dad thought the guy cut in front of him. It's just..." She squirmed. "It's scary. You know what I mean?"

"Yeah," Beth said softly. "I know what you mean." She bit her lower lip. "I hate to send you on your own to deal with him. But I think under all that anger he's not a bad man. And he's your father. If you grew up not knowing him, I bet someday you'd be sorry. I keep hoping that he'll realize how he's making other people feel and do something about it. But if he really, really scares you—"

"No, it's okay," Stephanie interrupted, looking older than her years.

Beth looked her straight in the eyes. "Will you promise to tell me if it's ever not okay?"

Lauren appeared in the doorway with a pile of books high enough to make Beth groan inwardly. Steph glanced toward her, but Beth insisted, "Promise?"

"Uh, sure."

Beth smiled shakily and gave her another hug. "It's not fair, is it?"

"What's not fair?" Lauren asked.

At the same time as her sister snapped, "None of your beeswax!" Beth said, "Just something Steph and I were talking about. Let's see, what did you pick out?"

Lauren stuck out her tongue at her sister, but didn't insist on an answer.

Normalcy, Beth thought, as Stephanie retreated with her own book to her chair, where she appeared to become completely absorbed in her reading. Beth might almost have believed it if only Steph had turned a page more often, and if she hadn't given a heavy sigh she apparently didn't realize anyone else would hear.

Not fair. But what could she do? Beth wondered with familiar despair and even panic. Go on in this constant state of tension? Or wait until Ray got caught playing his nasty games?

Of course, he wouldn't get caught unless she called the police, and she had a suspicion the only policeman who would be interested in her problems at this point was Sheriff Jack Murray—and he represented danger of a different kind.

JACK GLANCED AROUND the crowded gymnasium and felt familiar regret that he hadn't known his own son in time to be more involved in everyday things like the PTA. He'd had time to become good friends with his son, which was something, but he still resented all he'd lost. Will had walked into his life at fourteen years old, and now, in a blink of the eye, he was gone to college.

The pangs were old ones, and Jack was able to ignore them as he tuned in to the welcoming speech being delivered by the president of the middle school parent group.

''And so it's really a pleasure to see so many of you tonight.'' A stylish woman who probably never wore jeans or sweatshirts, the president beamed as she looked around. ''Let me start by introducing this year's officers.''

Jack was tuning out again when a name snapped him back to attention.

''And Beth Sommers, our treasurer. Beth, where are you?''

Jack's head turned along with everyone else's. Near the back, Beth stood briefly, smiled and waved to the perfunctory applause. Her curly dark hair was knotted on top of her head and she was dressed in a pretty but casual jumper over a white T-shirt. With the one glimpse he hungrily realized how good she looked: the delicate sculpting of her cheekbones, the graceful line of her neck, the chin that she could set so mulishly. Once she sat back down, he lost sight of her without making a fool of himself by half standing and craning his neck.

His intense reaction to her presence made him feel fool enough. Damn it, she'd turned him down as firmly as a woman could. Maybe it was personal— she wasn't attracted to him or just plain didn't like him; maybe it wasn't. She'd said she wasn't ready to try again. Either way, it spelled *no,* however much he wished it didn't.

His job was to protect her, whether she lived in his jurisdiction or not. He hoped she would call if she needed him, in which case he had to separate attraction from obligation. He might ride to her rescue, but she wasn't going to fall into his arms afterward.

The president introduced him and he went to the front. Jack took a moment to raise the microphone to suit his six-foot-two height, then looked around to take stock of his audience. Mostly women, not unusual for these school functions. When he'd shown up as a determined father, Will's last couple of years of high school, he'd occasionally been the only man at meetings. Jack thought that was a shame.

"Hello, folks," he said, nodding. "I see familiar faces, so some of you will have heard what I'm going to say tonight, but I figure that's okay. It's important that you know what to expect of me, and what I expect of you."

He had deliberately not looked in Beth's direction at first. He was taking the care he would with a skittish animal, not making any sudden moves, keeping his voice even, pretending disinterest.

And there was an element of anticipation, too. Until that moment when their gazes locked, he could imagine that her expression wouldn't be indifferent. He could hope for a spark in her eyes, guarded but still there, a hint of something to let him hope that her refusal to have dinner with him wasn't personal, that someday she would be ready.

He paused, let his eyes linger for a moment on the young mother who sat beside Beth, jiggling a toddler on her lap. She looked about sixteen, too young to have a child in middle school.

Beth could have avoided him—gazed down at her hands, smiled at the toddler, glanced toward the exit. But that wasn't in her nature. Instead, her chin was already up and she was waiting. He was interested to see the pink that washed her cheeks and the challenge in her blue eyes. No indifference here, though what she did feel, he couldn't guess.

Without a pause, Jack looked at her neighbor on the other side and continued his short prepared speech.

The way he talked to a group like this was as important as anything he said. He didn't want to be intimidating, though he still believed there was a time and place to scare the crap out of someone. But he'd learned these past years how wrong was Ed Patton's brand of law enforcement. Prevention and intervention were a thousand times better than throwing an eighteen-year-old kid in the slammer. By the time you had to do that, there was already a victim and the kid's life was ruined. Jack knew he had a well-deserved reputation for coming down like a crack of doom on criminals, but what he was working hardest on was finding money for programs aimed at troubled teenagers.

Ed Patton, he thought, had been like a dentist who liked to wield the drill without anesthesia. Jack preferred sealant when the adult teeth were still pearly white.

"I expect to see your kids on the basketball court, the soccer field, the stage right here behind me," he concluded into the microphone. ''Anywhere but in the police station.''

Some of the audience chuckled, and Jack, well satisfied, asked for questions. The few he got were friendly enough, the round of applause enthusiastic.

Strange, the things he'd found himself doing. Speechifying hadn't been covered in the police academy.

Instead of retreating to his seat, Jack strolled to the back of the gym and took up a station near the double doors leading into the central hallway of the two-year-old middle school. Just out of curiosity, he'd stuck his head into the boys' john earlier. Where you'd expect graffiti, here was gleaming tile. The carpet in the hall wasn't dirty, the lockers weren't scraped and dented and scrawled all over with obscene remarks. Inner-city junior highs were armed camps these days; he doubted a single gun was hidden in any of this long bank of lockers.

Folks were lucky in Elk Springs. As a law enforcement officer, *he* was lucky.

As a man, he was obviously a hell of a lot less so, Jack thought wryly. Beth Sommers was the first woman who had seriously interested him in some time, and he'd struck out.

He propped one shoulder against the wall, crossed his arms and listened to plans for a Christmas bazaar and a fund-raiser to buy new books for the library. Beth stood to give a brief treasurer's report; since she couldn't see him, Jack allowed himself the luxury of admiring the straight line of her back and the fine dark hair that had escaped to curl on her nape. For just an instant, he imagined his lips traveling down her neck. The hairs would tickle his nose, but her skin would be silkier than anything he'd ever touched, and her pulse would beat like tiny birds trapped under his mouth.

Hell. It was just as well when she sat back down, putting him out of his misery.

A minute later the meeting broke up and the crowd began filtering out. A few stopped to chat or shake hands and thank him for coming. He was a patient man; except for some emergency exits, this was the only way out. Sooner or later, Beth would pass within a few feet of him.

She was deep in conversation with the president of the parent group as the two women approached the door. It was galling to have Beth glance his way and look vaguely surprised to see him; he was so aware of her, he knew where she was at any given moment. Apparently she didn't feel the same.

Which she'd made clear enough, Jack reminded himself, irritated. Was he such an egotist, he couldn't believe a woman wasn't interested in him?

Answer: no. He'd philosophically accepted refusals before. Meg Patton walking out on him—now, that had been tough. Worse than tough; he knew the one day had changed him in ways he didn't yet understand. But since Meg, he'd asked out women who weren't interested. He'd even been dumped a time or two without going into a black depression.

Beth was different. He had trouble believing his own response to her could be so strong if it wasn't two-way.

He was pretty sure Beth would have nodded and

walked right by him if the president hadn't stopped to hold out her hand.

"Thank you, Sheriff Murray. It was so good of you to take the time tonight to talk to us. I'm really delighted with what you had to say, too. By the way, have you met Beth Sommers?"

He let a trace of a smile touch his lips. "As it happens, I have. Hello, Beth."

Her answering smile didn't touch her eyes. "Sheriff. How nice to see you again. And hear you. I really like your program pairing kids with police officers."

"I'm glad to hear it." Mentally he cursed the president who hadn't budged from his side and was beaming impartially at them. There were things he wanted to say and couldn't in front of her. He did the only thing he could think of. "Can I walk you out to your car? I've been meaning to ask you something."

The alarm in her eyes was quickly masked. "Could you call me at work instead? I really need to rush—I don't like to leave the kids with a baby-sitter any longer than I can help. And there are obviously people waiting to talk to you."

He turned his head and saw that it was true; half a dozen women and one man were hovering. And Beth had damn good reason to be nervous about leaving her kids alone with some fifteen-year-old. How would a sitter cope if the girls' father came hammering on the door?

"No problem," he conceded, stepping back.

"I'm sorry to run off like this," she was saying

to the president as they passed out of hearing. "I'll check on those figures and give you a call...."

Something told Jack that Beth would be unavailable if he called her at work. She had just made her refusal that much more emphatic.

WHY COULDN'T Jack Murray look like the last Butte County sheriff, who'd had a tic under one eye and had spent a good deal of time heaving his belt upward to try to contain his belly?

But no, Murray moved with the contained grace of a man aware of his strength and able to use it. Despite a sexy mouth, a permanent crease over the bridge of his nose should have given him a Scrooge-like appearance, but instead lent him a brooding air guaranteed to attract the least susceptible of women. Her.

Was she an idiot to refuse to have dinner with the man? Beth wondered, unlocking her car. Maybe it was unfair to assume he was like Ray under the skin, when she had never heard him raise his voice or seen him show even a flicker of anger.

Chances were, it would turn out that they didn't even like each other, and then she could quit waging this internal war.

Of course, she thought ruefully, maybe he'd had no intention of asking her out again. Maybe he had only wanted to know whether Ray had been behaving himself.

At home, Beth let herself in the kitchen door and found the baby-sitter in the living room, glued to the flickering television.

"Oh, hi, Mrs. Sommers." Half her attention was

still on the screen, until a commercial suddenly blared and Tiffany turned the set off.

"How did things go?" Beth asked briskly, counting out dollar bills from her wallet.

The teenager gave a blithe shrug. "Fine. I put them to bed a while ago."

"Oh, good. Did, um, anybody call this evening?" Beth felt a little guilty about not warning Tiffany. But there were days when the phone didn't ring at all, days when Ray was probably on the road hauling freight. She'd been afraid if she warned the teenager, Tiffany would tell the older sister raising her and she might refuse to let the girl baby-sit for Beth. A decent sitter was hard enough to come up with as it was; she didn't dare scare off the two girls she used. As a single parent, she was too dependent on them.

"No, but Lauren told me you were getting lots of calls where somebody hangs up." Tiffany's eyes were bright with curiosity. "Maybe you should call the police or something."

If one more person told her that, Beth thought she might scream. But she managed an offhanded smile. "Oh, if we ignore the whole thing, whoever is making the calls will give up."

"You could get Caller ID," she added helpfully.

"I am considering that."

"You know, the sheriff for the whole county lives only a couple of doors down from us." Tiffany marveled at the idea. "My sister said he was talking at the middle school tonight. You heard him, didn't you? Isn't he cool?" Despite the fact that Beth was now holding the front door open, the ponytailed teenager made no move to leave. She continued enthusiastically, "He was there talking to the principal when one of the chaperons for the dance caught a couple of guys spray-painting the administration building Friday night after the game. I don't know what he said to them, I mean, they wouldn't tell anybody, but everybody says he really scared them. I bet *he* could help you."

Her open admiration made Beth grit her teeth. It also hardened her sagging resolve. She was *not* interested in a man who scared anybody—even teenage boys who probably deserved it.

"Thank you for your suggestion, Tiffany," she said, in a tone that she hoped was both pleasant and dismissive. "I'll watch until you get home."

"Thanks, Mrs. Sommers." Her feelings apparently not hurt, Tiffany bounded down the porch steps with all the grace of a puppy, and cut across the lawn. In the middle of the street she turned and cheerfully waved.

Beth waved back, waiting until the girl disappeared inside the brick house kitty-corner to her own. Only then did Beth close and lock the front door, her hand still fumbling on the unfamiliar brass dead bolt.

Every time she touched the shiny new locks, Beth was reminded of Ray. As she made her way up to bed, she acknowledged the sharp feeling of dread lodged in the pit of her stomach. This was Thursday night; tomorrow evening Steph and Lauren's weekend with their dad began.

She lay in bed, sleep hours away, and prayed: Please let him be in a good mood. Please please *please* let him bring them home on time.

CHAPTER FOUR

STANDING IN the living room where she could keep one eye on the clock, the other on the empty street, Beth clutched the cordless phone in a grip so tight she felt as if the plastic case should crack.

Ray was now four hours and thirty-two minutes late bringing the girls home. *Call the police,* everyone had said. Finally, in terror, she'd known she had no other choice.

And look what good it had done her.

He's how late? they'd asked. *Only a few hours? Perhaps car trouble...*

"Ma'am," the officer on the other end of the line said patiently, "has your ex-husband threatened to take the children?"

Any other time, Beth would have been annoyed; tonight, his condescension only quickened the panic beating in her breast. He wasn't going to help her. She could tell already.

"Not...explicitly." She explained about the other weekends, when he had kept her waiting and laughed at her fear. Swallowing her shame, she told the officer about the shouted voices and the flowerpots shattering against her front door.

He listened, she had to give him credit for that much, but at the end he explained, "It doesn't sound to me as if kidnapping is a real concern at this time.''

Kidnapping. The very word sent a shudder through her.

"When will you consider it a real concern?" Beth asked sharply.

"After twenty-four hours…''

"They'll be long gone.'' Through the state of Washington across the Canadian border. Down I-5 to Mexico. Would Ray be able to take the children out of the country without identification of any kind? A memory flickered, from long ago when they had been a family who took vacations together: a customs guard bending over to glance incuriously in the driver's side window as he asked by rote how long they planned to stay in Victoria, B.C. Would he have asked any more questions if Ray or she had been alone with the children?

Oh, God.

Beth ended the call hastily and probably rudely; she didn't care. She only knew that another ten minutes had passed, and Ray's pickup hadn't appeared. He'd had the girls for two nights this weekend, and was supposed to have had them home at one this afternoon. It was now…5:42. Dinnertime. She hadn't even started the chicken casserole she'd intended to make tonight. Hadn't thought of it. Didn't know whether the chicken was spoiling on the kitchen counter or whether she'd put it back in the refrigerator.

What now?

She could drive over to Ray's apartment. She'd done that once, two and a half hours ago, but his pickup hadn't been in the slot and nobody had answered the doorbell.

He wouldn't take the girls, Beth told herself for the hundredth time. The thousandth time. He couldn't go and keep his job. He loved long-haul trucking; he owned his own rig, a huge investment. What would he do? Leave it? Anyway, he didn't *want* to be a full-time parent.

No, he was just trying to get a rise out of her. Pacing, wringing her hands, Beth tried to convince herself that he wanted to upset her, but he hadn't become unbalanced enough to destroy his own life just to destroy hers.

What were a few hours? If he'd asked, she wouldn't have minded if he took the girls somewhere special this afternoon. If, when he brought them home, he saw that she wasn't scared, only irritated, he'd quit doing this. Her fear fed him. She had to—somehow—hide it.

The old-fashioned mantel clock ticked, the tiny sound magnifying the silence, italics emphasizing a stark word. The tick was like her heartbeat as she tried to sit but somehow ended up standing at the front window again. How could it beat so hard and fast and yet the minutes pass so slowly?

Jack Murray would do more than listen. The thought tapped insidiously on her consciousness, a temptation so great she almost groaned aloud.

He'd told her to call if she needed him. She remembered his patience, his solid presence, the way he had so effortlessly cowed Ray. He hadn't had any obligation to stop that night, or come to see her later. He did seem to sympathize.

Beth pressed her forehead to the glass and closed her eyes. Ray would be so angry if Jack Murray were here when he brought the girls home. She might as well wave a red cape.

But it wasn't her fear of angering Ray that kept her from snatching up the phone again and dialing. It was the fact that the sheriff had asked her on a date....

No. Her breath clouded the windowpane. She had to be honest with herself. What really bothered her was the expression in his dark eyes when he looked at her, and the way that made her feel. She was bruised inside by her marriage and divorce. She didn't want to be aware of a man. She wasn't ready.

Would never be ready for the Butte County sheriff, a man who had to be as capable of violence as Ray was.

Beth held out for another fifteen agonizing minutes. She called Ray's apartment and listened to his curt message: "If you want me to call, leave your number."

"Ray," she said, "I expected Steph and Lauren home some time ago. Please phone me."

When the clock chimed softly six times, Beth knew she couldn't bear the silence anymore, the relentless tick of the second hand, the empty street. She reached for the phone. Only then did it occur to her that Jack Murray might not be at home waiting for her call.

Painful relief surged through her when he picked up after the third ring and said brusquely, "Murray here."

"Sheriff, this is Beth Sommers. Your neighbor. Um, the one who..."

"Has troubles with her ex-husband. I know who you are, Beth. Is he there now?"

"No." Her chest felt as if it were being crushed. "Ray had the girls this weekend. He was supposed to bring them home at one today. He's...he's five hours late. I called the Elk Springs police, but they can't do anything until twenty-four hours has passed. I could tell they thought I was being hysterical. Maybe I am...." Her voice was rising and she had to swallow a sob.

"I'll be right over." She heard a click and more silence, but a different brand this time.

He was coming. He would find Ray and the girls. Her anger had long since been swamped by fear, but tears hadn't threatened until this minute, when she no longer felt so helpless and alone.

The sheriff arrived in an unmarked dark blue sedan. Beth rushed to unlock the front door. At the sight of the tall, dark man striding up her walkway, she was shocked by her desire to throw herself into his arms and cry against his shoulder. She had always been so independent—too much so for Ray's taste. Even when times were toughest, she'd never been so tempted to trust a man to take care of her.

He took the porch steps two at a time. "Any word?"

Beth shook her head, her lips pressed together. *Hold me,* her heart cried.

She stood back and said stiffly, "Thank you. For coming."

"I told you to call me." He stopped on the doorstep, his brown eyes searching her face. "Why did you wait so long?"

"I was sure he'd show up. It's a game for him. No, it's not," she reversed herself. "He hurts, and somehow that's warped him. He wasn't like this. He loved the girls!"

Without a word, Jack stepped forward and enfolded her in his arms. Off balance, she had to wrap hers around his waist. It felt so natural to lean against him and lay her cheek against his broad chest. His heart drummed beneath her ear and for just an instant she felt...safe.

But she wasn't. Steph and Lauren weren't. She couldn't assume some man would fix troubles made by another one.

Beth stiffened and drew away.

Briefly his arms tightened, then freed her. Without comment, Jack said, "Give me his address and phone number. We'll start there."

Beth led him into the kitchen. "I just left another message ten or fifteen minutes ago."

"I'll send a deputy to his place."

"Thank you." She swallowed and willed herself not to cry. "I don't think he's there, but...thank you."

He reached for her but stopped himself. "You're welcome."

She listened as he made the call. Brewing coffee gave her something to do while they waited. When she put the cup in front of him, he looked up.

"Where else does he take them?"

Beth sagged into the chair. "Not much of anywhere. Just recently Steph was saying that he's always promising something special and then reneging. They mostly hang around at his place. Play computer games and watch TV. They get bored.''

He watched her steadily. ''Do they go fishing? For walks? To the softball field?''

A spark of hope flared to life. ''Wait. A friend of his has a cabin on the Deschutes. I wonder…''

The phone rang. She pounced on it, her heart drumming. ''Hello?''

''Sheriff Murray handy?''

Almost holding her breath, she passed the phone to him.

''Yeah?'' He frowned. ''Okay. Let me call you in a minute.'' Setting down the phone, Jack shook his head. ''No sign they're there.''

''Oh, no.'' She twisted her fingers together and tried desperately to think. ''The friend's name is Bill. Bill… Oh, what is it?'' she exclaimed in frustration. ''Why can't I remember?''

Jack's big hand covered hers. ''Hey.'' His voice was a soft rumble. ''Calm down. It'll come to you.''

''Yes.'' She closed her eyes and made herself take a deep, slow breath. ''Of course you're right. Just give me a minute….''

The chair was already tumbling back even before she consciously realized she'd heard a car—a pickup—out in front. ''He's home.'' She raced for the front door. ''Oh, God, let it be him.''

Jack was right behind her when she opened the door. Ray's pickup sat square in front of the house. Steph and Lauren were scrambling down, Lauren running toward the porch.

Beth stifled a sob and met her youngest halfway

up the steps. The convulsive hug gave away her feelings; her voice didn't. She prayed it didn't.

"You guys are late! What have you been up to?"

Stephanie was grinning, her dad right beside her, his hand on her shoulder. "Dad took us to a movie this afternoon, and then to the arcade. It was so cool! Look what I won!" She held up a pink and purple stuffed unicorn with a drooping horn.

"I threw up," Lauren confessed. "Dad bought all the candy we wanted, an' I had these huge Junior Mints and then red licorice, but my stomach got upset."

"No kidding." Beth marveled at her outward calm. She couldn't bring herself to look at Ray, at the smirk she knew she'd see on his face. Never in her life had she been so angry she wanted to hurt someone, but right this minute she hated him with all the ferocity of a feral mother protecting her young from a predator. She didn't care that he was their father; he threatened them.

"Girls," Jack said calmly, "please go in the house. I need to talk to your father."

Ray spit out an obscenity. "You have a *cop* here?"

"Don't you talk like that in front of them!"

Jack squeezed her shoulder. His warm grip steadied her. As the girls hurried into the house, she stared at the man she had once loved, and wished she never had to see him again.

"Mr. Sommers," Jack said, "Beth says that your visitation extended only until one o'clock today. Are you aware that you're breaking the law in violating court-ordered visitation?"

Ray had once been handsome. He'd acquired new lines in his face, new puffiness under his eyes, a sneer to his mouth. He spit out another obscenity. "A few goddamn hours, and she's calling the goddamn cops? Steph and Lauren are my kids, too. We did something fun today. Yeah, sure. That's a crime." He gave an ugly laugh.

"Yes, in fact it is." Jack's voice held no emotion whatsoever. "Mr. Sommers, I doubt Ms. Sommers would be distressed if occasionally you were a little late, especially if you called to let her know. In fact, however, you've demonstrated a pattern of not bringing your daughters home when you promised to. If you don't want to lose visitation, you'd better stick to the letter of your agreement."

Ray took a bullish step forward. "Who the hell are you to tell me what to do?"

They were going to fight, right here on her front walk. She should never have called Jack, Beth thought in horror. This was all her fault.

Muscles tightened in his jaw, but he continued to sound dispassionate. "I'll be happy to show you my badge."

"Yeah, and it doesn't say Elk Springs P.D., does it?" Ray spread his hands and turned to look around the neighborhood with exaggerated surprise. "Gee, we're inside the city limits, aren't we? So, I'll say it again—who the hell are you?" Eyes furious slits, he leaned forward so the two men's faces weren't more than inches apart. "You're not the law. Not here."

In the hand that still rested on Beth's shoulder,

she felt the tension that quivered through Jack, belying his outward relaxation.

"I'm giving you some friendly advice," he said calmly. "The Elk Springs P.D. are aware of the situation here. As I'm aware that you have a court date approaching. I'm sure the judge would be interested in knowing that your anger toward Ms. Sommers extends to violating an earlier court order."

"Damn," Ray said incredulously. "You're threatening me. You son of a..."

"Not threatening. Advising you."

Ray growled and lunged forward. Jack gripped his shoulder. His voice was dangerously silky. "Assaulting a law enforcement officer won't help your cause."

Face purple, a vein in his temple throbbing, Ray stepped back. He turned his glittering gaze from Jack to Beth. "You shouldn't have called him."

She was horrified by the apology that wanted to tumble out. She wasn't sorry! She refused to be the classic abused wife who believed everything that went wrong was her fault.

Gaze steady, chin high, Beth said, "If you don't bring the girls home on time, I'll keep calling the police. Every time. Think about that."

"You want war? Then you've got it," snarled her ex-husband, before he stalked to his truck, got in and drove away.

Beth's breath rattled out and her knees sagged.

Jack took her arm. "The girls are okay. He won't hurt them."

"He already has," she whispered. Pulling away, Beth said, "I need to talk to them."

The sheriff followed her back into the house. She wanted to ask him why, but couldn't be so appallingly rude. She had begged for his help, and he'd given it. She couldn't expect him to conveniently disappear now that she was once again reluctant to face him.

"Mom?" Stephanie was waiting in the front hall, her expression anxious. "Where's Dad?" She peered past the two adults. "Is something wrong?"

"No." Beth forced a smile. "Not really. I was annoyed at your dad because he didn't let me know he'd be bringing you home late today. That's all. It's not your fault."

"But he said..." She stopped.

"Said what?" Beth prompted, painfully aware of Jack, silent, behind her.

Looking flustered, the eleven-year-old said, "I thought you knew. But...but it was okay, wasn't it?"

Beth gave her a quick hug. "I'm glad he took you somewhere fun. I just want to know ahead of time, that's all! Now, where's Lauren?"

"I made her take her stuff upstairs. In case..."

In case her parents started screaming at each other again. In case flowerpots shattered against the front door.

Suddenly ashamed, Beth managed a twisted smile. "You're a good big sister. Thank you. Now, why don't you take your own bag up? Make Lauren unpack. Tell her Mom said to use the hamper."

"Okay." Steph grabbed her duffel bag and started up the stairs. "I've got to work on my Kenya project."

"Oh, no! Is it due tomorrow?"

"I'm almost done." Steph waved a reassuring hand as she disappeared from the landing.

Thank God for one organized kid. Left to her own devices, Lauren wouldn't worry about her homework until tomorrow morning when she was trying to find her book pack. Beth wondered if Ray remembered that much about the two girls. Did he care about things like their schoolwork anymore? Why couldn't he see that they were more than weapons he could launch at her?

Forcing a rueful smile, she turned to Jack Murray. "Well, I'm having a feeling of déjà vu."

He leaned against the newel, to all appearances completely relaxed. "Ah, but this time's different. I didn't invite myself to this party."

For the first time, Beth realized he wasn't wearing his uniform. This was not a cop who lounged at the foot of the staircase, but rather a man. A formidably attractive man, she thought, understanding her unease.

Blue jeans, comfortably faded, molded to the long muscles in his thighs. Over an equally faded T-shirt that had once been blue, he wore a windbreaker. To hide a gun? Beth wondered. On his feet were grass-stained running shoes.

For some reason, Beth's gaze snagged on those shoes. Had he actually been mowing his lawn when she phoned? Did the county sheriff do something so mundane as mow and edge and fertilize his own grass?

She blinked and looked back at his face to find

that he was watching her quizzically. He'd said something: *I didn't invite myself to this party.*

"No," she said quietly. "I got you into this. Unnecessarily, it would appear. I'm really sorry. There's a good reason the policeman I talked to wanted to wait twenty-four hours, isn't there?"

His brows drew together, deepening that permanent crease. "Yeah, but that doesn't mean you were wrong to call them. Or me. You had every reason to be anxious. Your ex is keeping the kids a little longer every time, isn't he? Upping the ante. What's it going to be next week? Not bring 'em home until Monday morning? And after that, what?"

She shuddered.

Jack's expression changed and he muttered what was probably a swear word. "I'm scaring you for no reason. We'll deal with what comes. The fact that you called me today may give him pause."

"You didn't scare me." Beth hugged herself, quaking inside. "How could you? I've already imagined everything. Just this afternoon alone, I've pictured him taking them to Mexico, or having a car accident, or hiding out, or…or even…"

He straightened. "Don't say it."

She had to. Just once. Her worst nightmare, the one that seeped like toxic gas into her dreams and waking fears alike, needed to be spoken aloud once, at least.

"The cases you read about in the newspaper." She was surprised she sounded so…normal. As if she were arguing an abstract point. "Nobody ever expects a man to kill his wife and children and himself. They're always regular people. Neighbors. You know how the pictures of the children always look like they must be their school photos? The kids are so well scrubbed, with these big grins, and you think—how could he? But you see, I'm already thinking that. And I wonder if those other women weren't, too. If…there weren't some kind of warning. If he didn't…up the ante. That's how you put it, right? Because Ray either has to give up, or do something dreadful. And I think—'' she no longer sounded so steady ''—I think his pride won't let him give up, no matter what.''

''The vast majority of custody disputes don't escalate into tragedy.''

''But you see, Ray and I don't have a custody dispute. We agreed right away that Steph and Lauren would live with me, and we had no problem over visitation. This…this has to do with me, not them. That's what scares me.''

He swore and pulled her into his arms again. She went with a ragged sigh, grateful for his warmth and strength and comfort.

''Not all men are like him,'' he said roughly, mouth against her hair.

She felt so very safe, though she knew it was an illusion. He couldn't stay twenty-four hours a day and guard her or her children. He couldn't trail at Ray's elbow the next time he took Lauren and Steph. She still didn't know whether his presence today had made things better or worse. She knew only, gratefully, that it felt so good for once to lean on someone else. To know that he was capable of coming to her defense, that he would if he could, that she wasn't totally alone.

"I'm...not feeling very trusting right now," she said, cheek against his chest.

His arms tightened, his voice a rasp in her ear. "I won't ask you again right now. That's not why I came. Just...think about it. Okay? I'm not like him. Nor are most men. Don't let him scare you off."

Now she did draw back. He didn't try to hold her.

"Why me?" Beth asked, studying him in perplexity. "I'm not beautiful. My life is a mess. I don't understand what you see in me."

"I could argue about whether you're beautiful."

"I have a mirror. I'm...pretty. Maybe. You..." She gestured. "If *Playgirl* chose a Bachelor of the Month from Butte County, you'd be their choice."

He gave a grunt that wasn't amusement. "I'm ugly as sin."

"You're sexy, and you can't tell me you don't know it. You must have women...."

"Falling all over themselves? No." He shrugged. "I can find dates."

"Then...why me?" she asked again stubbornly, knowing the answer mattered.

The shift of emotions across his face showed that he didn't want to answer, but at last he said, "You *are* beautiful, to me. But you're right. That's not what interests me."

"Then what does?"

"The way your chin comes up when you're afraid. It...reminds me of someone who was important to me. Your refusal to be petty. Most women would try to protect their kids from their dad. But they wouldn't protect their relationship *with* him. You put them ahead of your anger. That's rare,

Beth.'' His eyes were heavy-lidded, his voice velvety. ''Rarer than you know.''

''Because I want them not to hate their father?''

''Yup. Do you know how many parents use the kids as terrain on a battlefield?''

Yes, she realized. That was exactly what Steph and Lauren had become to Ray. Not weapons, as she had earlier thought, but terrain: an advantage sometimes, a disadvantage sometimes. They could have been hills or trees or rivers in a faraway landscape of war.

''Yes.'' She closed her eyes briefly. ''I swore I wouldn't.''

''That, Beth Sommers, is why I'd like to know you better. You have guts and heart. I'd be a fool not to notice.''

His voice was rich, dark and unsettling. It excited a thrill in her belly she didn't remember having felt in years. He wasn't just attracted to her. He saw something unusual, something special in her. How could she resist?

''Then,'' she said on an indrawn breath, ''I'd enjoy having dinner with you sometime. If you still want to take me.''

His eyes darkened, though he didn't move. ''Oh, yeah. I'd still like to take you. So long as you aren't agreeing because you think you owe me. Or because you'd be reluctant to call me again if you say no now, and you're afraid you'll need me.''

''You said you'd come no matter what.'' Beth squeezed her hands together before her. ''You did today. You didn't even hesitate.''

''And I won't next time.''

She nodded. "So…no. That's not why I'm agreeing."

He didn't ask why, for which she was thankful. He, at least, had been able to answer. How could she have admitted, *Because you make me feel safe?*

Gruffly, he said, "Name the day."

"Weeknights aren't the greatest. Friday? I can get a baby-sitter."

"Friday at six, then." He backed toward the front door, his dark eyes holding hers. "Do you like Italian?"

A smile broke through Beth's tension like a sunrise over the high desert ridges. Getting dressed up, flirting with a handsome man, dining out on something besides burgers and fries… Why, it might actually be fun.

"I love Italian."

"Good." He nodded and opened the front door. "Friday."

"Jack?"

Filling the doorway, he glanced back. "Yeah?"

"You will tell me who I remind you of, won't you?"

Another play of emotions on a face she'd have sworn was imperturbable intrigued her.

"I shouldn't have said that. I didn't even realize…" His abrupt stop lent punctuation to his obvious discomfiture.

"Neither of us is eighteen years old. I don't mind hearing about an old girlfriend." Did she?

His brows lifted briefly. "Then I'll tell you about Meg. And our son."

"Son…?"

''Friday,'' he promised, amusement lifting one corner of his mouth.

Beth found herself smiling at the closed door. She felt suddenly young, fizzing with excitement. She'd lied to herself. He did make her feel safe, but that wasn't the only reason she'd agreed to the date.

Jack Murray was a sexy man whose warm gaze and husky voice reminded her that she was a woman. She *wanted* to remember. She wanted another chance at love and forever. Jack knew what she was, even admired her for being ''gutsy.'' To paraphrase him, she'd be a fool not to grab for a man who liked a strong woman, instead of feeling threatened by her as Ray had been.

Now she had something to look forward to. She could focus on *this* Friday, and not the next one.

When Ray was entitled to take his children again, and she would have to live with the fear that he wouldn't bring them back.

CHAPTER FIVE

HE SHOULDN'T HAVE TOLD her she reminded him of Meg, Jack thought, casting a glance at Beth. She would have questions tonight, and what could he say? *I haven't yet found a woman who measured up to my teenage lover, but I'm thinking you might?* Wouldn't she figure he was looking for a stand-in?

Hell, was he?

Beth Sommers sat in the passenger seat of his Dodge 4×4, her hands neatly folded on her lap, her back so straight he wasn't sure it was touching the seat. Her face in profile was fine-boned, delicate and coolly reserved. Did she wish she hadn't agreed to this evening?

"I've seen your baby-sitter before," he said casually, stopped at a red light. "Isn't she one of the Shaefer kids?"

"Yes, that's Tiffany. She says she lives a couple of doors down from you. I'm not sure which house is yours."

"Mine's the glow-in-the-dark lime-green one." Jack watched a beat-up VW bug sail across the intersection just as his own light turned and his foot moved to the gas. Seemed like everyone was pushing it these days. He ought to slap flashers on his roof and ticket the jackass, but he had a suspicion

Beth wasn't crazy about his profession. No point in rubbing her nose in it.

For the first time, her face lit with amusement. "I know the house! It's not lime-green. More of a…a sage-green. I like it with the white and cream."

"My son helped me paint last summer. The color looked okay on that little bitty paint chip. Came out brighter than I'd intended. Mrs. Finley next door told me I'd lowered everybody's property values for a block around."

"Oh, pooh." Beth scrunched up her nose. "Mrs. Finley's house has been white with black trim for forty years. She has no imagination."

"Yours is white."

"Yes, but that's because we haven't painted since we bought the house four years ago. We'd talked about this summer, but…"

A small thing like divorce had intervened, he read into her trailed-off explanation.

"Next year," she finished more strongly. "I've always wanted a yellow house. A sunny lemon with a white porch and eaves. What do you think?"

"Sounds beautiful. Mrs. Finley will have a heart attack."

Traffic in Elk Springs was getting worse all the time. Though they were a month from the opening of ski season, when the population of Butte County came close to doubling, still traffic crept down Main Street as if this were downtown L.A. Not enough parking, he thought for the thousandth time. The boutiques and art galleries, the bookstore and espresso stands drew tourists who had to fight for street parking.

This eastern Oregon town had been a sleepy ranching community when he was a boy; Jack's father owned a furniture store. Those were the days before the mall, when the hardware store had been in the brick building right up ahead that had been gutted and now held small shops and a French restaurant. Jack skied himself, but he hadn't minded the drive to Mount Bachelor. He sometimes regretted the new ski resort built just a few years before up on Juanita Butte outside town. Life would never be the same in Elk Springs, especially for the county sheriff, who had to find enough manpower and tax dollars to control crime.

At Trattoria Ginelli's, an Italian place new to Elk Springs just the previous fall, he and Beth were seated immediately at a small table nestled in the curve of a bay window overlooking the Deschutes River. In the fading light of dusk, the water was a deep purple, the overhanging willows indistinct, graceful silhouettes. The restaurant was lit by copper fixtures and candles in wall sconces instead of on the tables. Jack liked the warm, rustic atmosphere created by a floor tiled in terracotta and mismatched antique tables and chairs scattered in nooks and crannies created by folding screens. Perusing the menu, he and Beth chatted about Elk Springs and what the future might bring.

"Ray and I moved here from Beaverton, over near Portland," Beth said. "To us it felt as if Portland was just spilling over, and what had been a small town was getting too urban. Ray could work out of the eastern part of the state, and this looked like a great place to raise kids. We'd been keeping an eye out for the right kind of business for me, and the stationery store was up for sale. I haven't regretted the move, even since the divorce. My parents are in Portland, but I'm just as happy to have a few hours' drive between us. Visits are great, but…''

He talked about his own parents as he and Beth sipped wine and nibbled on bread. He had to admire Beth's restraint. Their entrées came before she asked about Meg and Will.

''How old is your son?'' she asked casually, picking up her fork.

''Nineteen,'' Jack said, having trouble believing it himself. ''Let me show you a picture.'' He whipped out his wallet and passed over a snapshot taken on a camping trip that summer. Will was a good-looking kid, if Jack did say so himself. Jack was six foot two; his son had an inch on him now. Who knew if he was still growing?

''Why…this could be a picture of you.'' Beth looked up in astonishment. Her next words seemed to slip out. ''He's very handsome.''

He gave a slow smile. ''I'll take that as a compliment.''

Her cheeks grew pink, but she teased, ''Of course, he *is* younger. Lots younger. No lines beside his eyes.'' She pursed her lips and looked from him to the photo and back, her expression not quite as innocent as she imagined. ''Isn't it a shame that we can't stay looking the way we did at nineteen forever.''

''Okay. You've bruised my ego enough.'' Laughing, Jack took the photo back and tucked it carefully into a plastic sleeve before restoring the wallet to his hip pocket.

"What's really a shame," Beth said thoughtfully, "is that men age better than women. Why do you suppose that is?"

"Lady—" he let his gaze caress her face "—if you're an example of how women wear their years, I'd have to argue with your point."

She didn't flatter easily. "I'm thirty-four. I look it."

"When I see a sexy young thing, I imagine Will turning to gawk. Women my son could date don't interest me."

Now a smile blossomed. "You don't hanker to convince your son that you can attract sexier young things than he can?"

"Never crossed my mind." He buttered a slab of Italian bread.

Her smile faded; her gaze became grave. "Are you divorced from his mother?"

Moment of truth. "No. We were never married. She took off when she was seventeen. I didn't know she'd been pregnant until she came back to Elk Springs with a fourteen-year-old son," he said baldly.

Beth gaped. "She never told you?"

"Meg had good reason." More reason than he ever intended to tell anyone, much less this woman who needed to trust him. "Her father was abusive, and she was afraid of what he'd do to her when he found out. I think she was even more afraid of him taking her son from her." Jack concentrated on tear-ing the bread in half. "I was a kid, too. I couldn't have stood up to him."

"Well, of course you couldn't, but..."

"But what?"

Not until he saw her shrink back did he realize how fierce his stare and voice were.

"I'm sorry," she said quietly, face remote again. "This is none of my business."

His jaw muscles clenched. Voice rough, he said, "No. I'm the one who's sorry. I volunteered the story. I wanted to tell you about Meg and Will. I'm just having trouble dealing with the knowledge that I helped create a child, but I wasn't man enough to protect him or his mother."

"From what you say, she wasn't old enough to be a mother, either."

"Meg might have been seventeen, but she had the guts to take off on her own, and she made it. Somehow she raised a hell of a kid. She was stronger than I was."

"But you don't know." Beth studied him. "She didn't give you the chance to find out."

Yes. God, yes, she had. But he couldn't say so. He hated admitting even to himself what a gutless wonder he'd been. "Crawl," Ed Patton had demanded, and he'd crawled. If he'd known Meg was pregnant, would anything have been any different? Jack wanted to think so, but he couldn't be sure.

Jack finished demolishing the bread. "I'd like to believe I would have grown up fast, the way Meg had to. But how the hell do I know? Teenage boys aren't known for their maturity."

Those grave eyes were still fastened on him.

"This Meg. You sound as if you…love her." She said the last delicately, but with an air of discovery, as if she'd just realized something about him.

He nipped that one in the bud. "No. We've become friends again, but love…" Jack shook his head. "Whatever spark we had was long gone. I was pretty steamed that she hadn't told me about Will sometime in all those years, and we had to work that out. Meg married Scott McNeil, the general manager of the ski area. Nice guy. They're crazy about each other."

Beth's scrutiny continued, and he could hardly blame her. Men and women their age carried emotional baggage. That was expected. But she wouldn't want to date a man who was still in love with the mother of his child.

"I admire Meg," he said, in the face of Beth's doubtful silence. "I like her. Hell, she's one of my deputies. I did love her, when we were seventeen, as much as a kid that age can really love a girl. But I gotta tell you, that was twenty years ago. People change."

"Yes." Her smile was rueful, even apologetic. "Sadly enough, they do."

"Sadly isn't the word I would have used." He heard the momentary hard edge to his tone. He didn't like the boy he'd been, although sometimes he wasn't sure he liked the man he'd become because of that bitter day, either. Making sure his voice had become gentler, he said, "You're thinking of your ex-husband."

Grief flitted across her face. "Both of us, maybe.

We both changed. Maybe we each let the other one down.''

Picturing the SOB smashing clay pots against her front door even when he knew damn well not just Beth but his children were on the other side of it, Jack had trouble feeling pity for Ray Sommers. But he understood what she was saying.

"What do you think he wanted in a woman?"

She played with her wineglass. "A traditional wife. Someone who would...support him. Admire him. Obey him, although he wasn't a tyrant." Her brow crinkled as she considered her words. "He just...needed to feel big. Once, when we were fighting, he said I made him feel small." She looked almost pleadingly at Jack. "I didn't on purpose. But he didn't like me making more money than he did, or being too busy with the store to stay home days when he was between runs, or...or contradicting him with the girls. That's what some of this is about. He didn't want custody—*couldn't* have it, since he's on the road so much of the time—but he hates the fact that the visitation is laid out in the court order, that we're not just going on trust." She heaved a sigh. "The way he sees it, I'm still giving him orders.''

"And a woman isn't supposed to give the orders.''

"Right." Her mouth twisted into a semblance of a smile. "His parents are old-fashioned, his mom a housewife, and I was supposed to be like her, I guess.''

"*Were* you like her?" Jack found he really wanted to know. It was easy to imagine her as a girl or young woman, slender, quick moving, dark hair glossy and her sparkling blue eyes unwary. In those days, her face would have glowed with innocence and her sweetness wouldn't have been laced with regrets, disillusionment and hurt. She'd have been gentle, perhaps even timid, without the grit that brought her chin up in that distinctive gesture of strength and defiance that had resonated with him.

At seventeen, Beth wouldn't have been able to do what Meg had done for the child she carried. But then, Beth hadn't been deserted by her mother when she was fourteen. She hadn't had to protect her younger sisters from a cruel father. She hadn't had to pretend she was clumsy to explain all her bruises and broken bones. She hadn't yet been honed by fire.

Meg had had to prove herself young. Beth's turn came later, but she was measuring up in a way he admired just as much.

In response to his question, Beth made an unhappy sound. "When Ray and I met, I was…unformed. I wasn't anybody in particular. I still had to become somebody. Ray just didn't realize that. He thought who he saw was who he got."

"Did you get who you saw?"

"Well…more so. I just didn't know that wasn't what I wanted. So you see, I hold some blame."

"In the failure of your marriage?" He tried to sound matter-of-fact. "Maybe. It takes two to tango. But in the aftermath?" Jack shook his head. "You aren't the one throwing things or trying to scare him by letting him think he might never see his girls again. That's low."

"Yes." Beth's mouth firmed. "Yes, it is. Ray and I may have misjudged each other, but I never would have married him if I'd seen his temper." Her eyes were unfocused as she looked into the past. "He wasn't an angry man. Not then. It…crept up on us both. The less compliant I was, the madder he got. Which brought out the stubborn streak in me he hadn't known I had." She grimaced. "A vicious circle. The sad story of a marriage."

"One I've heard plenty often." Every cop dreaded domestic disturbance calls. Often neither party really wanted help. The vicious circle Beth described was like a whirlpool, sucking people down. Even the battered wives often wouldn't reach for a buoy tossed to them. Jack didn't get it, but he'd seen it plenty of times.

"Have you ever been married?" Beth asked.

"No. Just never happened."

"Not because of what you see on the job?"

Surprised, he said, "I see good marriages, too. It's tough for cops, but I know plenty who have supportive spouses. Meg is a deputy, for example. Her sister Renee is the police chief here in Elk Springs. They're both happily married, far as I can see. My own parents don't seem to have any regrets. So no. Like I said, things just never came together."

She nodded. "Are you sorry? You sound as though you've really enjoyed Will. You don't wish you had other kids?"

"Sometimes," Jack admitted. "But, you know, Will is nineteen. Think how disconcerting it would be if he and I became fathers at the same time."

Her gentle chuckle was as good as a soft brush

of fingers. "Maybe. But you *were* awfully young when he was born. And don't forget, when he becomes a father, *you'll* be Granddad. You'll need a pick-me-up to keep you from feeling old."

"You're making me feel better," he groused, delighted by her fresh laugh.

While they finished dinner and sipped coffee, they steered clear of any topics that were too personal. Enough was enough for one night, he figured. He'd wanted to know what went wrong with her marriage. She'd needed to hear the basics about his son and marital status. Okay, they'd done that. Now the conversation came easily, just small stories about eccentric customers at the stationery store and oddball cases he'd investigated as a cop.

He told her about the old guy who shoplifted a candy bar at least once a week from the 7-Eleven, then took it back and apologized. When Jack talked to him, he confessed, "I don't mean to, but I see the clerk watching me, and I start wondering if I could pull it off, and... Well," he'd finished apologetically, "it's not as though I would ever *keep* anything I took. Why, that would be stealing! It's just the challenge, you see."

She countered with stories about an old lady who had pretended she worked at the stationery store. When Beth turned her back, the woman had whisked behind the counter and start ringing up purchases. "Which would be okay," Beth said, making a face, "except that she wanted to give discounts. 'Oh, that's fifty percent off today!' I heard her carol. Fortunately, her daughter came in and collected her."

Somewhere as the evening wound down, Jack realized he'd left the impression that his career hadn't involved a hell of a lot more than a series of traffic stops, with the biggest case he'd ever cracked the serial theft of automobile hood ornaments in the Safeway parking lot. The SWAT team, drug busts, rape and murder didn't figure in their conversation. He wasn't even sure whether that was deliberate on his part, an effort to avoid reminding her that he was the cop she'd called in fear for her children.

Hey, he told himself. She was a big girl. She knew evil walked out there. Sooner or later, if they dated seriously, she would want to know what he'd seen and felt and done. It was something they had to talk about. He had blood on his hands, figuratively speaking. Either she could deal with that, or she couldn't. He'd discovered long since that some women couldn't.

He hoped Beth Sommers wasn't one of them.

During the drive home he was very aware of her beside him, her knees primly held together, her elbows close to her side. She stole a few glances his way, too, and when their gazes intersected once or twice, she was the one to look away. She was getting nervous, he figured, thinking about the same thing playing through his mind: him kissing her.

He'd held her in his arms twice now, for comfort. Most cops, male and female, offered that kind of comfort in the line of duty from time to time. Jack couldn't remember ever having sexual thoughts when a woman trembled in his arms from fear or relief or terrible grief. But with Beth resting against him, he'd felt not just rage at her jackass of an ex-husband and pity for her. He'd also been painfully conscious of the swell of her breasts pressing against his chest, the curve of her back under his hands, the scent and tickle of her hair, the delicacy of her neck. He'd have given hell to any of his men who admitted to lusting after the victim at a domestic abuse scene! But, by God, that was exactly what he'd been doing.

He had wanted Beth Sommers from the minute she flung open her front door. And tonight he was going to kiss her. She knew it, and he knew it. Which didn't make conversation easy.

In her driveway, Jack put the 4×4 into park and set the emergency brake. He laid his arm along the back of her seat and turned toward her, feeling suddenly clumsy and about as subtle as a kid Will's age. Getting this kiss right was too important. He wanted to be smooth, seductive, tender, not heavy-handed or pushy. It didn't take a mind reader to know that she hadn't kissed a man since her divorce, which explained why she gasped faintly at even this first overture.

"Hey. I won't attack you," he murmured.

"No." The whites of her eyes showed. "I know," she said hurriedly. "That's not why..."

Humor sanded the rough edges from his voice. "Pants on fire."

She let out a puff of air that took some of her starch with it. Her spine relaxed enough that her nape almost touched his arm. "All right! I'm a little nervous, okay?"

The amusement fled, leaving an ache like heartburn beneath his breastbone. "Me, too."

"Really?" Beth whispered.

A fraction of an inch from her bare neck, his fingers curled into a fist. "Yeah. I don't want to scare you."

In the dim light from the dashboard, he saw her nibble on her lower lip. "I guess you can tell I haven't dated in a long time."

Jack had to clear his throat. "I can tell."

She moved enough that her hair brushed his hand. The single curl had the feathery texture of down. He wondered whether handfuls of her dark hair would have the weightlessness of down, too, slipping through his fingers.

"Now I feel a little silly." Her breasts rose and fell; she trembled when his fingers flexed and touched the bump of her vertebrae. Even her voice became tremulous. "I'm sorry. Maybe I should...should just say...good-night." The last came out on a sigh as his hand wrapped her nape.

"I would really like to kiss you," he said huskily.

Her eyes were huge and shadowed, her mouth soft and parted. "I think," she said, so low he could just hear her, "I'd like it if you would. Kiss me, I mean."

He gave a laugh that might have been a groan and drew her toward him, cursing the console between the front seats. Tension quivered through her, making the shoulder he gripped feel brittle. And yet she lifted her face willingly.

Their noses bumped as he bent his head. Her giggle lightened the moment. "It looks so easy in movies," she breathed against his mouth.

He felt her smile when he closed the last distance. Her lips were incredibly soft, her scent a trace of something once familiar but almost forgotten. His mother might have used the same shampoo or soap. Lavender. Why did he think lavender?

This kiss had to be gentle, tentative; he couldn't let himself demand more than she offered. Their mouths brushed, tasted, nibbled. She made a throaty little sound that sent a rush of pure heat to his groin and tightened his fingers on her upper arm.

Her lips parted, and for just a moment he deepened the kiss, touched her tongue with his, nipped a little harder. Then Jack made himself ease away, trail his mouth over her cheekbone, nuzzle her ear, lay his cheek against that cloud of dark hair.

"Oh!" she murmured, in a tone of wonder that had him gritting his teeth on a surge of hunger.

If his tone was gravelly, he almost managed to inject some amusement in it. "Not so bad, eh?"

A chuckle rippled through her. "Did I hurt your feelings by implying a movie star would be a better kisser?"

"I looked at it as a challenge."

"Somehow, that doesn't surprise me." Beth sighed and straightened away from him. "Now, I will say good-night."

"I'll walk you to your door." He was out and around to her side before she had done more than step onto the running board.

He took her hand to help her down, and kept it clasped in his as they climbed the steps to the front porch of her old house. Canned laughter from the television drifted from inside. Under the porch light, Jack could see her face better than he had since they left the restaurant.

Her expression was grave again, questioning, although she said only, "Thank you, Jack. I had a good time."

"Yeah. Me, too." He bent and kissed her again, quick and hard, letting her feel some of the heat that would have him heading home to a cold shower.

The throatiness in her voice told him he wasn't alone, which was some comfort.

"Good night, Jack."

"I'll call." He let her go reluctantly, stood there when she slipped inside, gave a final uncertain smile and shut the door.

He wanted to pump his fist and exclaim, "Yes!" Or maybe hammer on the damned door and beg her to let him in. He hadn't felt like this since he was a teenager, somebody else altogether named Johnny Murray, who couldn't get enough of his girlfriend.

That teenage boy had been a stranger to him for almost nineteen years. In one day he had become someone else and taken to calling himself by another name. Jack Murray was a hard man who didn't beg and who had forgotten how a simple kiss, a certain soft voice, the memory of a scent, could exhilarate.

Making himself back away from her front door and finally stride to his Dodge, he was shaking his head over himself. How the hell had he gotten in so deep, so quick?

CHAPTER SIX

BETH STARED at herself in the mirror with disgust.
For Pete's sake, she was going to a backyard barbecue, not dining and dancing. She was supposed to
be dressing *down* from church. The kids would wonder if she reappeared in a dress she usually saved
for Rotary Club events.

Pulling it over her head, she called, "You guys
almost ready?"

"I am." Without knocking, Stephanie opened the
bedroom door. "Oh. Sorry. You're *still* not
dressed?" Her gaze went to the dress, lying on the
bed. "You're not going to wear that, are you?"

"Of course not! I was just trying it on. I feel fat,"
Beth lied. "I figured I could tell if I've put on
weight."

"Is the scale broken?"

"The scale?" She could see it through her bathroom doorway. "Um…I thought it might be weigh-
ing light. Do you know your weight? Why don't you
try it?"

Stephanie rolled her eyes but went into the bathroom and stepped on the scale. "One hundred and
ten!" she wailed. "I was only ninety-nine pounds
last time. *I'm* getting fat!"

Beth buttoned the jeans she'd hastily grabbed.

"Sweetie, you've grown at least two inches in the past few months. Of course you've gained weight. You're *not* getting fat."

Almost twelve, Stephanie was only a couple of inches shorter than Beth and gaining fast. She was at that gawky, ugly-duckling stage where her legs were too long and her feet too big, her face all eyes and cheekbones. More than Lauren, Stephanie would be beautiful when she'd matured and everything fit together. Right now, she was skinny and long.

"But eleven whole pounds?" Stephanie rushed from the bathroom to stand beside Beth and examine herself anxiously in the full-length mirror on the closet door.

Beth laughed. "I defy you to find enough fat to pinch."

"Rochelle only weighs eighty-six pounds," Steph said gloomily, turning from side to side to see herself from every angle. "She was bragging the other day."

"Rochelle's mother is barely five feet tall. I don't even want to think about what she weighs. The whole family is miniature. You can't compare yourself." Beth held up a cotton twinset in a soft shade of sky blue. "What do you think?"

Stephanie glanced and shrugged. "It's okay. If you don't spill barbecue sauce down the front."

"And I always spill something. Great." Beth shook her hair out after pulling the sleeveless sweater over her head. "I need a bib."

Her daughter giggled, sounding more like a friend

than a child. "Sheriff Murray would wonder about you, wouldn't he?"

If he didn't already wonder about her, Beth thought wryly. But he must have enjoyed their Friday night date, or he wouldn't have called the very next day and casually invited her to bring her kids for an afternoon barbecue at his house.

"Will surprised me last night," he'd said. "I got home and here he was. With company. He has a new girlfriend he wanted me to meet. She'll be here Sunday, too."

Beth had never expected to have so much in common with some boy's college girlfriend: the one was there to be approved by the dad, the other to be approved by the son. At least Will's girlfriend didn't have to hope her children were on their best behavior, too.

"Okay." Beth took one last glance at herself in the mirror. The makeup she'd put on earlier for church had stood the test of time. She fluffed her hair, decided she'd do and asked, "Do you know where Lauren is?"

"I think she's downstairs already."

The phone rang. Beth circled the bed, but the second ring was cut off as Lauren apparently picked up one of the downstairs phones. Beth quelled her brief moment of disquiet. The Caller ID she'd finally added had ended the reign of nerves imposed by their anonymous tormenter. When the phone rang these days, the caller was always someone they knew.

At the foot of the stairs, she heard Lauren chattering happily in the living room. She was talking about the barbecue and how Mom wasn't ready yet. Hearing the footsteps, she turned, her freckled face cheerful.

"Here comes Mom. I gotta go, Dad. Unless you want to talk to Steph?"

"It's Dad?" Stephanie said from behind Beth. She sounded almost as appalled as Beth felt.

How could she ask the girls to censor what they told their father? How could she even explain why they should? His anger was scary to them as well as to her, but Lauren especially wasn't old enough to have to watch every word she said to him.

But instinct obviously kicked in with the advent of teenage years, because the moment Lauren hung up the phone, Stephanie exclaimed, "Jeez! Why are you telling Dad all about who Mom is dating? You know he didn't want the divorce! And he's always talking about how maybe he and Mom can fix things."

Her younger daughter was crestfallen. "Dad just wanted to know what we were doing this weekend. It's not some kind of secret, is it?"

"No." Beth came down the last steps. "Your dad may not like the idea of me seeing somebody else, but he'd hear sooner or later anyway. Besides this isn't exactly a date."

"Then how come you were so worried about what you were wearing?" her oldest daughter wondered aloud.

Beth gave her a look. "Just because I wanted to look nice..."

"Tiffany says he's a babe. For an old guy."

Lauren's eyes widened. "But he's not Mommy's boyfriend or anything."

"He might be," Steph said blithely.

"But what about Dad?"

Beth gave a gentle tug on her daughter's ponytail and then urged her out the front door. As she locked behind them, she said, "Your dad and I are *not* getting back together, whatever he tells you. Remember how much we all yelled. That's no way to live. He's just…having a little trouble adjusting. But someday he'll meet a woman who is right for him."

"And we'll have a stepmother?" Steph trailed her mom and sister down the stairs. "What if she's wicked?"

"What if she's really, really nice?" Beth countered.

Steph dropped the subject. "Are we walking?"

"You thought we'd drive? Two blocks?"

"The neighbors will all see us. Everybody'll talk about you and the sheriff." She said it in a singsong voice, finishing with, "'First comes love, then comes marriage….'"

"Stop!" Lauren said fiercely. "Mommy's not gonna get married!" She grabbed her mother's hand. "Are you?"

Beth managed an easy laugh. "You'll be the first to know. I had a nice dinner with Mr. Murray, and he invited us over today. There might even be other neighbors there." Uh-huh. Sure. "And that is all," Beth concluded, her firmness as much for herself as for the girls.

"See?" Over her shoulder, Lauren stuck out her tongue at her sister.

"Mom!" Steph complained. "She's being a brat."

Beth stopped dead on the sidewalk. "When we get there, you will both make me very happy by being incredibly polite, eating at least a little bit of everything offered to you including foods that look disgusting, not squabbling and not interrupting when other people are talking. *Very* happy."

They both mumbled assents. Beth took a deep breath and marched on. Two neighbors, including the infamous Mrs. Finley, were working in their yards. Beth exchanged polite greetings with both and was aware of their stares following her and the girls down the street. Both, she was sure, saw them stop in front of the sheriff's riverfront Queen Anne home.

Taking a deep breath, Beth didn't let herself pause, turning up the walk between narrow hedges of boxwood. To distract herself, she studied the paint job. The color wasn't quite as soft as sage, she would have had to admit. Grass-green, perhaps.

"It's awfully bright," Steph whispered.

"I like it," Lauren said in her usual penetrating voice. "It's like a…a big playhouse."

A deep male voice said, "It's cool, isn't it?"

All three spun to face the man who let the wooden screen door bang behind him as he stepped onto the porch. No, not man, Beth realized, even as she stared in shock: teenager. Jack's son, unmistakably. In person, the resemblance was even more stunning. Dark-haired, broad-shouldered, with a face that should have been homely but was instead masculine and even sexy, Will Murray—or did he have a different last name?—must be breaking hearts wherever he went.

"You look like Mr. Murray," Lauren decided.

"Yeah, he's my dad. You must be Ms. Sommers and her daughters."

"I'm Lauren. And this is my sister, Stephanie."

Cheeks pink, Steph mumbled, "Hi."

"Nice to meet you, Will," Beth said. "Please, call me Beth."

"Okay!" He grinned. "Come on in. Everyone else is in back. We can cut through the house. Dad's been wondering where you were. He was about to send out a search party."

"We only live two blocks away." Trust Lauren.

"That's what *I* said." He lowered his voice to a very loud, conspiratorial whisper. "But Dad is the sheriff, you know. He sees bad guys behind every bush."

Will and her youngest seemed to be great friends already. Steph was suffering from an attack of shyness, probably because she was old enough to notice that *he* was the babe his dad was too old to be. Amused, Beth speculated on what Tiffany had had to say about *him*.

She forgot Will and even his father the moment she stepped through the front door. Rays of sunlight fragmented by beveled glass made intriguing patterns on gleaming inlaid wood floors. A wonderful steep staircase with a Persian runner and glossy banisters led to an upper landing. Her wondering gaze lingered on the chandelier above, until she realized she was falling behind.

Through open French doors was a living room—

no, a parlor. Several rugs in deep shades of ruby and
teal and rose defined sitting areas. The couches and
chairs were modern, deep and relaxed, but so simple
the eye passed on to the wonderful woodwork and
the turned-leg tables and the Tiffany lamp. Oh, and
the fireplace, with marble hearth and white-painted,
carved mantel.

Dazzled, she passed through the next opening into
a library with leaded-glass-fronted oak bookcases, a
huge desk and two leather chairs. Through more
French doors was a brick patio with wrought-iron
Parisian style furniture and huge terracotta and stone
pots full of late annuals. Not even her peripheral
awareness that Jack stood beside a mundane kettle
grill from which smoke and wonderful smells ema-
nated kept her from gaping at the view. The backyard beyond didn't have to be landscaped; smooth
lawn led down to the river, low at this season and
overhung by an ancient weeping willow.

"Hey."

She blinked and turned to Jack, who was smiling
crookedly at her.

"I'm in love," Beth said simply.

His dark brows quirked. "With my son?"

"Son?" She blushed at her vague tone, which
suggested that Will was a nonentity. "I'm sorry!
Will was wonderful. But...no. It's your house. Why
didn't you say?"

"I figured you'd been inside. Didn't you know
the Fullers, who I bought it from?"

"No. And, if the outside is any example, I'll bet
the inside has changed anyway."

The handsome young man beside him grinned.

"Oh, yeah. You can say that again. Dad shanghaied me into helping strip woodwork." He made a face. "Gee, that was fun."

Jack lightly cuffed his son's shoulder. "What are kids for?"

Beth was charmed by the easy camaraderie between the two, by the smile in their eyes when they looked at each other. And, oh, yes, if she was to be honest, by the sight of two such handsome men.

"Hey," Will said suddenly. "You haven't met Gillian yet." A pretty young woman with pale, boyishly short hair and spectacular green eyes had been hovering to one side. When he held out a hand, she stepped forward. "Gilly, this is Dad's friend Beth Sommers and her daughters, Lauren and Stephanie." He laid an arm across his girlfriend's slender shoulders. "Everybody, Gillian Pappas."

This time, Beth was proud of her daughters' manners as adults and kids said all that was polite once again. When Jack announced that the steaks and chicken were almost done, Gillian and Will took Steph up on her offer to help bring the rest of the food out. Lauren wandered toward the river as if drawn by the song of a siren. Beth didn't blame her. If she'd been a child, the hidden depths inside the overhanging branches of the willow tree would have called to her, too, the secrets and the shifting green colors and the murmur of river currents somehow magical.

"You must have spent a fortune remodeling this place!" She felt gauche the minute the words were out. Jack was the Butte County sheriff. Of course he had money!

"More elbow grease than bucks." He nodded toward the table. "Would you hand me that plate?"

"You should have let me bring something." Their fingers touched briefly; their eyes met, and goose bumps galloped down her spine at the expression in his.

First comes love.... Beth shook off the recollection of her daughter's ditty, as if it were a taunt that made her shiver. Not love. Not yet.

"I wanted to feed you." Jack's voice was a shade huskier than usual. "Besides, believe it or not, Will likes to cook. He makes a mean potato salad."

"And wait'll you taste Dad's lemon meringue pie," his son said, setting bowls down on the table and turning to head back into the house.

"Oooh." She smiled at Jack. "I'm impressed."

"Don't give me a hard time." His grin speeded her pulse. "I've been a bachelor for lo these many years. Whaddaya think, I had fast food every night?"

"I...hadn't gotten so far as to speculate about your diet," Beth admitted. Only about his former girlfriends, his reasons for never marrying, what he had done—or not done—that brought that grim set to his mouth when he talked about Will's mother not being able to depend on him.

Just a few little things like that.

"I'll bet you're a good cook." He heaped meat onto the plate. "Even a little adventurous."

She risked touching him again and took the plate. "Now how would you know that?"

"I saw your kitchen." His mouth had a wicked curl. "I'd swear that was a crepe pan hanging above the stove." His tone changed as he took a bowl of fruit salad from Steph. "Thanks."

"Um…you're welcome. Gillian is bringing lemonade, but she said to ask: do you want beer?"

"Nah. Unless?" He lifted his brows.

Beth shook her head. "Lemonade sounds good."

They all ate at the long, wrought-iron table. Steph hugged Beth's one side while Jack was on her other. Lauren cheerfully sat between Gillian and Will, who treated her like a little sister.

Conversation was light and general. Will grumbled about a professor who seemed to think his students had no other classes; Gillian talked about a field trip in Oregon's John Day country hunting for fossils with other paleontology students. Lauren, wide-eyed, asked if they'd found dinosaur bones.

"No, but I found the imprint of a fish. It's really cool."

Beth told stories about the oddball things people wanted to have run off on the color copier, and Jack grumbled about the makeup of the county council, which was resisting the necessity of hiring more deputies.

She was having fun, she realized as she finished her slice of pie and helped carry dirty dishes into the kitchen.

"We'll clean up," Will insisted, making shooing gestures. "Get. Gilly and I can do this."

Outside, Lauren dragged Stephanie off to the riverbank, where they shortly disappeared through the canopy of willow branches.

"This was nice, Jack," Beth said contentedly,

from her lazy position on a redwood chaise longue. "Thank you for having us."

Sitting only a few feet away on one of the wrought-iron chairs, he stretched out his legs. The denim pulled over powerful muscles. "You know I wanted to see you again."

She was not a shy woman by nature, but he made her feel that way. "I...I'm glad."

He nodded toward the river. "How do your girls feel about you dating me?"

First comes love....

She brushed off the memory of her daughter's teasing as if it were an insistent mosquito. "I think Stephanie understands. Lauren still thinks her father and I might get back together, a notion he encourages."

Jack shook his head, his gaze pinning her. "You're open with her?"

"Of course I am! It's just...difficult."

He grunted his agreement. "Does he know you're seeing me socially?"

"If he didn't guess, he knows now." The reminder edged a knife blade of tension into her peaceful afternoon. "Right before we left, I overheard Lauren telling Ray all about how we were going to the sheriff's house for a barbecue."

A frown gathered between Jack's dark brows. "Do you expect trouble?"

"I don't know," Beth said slowly. "Did I ever tell you about the phone calls?"

Expression arrested, he leaned forward. "Phone calls?"

"We'd pick up, and hear someone breathing.

Usually when the kids answered, he'd hang up."
Catching herself, she gestured. "Listen to me. I
don't know that it was Ray, but I assume. And yet,
it was so petty."

"Past tense?"

"I added Caller ID. With the block on anonymous
calls."

"You should have told me." Jack sounded per-
turbed. "If your ex-husband was making those calls,
it suggests he's waging a real campaign to scare the
hell out of you."

With some indignation, she asked, "You didn't
believe me when I said that's why he was keeping
Steph and Lauren late?"

"Sure I did."

Had he spoken too hastily and therefore insin-
cerely? She didn't have a chance to ask, because her
daughters were coming. Lauren, Beth saw immediately, had managed to get her shoes and jeans up to
her knees soaking wet.

"I slipped," she explained.

"So I see," her mother said dryly. "It's going to
be a squishy walk home. One we'd better start."
Why she was suddenly anxious to leave, Beth
couldn't have said. All she knew was that her mood
had been shattered by talking about Ray.

"You don't have to go." Jack sounded merely
polite, but the frown still lingered on his brow.

"Yes, I think we do. The girls have homework,
and I have laundry to get done to be ready for the
week." Beth stood.

He towered over her as he did the same. "I'll
walk you out."

"Let me say goodbye to Will and Gillian."

They didn't have to detour into the kitchen; the tall young man and his girlfriend were just coming out of the house.

When told Beth and the girls were leaving, Will said, "Yeah, we have to hit the road, too, Dad. Gil has an eight o'clock class tomorrow morning."

His father said, "You, of course, never sign up for one that starts before ten."

Will's grin was more lighthearted than any expression Beth had seen on Jack's face. "You got it. I figure, I wouldn't learn anything anyway. Now, by ten, the old brain is in gear. You know?"

Beth didn't. At Will's age, she'd been married, pregnant the next year. Not until the girls were three and six did she start taking evening classes at the community college in accounting and business. Ray had liked the idea, but his enthusiasm quickly cooled. He didn't want to baby-sit evening after evening. He didn't want to hear about what she'd learned. "Come on, we don't really need the money," he'd wheedled. "You don't have to do this."

"But I want to," she had said quietly, really standing up to him for one of the first times ever.

Beth knew that if she had quit school then, she would likely still be married.

Shaking off the memory, she said her goodbyes, poked Lauren who piped up, "Thank you for dinner," and ushered them ahead of her down a brick path that led through a side yard with a mature maple surrounded by a bed of glossy green ivy. Jack was just behind her.

On the front walk, Beth turned. "I really enjoyed this afternoon. I mean it. Thanks."

"Hey!" a girl's voice yelled from the street.

Beth waved at their teenage baby-sitter, who sat on the handlebar of a boy's mountain bike. She was laughing, but her gaze was avid.

"Hi, Tiffany," Steph and Lauren called, then, "Watch out!"

Jack made an abortive step toward the street as a car passed. The bike wobbled and righted itself. Both adults winced.

"Damn fool kids," he muttered.

"Steph has given up riding her bike," Beth said in an undertone, "because I won't let her unless she wears a helmet. *Nobody* wears a helmet, she says."

"She's right. They don't." He shook his head in disgust, looking up the street after the zigzagging bicycle.

"Do you see many head injuries?"

"Constantly. If as many children died or were permanently disabled from a disease, the government would be pouring money into research and treatment. Bike helmets aren't glamorous enough, apparently."

She liked him when he talked that way, with passion and caring. It gave her hope that he hadn't become a cop because he craved the adrenaline rush or the sense of power over others, that in fact he despised violence as much as she did.

As though he read the softening in her, he took a step closer and said in a low, intimate voice, "How about if I stroll over later and meet you on the front porch for a good-night kiss?"

The idea was deliciously provocative. In a rush she saw herself opening the front door quietly, slipping out into the cool night, leaning against the big square porch pillar as Jack threaded his fingers through her hair and bent his head slowly.... His face was in darkness, his heartbeat heavy under her palms....

After a quick glance to be sure Steph and Lauren were out of earshot, Beth said breathlessly, "Are you suggesting I sneak out after my kids are in bed and neck with you?"

His grin was wicked. "Something like that."

"Well." She tried to sound shocked and failed. "Are you serious?"

"Oh, yeah." His tone held something unreadable. "I'm serious."

"What if one of the girls came looking for me?" Oh, how tempted she was. "Or Ray were watching the house?"

Jack swore. "Does he?"

"I don't know," she admitted. "I'd say no, except somebody did ring the doorbell a few times, too. At the same time as we were having trouble with the anonymous phone calls. I'd open the door, and no one would be there. It was...creepy."

"Did you accuse him?"

"No." She searched Jack's suddenly tense face. "What if I'm wrong? Think how terrible that would be. It could be a teenage prank." She sounded so hopeful. "You know how many kids there are in the neighborhood. I even thought of a boy I had to fire at the store a few months ago. He was always late to work, and he kept forgetting to sign in or out, so

I wasn't sure how much he really had worked. At the time, I didn't think he was that mad. He seemed more ashamed, but who knows?''

Jack scowled. ''If you have even one more incident like that, you'll let me know. I don't like it.''

''Surely this county has enough crime to keep you occupied.''

''I have time,'' he said tersely. ''Call me. Immediately. You got it?''

Rebellion swelled in her chest like a hot air balloon, then soundlessly deflated. He was offering help out of the goodness of his heart. If he sounded a little autocratic, well, that was hardly surprising from a man who'd been in law enforcement for ten plus years. And it wasn't as if she didn't *want* to call him the next time something scary happened. She remembered how overwhelming the relief had been last Sunday, when he'd dropped everything and come the moment she asked.

''Okay,'' she agreed. ''I'll call.''

The grimness left his face, but she felt pinned by his intense dark eyes.

''Do we have a date tonight?''

''Can I, um, take a rain check?'' She felt like an idiot—no, what she felt was very young and naive, a Goody Two-shoes who didn't dare sneak out at night the way all her friends claimed they did. ''Until the girls are more used to the idea of my dating,'' she added, knowing how feeble that was as an explanation.

Jack just looked at her for a moment, but at last he nodded as if he understood more than she'd said.

"Deal," he murmured, then raised his voice. "Hey, girls, thanks for bringing your mom."

"You're welcome," Lauren said impudently.

Steph thanked him again.

Beth smiled one more time, blushed at the way his eyes narrowed and focused on her mouth, then turned away.

"Did you get sunburned?" her youngest asked, as she joined them on the sidewalk.

"I don't know. Am I red?" she asked, and was horrified at how easily—and often—she seemed to be lying today.

But then, how did you tell your children: *A man just looked at me as if he wanted to rip my clothes off, and I would very much like it if he would?*

No. Some little white lies were a good thing.

She just wished an almost twelve-year-old was as innocent these days as she'd been at that age. Steph's knowing expression was enough to deepen Beth's blush.

A week ago, she hadn't even thought about conducting a romance. Now, she was wondering how a woman did it when she had almost-teenage children.

Ah, well. There were worse problems. She just wouldn't think about those today.

RAY TOOK a deep swill of his beer. He was parked in front of the Blue Moon Tavern. Music and bright lights spilled into the dark parking lot, packed with pickup trucks and Harleys. Windows blinked with neon signs advertising beer. Beyond them he could see men clustered around a pool table and a few couples shuffling to Garth Brooks on the small dance floor.

He'd meant to go in and have a good time. Why not? His bitch of a wife apparently was. Hell, maybe he'd cut in on one of those cowboys in tight jeans and take the floor with the pretty blond girlfriend. About time he had a pretty blond girlfriend of his own.

Ray slapped his hands onto the steering wheel so hard his palms stung. He wanted his wife, not some blond slut! He didn't plan to start all over and then find out his sweet blue-eyed bride wanted to wear the pants in their marriage.

Ray still didn't know how it had happened. One day, she was meeting him at the door with soft kisses, cooking his favorite dinner, sewing cute dresses for the girls when she had time from being a wife and mother. The next day, she was talking about going back to school.

What he should have done was put his foot down right then, but he'd thought she just wanted to get out of the house a little bit, maybe pick up a skill that would let her get a decent part-time job once the girls were in school all day. Extra bucks would be nice. He'd been thinking maybe they could get a boat for fishing and waterskiing. Something nice.

Before he knew it, Beth was never home. When he saw her in passing as she slapped microwaved food down in front of him and waved goodbye, her eyes were glowing as she talked about small business administration or taking over his books. She did have a head for figures, so he indulged her. She'd get her degree in just another semester or two, she promised. Only, when she finally finished school she didn't take a regular part-time job, as he'd expected; instead, she became the manager of a stationery store. She didn't want to buy a boat, she wanted to have her own business.

Swallowing his beer and staring at a flickering Bud Light sign in the tavern window, Ray saw it clear as day, a series of little steps like a baby going from pulling up on the couch to running into the street. Beth had been working on leaving him from the day she enrolled for that first class at the community college. His role had been sugar daddy. He could hold her up, pay the bills, until she could do it herself.

Even then, he had really believed she would come running back once the going got tough or the kids cried about missing their daddy. Or she missed him. Once he'd been her whole world, or so she claimed.

Now he knew. She'd decided she needed a man, all right, but she'd found a new one.

"Maybe his gun gets her excited." Hearing his own voice surprised him. What was he doing, sitting here in the dark talking to himself?

"If I was any kind of man, I wouldn't take this sitting down," Ray mumbled. That was what he was doing. Sitting there on his ass while his *wife* let the county sheriff fondle her.

He'd had enough beers to feel alive and seriously pissed, but not enough to make him drunk. Not him! Why, this was a good time to let her know the world was a dangerous place for a woman and children living alone.

The phone calls had shaken her up, or else she

wouldn't have signed up for Caller ID. After a while the kids never answered, it had always been her. He could feel her terror even without hearing the gasp of breath, the sweaty sharpness with which she hung up.

He liked shaking her up when he had the kids, too. Maybe one of these weekends he just wouldn't bring them home at all. See how she liked that big empty house then!

Ray tossed the empty can into the grocery bag and groped for another. On the brink of popping the top, he hesitated. Maybe he shouldn't get drunk. *Just do it,* he thought.

Wasn't that an Olympic motto or something? Maybe it was a beer commercial. Hell, he didn't know.

"Just do it." He tasted the words and liked them.

Decisively, he started the engine and backed out. He didn't even have to go home. Everything he needed but a rock was in the toolbox in back. Conveniently, Ray himself had outlined a flower bed with softball-sized rocks.

Although he planned to make a quick getaway, caution made Ray park two blocks away. Damn, but nights were getting cold! He hated winter, a heartbeat away.

Ray dug out what he needed and then cut across lawns and through alleys to avoid streetlights. Plunging through a dark yard, fallen leaves crackling under his feet, Ray swore when vicious thorns snagged his pant leg. Still whispering obscenities, he turned and kicked at the shrub. Like a woman it lashed back and he let out a yelp.

He wanted to hurt something, and this was a good excuse. He found one long stiff cane with his questing fingers and then shoved the thorny arms down to a level where he could trample. Branches snapped and crunched under foot. He didn't quit until a dog barked and a porch light came on. Then he ran.

He cut through a neighbor's yard and came out in front. The rocks from the flower bed were just the size he'd remembered. One hefted in his hand, Ray crouched in front of Beth's house. No, goddamn it! *His* house. For a moment, he saw nobody in the lighted front window. Then his dear *ex*-wife, as she liked to remind him she was, wandered into view with the phone to her ear. She glanced out the window, laughing. She was looking right at him as if he didn't exist. Ray couldn't believe it! She was laughing at him. Probably talking on the phone with her new boyfriend.

A bloody haze spread over his vision and he shot to his feet. *Let her laugh,* he thought savagely, and threw the rock with all his strength.

The front window exploded in glittering, golden shards like Fourth of July fireworks. Fitting, because he'd been saving the cherry bomb since the Fourth. He lit the fuse and flung it at the jagged hole. Glinting like a tiny firefly, it spiraled through the air. Just as it went through the opening, his triumphant gaze saw a shocked face staring.

Lauren. God help him, his freckled younger daughter was right there in the room.

His anguished bellow was lost in the boom that scattered more glass and sent him to his knees with his head buried in his arms.

CHAPTER SEVEN

LAUREN SCREAMED and screamed even with Beth holding her tight. In desperation, Beth slapped her cheek just hard enough to sting.

The scream gurgled to a stop and Lauren stared with shock at her mother.

"Sweetie! I need to know if you're hurt," she said urgently. "Can you hear me?"

"I'm so scared!"

As patiently as she could, Beth repeated, "Can you hear me?"

Her youngest gave a jerky nod. Her pale freckled face was bleached to a pasty tint. Wet cheeks and runny nose didn't help. "With this ear," she whispered. "This one feels funny."

"Oh, God." Beth pulled her into a desperate embrace again. "We have to get you to a doctor."

"Mom." Stephanie appeared from the kitchen, looking scared. "The police are coming. I had to leave a message for Sheriff Murray."

"Thank you."

From where the three huddled in the entry hall, Beth looked through the arched doorway into the living room. Glass littered the hardwood floor in knifelike shards. She couldn't take her gaze from one nearly a foot long that protruded from the couch like a dagger. What if a shard had exploded point first into Lauren's tender skin?

Don't let Ray have done this, she prayed.

Her own ears felt as if she had cotton wool in them. She seemed to hear a faraway throb, like war drums. Nearer sounds, like her daughters' voices, were small and tinny, as if they came over the airwaves from a radio station she couldn't quite tune in.

But sirens…she did hear the distant wail that came closer quickly.

Beth let the two uniformed officers in and said, "Thank you for coming so fast."

It wasn't their fault that neither was Sheriff Jack Murray.

Both were men in their forties with pleasant faces and the beginnings of paunches. From their voices, either could have been the officer she talked to the day Ray had kept the girls so late.

The two examined the living room, poking the rock and bits of debris from the bomb. She and the girls waited without moving from the foot of the stairs while the two male officers searched outside and came back in with wordless shakes of their heads.

"We'll hope a neighbor spotted a prowler," one said. "Somebody might have made note of a vehicle parked briefly. That's our best hope."

They would canvass the neighborhood several blocks each way, he added. Did she have any idea who might have done this?

Beth hesitated long enough that one repeated, "Ma'am?"

"Girls," she said through the pounding in her ears, "go to the car. I'll be there in a second."

Stephanie put her arm around Lauren and led her toward the kitchen. After only a few steps, she paused. "Do we have to go outside without you?"

Beth's heart squeezed. She and Ray had moved to Elk Springs so their girls could grow up feeling safe and confident. If he had done this to them... Fury greater than she'd ever known stirred and lifted its head like a beast awakening.

"No. It's okay, Steph. Wait for me at the back door. I won't be long."

Her oldest nodded and they disappeared.

"You might talk to my ex-husband," she told the two officers. "I've called about him before. He's...angry."

They made notes about the phone calls and the ringing doorbell, about the sixteen-year-old she'd had to fire from his job. They suggested a company who would come and board over her front window until she could replace the glass. Beth hadn't known anyone could make a living boarding over shattered windows, but apparently there were plenty.

"Mainly after fires," one of the policemen said, seeing her distress and surprise.

At the hospital she and Lauren took audio tests and submitted to doctors peering into their ears. Eardrums were intact; they were very lucky. Their hearing would come back slowly. They might hear other, strange sounds in the meantime.

Beth discovered, walking through the lamplit hospital parking lot with her daughters plastered to each side, that she didn't want to go home. A hollow feeling opened in her chest as she pictured pulling into the detached garage and stepping out into the yard, unlocking the kitchen door—had they locked it at all?—walking into the empty house. She would have to search every closet, under all the beds, take her flashlight to peer into the black attic. Her solid old house, always beloved, suddenly didn't feel safe or altogether familiar.

The girls felt her shiver. "Mom?" Steph questioned, her voice high and panicky.

For the first time, Beth wished her parents lived in town. She wanted to go home and sleep in her childhood bedroom, *be* a child again instead of the parent who must always seem strong and assured.

She groped for other ideas. Maria. Of course, her friend would take them in, but Beth didn't even know if she had a spare bedroom.

And then what? Unlocking her car, she made herself face facts. They had to go home eventually. She couldn't afford just to walk away.

The anger waking inside her stirred again. No. She wouldn't give him that satisfaction.

Beth buckled Lauren into the car as if she were two years old again. Steph fastened her own seat belt and sat quietly and stiffly in the front.

Getting in behind the wheel, Beth said with false cheer, "Well, this was quite a night."

No response.

During the drive she rattled on about how mean some pranks were and didn't they remember the time the O'Learys' house was egged and the time all the air was let out of the tires on Tiffany's brother's car.

Stephanie had her head bent so that a curtain of hair hid her face. In the rearview mirror, Beth's eyes met Lauren's.

"Mommy? I'm scared."

"Oh, honey." She turned into their alley, wishing the hedges weren't so high and weren't evergreen, that the overhanging trees didn't block the streetlight with brown leaves hanging on. Wishing she had an automatic garage door opener. "There's nothing to be scared of. I really think this was the same kind of prank as those others. Someone thought it would be funny. They must not have seen us through the window. It's an awful mess to clean up, but that's all."

She heard a sniff from the back seat.

In front of the garage, she let the engine idle and got out herself to heave the door open. The backyard was a grotto of deep shadows to one side. Leaves rustled and she started. Trying to hurry but not be too obvious, Beth gritted her teeth. *Tomorrow I'm calling someone about installing an automatic opener.*

Then all she would have to worry about were the few steps to the back door.

And what might be waiting inside her house.

Back in the car, she didn't start it forward immediately. "You know," she said, "if you guys really are scared, maybe I should have a security system installed. That way we wouldn't have to worry at all." At least she'd gotten that "we" in there somewhere. Admit it. *She* was scared.

"Could you, Mom?" Steph said in a rush of heartrending relief. "It wouldn't cost too much?"

"Nope." She put the car in drive and eased forward into the garage. The very idea made her feel better. They'd get through tonight; *he* wouldn't come back, not so soon after the police had been here. And maybe she could get the security system installed tomorrow.

Sticking close together, herd creatures clustering, they all walked quickly from the garage to the back door. Inside, the girls stuck with Beth as she scanned the kitchen, glanced in the pantry and poked her head in the den.

"What if someone comes in the window tonight?" Lauren asked in a small voice.

"I called a company to come and board it up. Let's see if they have."

All three stopped on the threshold of the living room. Nobody wanted to go in. She was grateful to see that the window had been covered with ugly but solid raw boards. The fragments of glass shone wickedly.

"I'll clean this up after you guys go to bed," she said in that fake cheery voice.

"Can we sleep with you, Mommy?" Lauren asked.

Ding dong.

Beth jumped six inches at the deep chime of the doorbell. Both girls jerked, too.

Turning to stare at the door, she thought, *And a peephole, too.*

Yeah? And what good will that do, considering you have to let him in?

"Who is it?" she called.

"Jack. Let me in, Beth."

She almost fell against the door in her eagerness. The kids were still pressed to her sides when she got the dead bolt undone and swung the door open.

Jack shoved it wider to step across the threshold. He wore sweats. His hair was disordered, his eyes dark and tense as his gaze swept comprehensively over them. "You're all right." He sounded ragged asking what wasn't quite a question.

"You got Stephanie's message."

"Walked in the door five minutes ago. I called and you weren't here." A nerve ticked beneath his eye. "Scared the...dickens out of me."

Beth stepped back wordlessly, her ducklings shuffling with her. Jack followed and turned toward the living room. A profanity slipped out.

"None of you was in there?"

"I'd just started toward the kitchen to hang up the phone. Lauren was...about where you're standing. She fell back."

"A cherry bomb, the Elk Springs P.D. say." The hard note in his voice gentled when he looked at Lauren. "You can hear okay? Did the doctor check you out?"

She nodded like a small bird. "I can't hear so good out of this ear." She pointed. "You sound funny. But the doctor says it'll get better."

When he looked at her, Beth nodded. "Thank God, her eardrum didn't rupture."

"You didn't see anyone."

She shook her head.

"Did you just get home?"

"Yep. I was going to take the girls upstairs and

tuck them in.'' She squeezed both. ''In my bed,''
she whispered in Lauren's good ear.

Her daughter's sweet smile lit.

''I'm going to spend the night,'' Jack said, tone
making clear that he wanted no argument. ''On the
couch.''

Another wash of relief almost buckled her knees.
''You don't have to....''

Their eyes met. ''I couldn't sleep if I didn't.''

''Thank you,'' she said quietly.

''You're welcome.'' Jack nodded toward the
stairs. ''You been up there yet?''

Both girls shook their heads.

''Would you feel better if I check it out? Since
you've been gone? Maybe stick my head in closets?''

''Will you look under my bed?'' Lauren asked
hopefully.

''Especially under the bed.'' The smile softened
his harsh face amazingly. ''You guys brush your
teeth while I go see if I can rouse some dust bun-
nies.''

''Well!'' Beth said lightly. ''I think I'm in-
sulted.''

Any other time, she might have been worried
about how neat closets were. Tonight she didn't
care. Jack already knew everything about them. He
might as well see what it looked like under Lauren's
bed, too.

His presence made all the difference. Both girls
began to talk as they changed into nightgowns and
brushed teeth. Lauren kept saying, ''I'm talking too
loud, aren't I? I can't tell if I am.''

Stephanie admitted to screaming. "I wonder if anybody heard us?"

Passing in the hall, Jack said, "Yep. Five separate neighbors phoned the police. None of them was quite sure where the explosion had come from, but they reported hearing screams."

"Oh." Stephanie sounded satisfied. "I'll bet I'll be the only kid in seventh grade who had somebody throw a bomb through her front window."

"I should hope," Beth said with rolled eyes.

"All clear," Jack reported a moment later. He tousled Lauren's head. "Some spots clearer than others."

"Did you see any cassettes under there?" she wondered. "I have one that's Greek myths. I listen to it at bedtime, and I can't find it."

"I saw a few Garfield books, some jeans, a headless Barbie." He scratched his jaw. "A cassette now… I couldn't say."

"It's disgusting under there," Stephanie said with sisterly superiority. "She's a slob."

"Just 'cause *you* think you're a teenager now…" Lauren flared.

Beth turned them toward her bedroom. "Save it for tomorrow, okay?" Secretly she was relieved by their byplay; they sounded *normal*.

She was very conscious of Jack filling the doorway of her bedroom as she tucked the girls into her queen-size bed. She wasn't used to strange men seeing the lacy chintz pillows heaped on the window seat or the porcelain dolls sitting stiffly atop her dresser.

When Ray left, she had needed, on some deep

level, to redecorate this room, to stamp it as hers. Perhaps to pretend he'd never been an occupant. She'd stripped the tan plaid paper from the walls and replaced it with an old-fashioned flowered paper. Woodwork she painted white. Even the rag rugs were pastel colored, the bedspread a fluffy chenille in soft lemon yellow.

Alone, she was comfortable in this bedroom. It expressed a side of her that employees used to her brisk decision-making and insistence on organization and record-keeping would be astonished to know existed.

Jack was so intensely masculine, so rough-hewn and blunt, so terribly out of place in this bedroom, she wondered how he could attract her when she also was a woman who craved lace and flowery wallpaper. Or had she deliberately created a bedroom in which any man would feel out of place? One designed, even, to repel the male of the species?

Disconcerting thought.

She kissed the girls good-night and left on a bedside lamp. Each had brought a book to bed. Lauren, who was rather fond of scary stories, had chosen to read a collection of knock-knock jokes. Which she would no doubt want to read aloud and drive her sister crazy. Tonight, Beth suspected, Steph would be indulgent.

"I'll be up in a few minutes," she promised, and joined Jack in the hall.

Downstairs, she said, "I'm going to clean up the glass. I don't want Steph and Lauren to see it again."

He frowned but nodded. "We should take pictures for the insurance company. Do you have a Polaroid?''

Ray's parents had sent Stephanie one for Christmas. Beth took pictures from half a dozen angles and left them to develop on the hall table while she fetched two pairs of gardening gloves and a cardboard box to hold the shards of glass.

Jack picked up the big pieces while she gingerly swept the rest into a dustpan. Her gleaming hardwood floor had gouges and scratches; the fabric of the couch was torn seriously enough to need re-upholstering.

Beth reached out and fingered a tear in the tough material. ''Thank God we weren't sitting here.''

Jack lifted a couch cushion and shook it. Glass tinkled out. ''Do you think your ex-husband did this?'' His voice was hard.

Beth clutched the dustpan as if it were a shield and said helplessly, ''You know, I have absolutely no idea. I don't want to think he could or would, but…he's become a stranger. And perhaps he didn't realize what could happen. The police officers thought the bomb went off outside the window, which is why the glass exploded inward with such force. It was probably just supposed to make a big bang in the middle of the floor, not do so much damage.''

''If any of you had been right in front of the window, you could have been badly hurt.'' Jack's eyes were dark, his tone inflexible. ''Aside from the glass, you could have lost hearing permanently.''

''I know.'' She had to squeeze her lips together

and close her eyes against the burning. "For a prank…"

"This was one hell of a prank." Jack shook out the remaining cushions with suppressed violence. "Let me finish here."

"No. I'm okay." Beth went back to her sweeping in silence.

When they were done, Jack insisted on carting the glass out to the garbage can beside the garage.

While she waited at the back door for him, Beth was hit by a wave of dizzying exhaustion. She swayed and had to clutch the door frame. When he came toward her, his gaze sharpened and he let the screen door slam behind him.

"You are hurt."

"No." She managed a shaky smile. "Just tired. Listen, you don't have to stay. Really."

"If you kick me out, I'm sleeping on your doorstep."

"Then…we do have a spare bedroom. I'll make up the bed…."

His big hands gripped her elbows. "No. Tell me where I can find a blanket and I'll sleep on the couch. It should be fine if I turn the cushions over. I'd rather be down here just in case our friend comes back." His grip tightened and he swore when a shiver passed through her. "He won't come. Paranoia is an occupational hazard for cops. Just…indulge me."

"I think…" She felt herself leaning toward him, the weakness in her knees not altogether from weariness. "I think you're the one indulging me." Beth tried to smile again. "I wish I wasn't constantly needing your help and having to say this, but—thank you, Jack.''

His voice roughened. "I wasn't here when you needed me tonight.''

"Sure you were. You helped me clean up, didn't you? Or maybe I should say, you're here to pick up the pieces, in more ways than one. You can hardly sit at home waiting for my panicky phone calls.''

So why did she want to think of him doing just that? Why did she feel completely safe only when he was around?

Tonight, she was free to feel her acute exhaustion only because Jack would be sleeping on her couch. If he weren't here, she wouldn't have dared be tired. She would have slept lightly, or not at all, a fierce mother protecting her babies.

As a modern woman, she should dislike knowing she needed a man to make her feel secure. The disconcerting part was, she felt a primal satisfaction in his determination to keep her safe, in his tenderness and in the anger that lurked in his dark eyes.

"I could tell you were uneasy." Jack's hands slid up her arms; his fingers flexed. "We knew your ex had found out you were seeing me. I should have expected something.''

"*I* didn't expect this. Nothing like this.''

Don't let it have been you, Ray. Remember that you love your children, even if you hate me.

"I'd like to have a little talk with him tomorrow." Anger knotted Jack's jaw muscles. "I want to hear with my own two ears what he has to say.'' He grimaced at her expression. "You don't have to say it. I know the Elk Springs P.D. will follow up. If I went, it might provoke him further. I'm telling you what I'd like, not what I'm going to do.''

Now tears stung again. On impulse, Beth stood on tiptoe and pressed a kiss to his hard mouth. "Thank you," she whispered again.

He groaned. "This isn't the good-night kiss I had in mind.''

"Me, either." Tiredness and shock seemed to have swept away her inhibitions, because she heard herself saying, "But it is bedtime, and I'd like it if you kissed me.''

He said something in which, through the drumming in her ears, she heard only her name, but that was enough. "Beth," came out so hoarsely, with such longing, her knees finally gave way and she could only hold on to him as his head bent.

Jack kissed her with intense hunger but heart-stopping gentleness. Even as she melted against his powerful body, she felt his iron restraint and knew this kiss would lead no further. She could revel in these unfamiliar sensations without anxiety.

The urgent touch of his tongue brought cramps to her belly; the way his hands squeezed her upper arms made her yearn for him to cup her breasts. The scrape of his jaw against her cheek, the heavy thud of his heartbeat beneath her palm, were pure male.

A whimper slipped from her throat, shocking her. Sex had been...okay. She'd liked knowing Ray needed her; she liked arousing those feelings in him. Her pleasure had never equaled his, which he hadn't guessed. She had always made love silently.

It was the tiredness, the stress, muddying her emotions. Beth stiffened. Her swimming thoughts began to clear. Gratitude was a dangerous mix with romance. She didn't want to lie to Jack even wordlessly, with her kisses. She wasn't ready for…for more. How foolish it would be to wake up one morning and realize the only reason she was in bed with this man was that she felt safe when he was with her. There had to be more. So much more.

Jack felt her new hesitation almost as soon as she did. He gave her a last tender kiss and stepped back, still holding her as though he thought she might collapse if he let go.

"The…the blankets are upstairs." She ought to say something else, but what? Her mind's brief clarity had passed; her head might as well have been stuffed full of batting for all the good it was doing her.

But Jack didn't seem to expect anything else. "I'll walk you up. You look as if you're ready to collapse."

She nodded dumbly. He steered her to the staircase and she plodded up, one foot in front of another. At the linen closet, she stopped.

"In here, huh?" With those strong, competent hands, he gently propelled her into her bedroom and toward the bed. The lamp cast a golden glow on the girls, who were sound asleep and curled up close with their heads on one pillow.

"Wait. I should brush my teeth…" Beth whispered.

Voice a low rumble, Jack said, "You can do it in the morning."

"Oh." She could, couldn't she? She was the

mother. If she didn't want to brush her teeth, she didn't have to. "Okay."

His mouth found hers again for one quick, hard kiss. "Sleep tight," he murmured.

When he was gone and she heard the quiet snick of the hall closet door opening, Beth stripped. Careful not to wake the girls, she worked her nightgown out from under her pillow. It felt heavenly going on, cool and silky. She turned off the lamp, tumbled into bed and fell asleep nearly instantly to the sound of her daughters' soft breathing and to the fragrance that was them, more precious to her than her own life.

Why can't you feel the same, Ray? she begged, in her last conscious thought.

CHAPTER EIGHT

RAY GROPED desperately for a reason to blame Beth for the terror and shock he had seen on Lauren's face.

Dear God, what had he done? he would wonder one moment as he sat on the recliner that was the only piece of furniture he'd taken after the divorce. Head buried in his hands, he kept seeing her, his sweet, innocent Lauren with her cute freckled nose and penny-bright hair, Daddy's little girl since her first heart-melting smile at six weeks old.

But, goddamn it, everything *was* Beth's fault! he reminded himself in a conscious effort to shore up his defenses. They should be a family. It was Beth who'd kicked him out, not because he'd been a bad father or husband but because she wanted to rule the roost. The kids wanted Daddy home. Beth was the one who wouldn't listen. What alternative did he have but shock tactics?

He didn't sleep at all. With sobriety came remorse. He lay in bed and stared at the dark ceiling, seeing the cherry bomb arcing toward the window and then hearing the boom, the glass exploding. What if Lauren was hurt? He didn't know; he'd tried calling later, prepared to play "Dad just wanting to talk to his kids,'' but he'd gotten the answering machine. What if Lauren was in the hospital?

My fault, he told himself dully.

Hollow-eyed, heartsick, Ray got up in the gray light of dawn and knew he had to go see Beth. Confess, even.

She was always up early to get the kids ready for school and herself for work. The two hours he had to wait crept like soldiers on their bellies penetrating enemy lines. The painful slowness came from the near-unbearable tension.

At eight o'clock, Ray drove over there. Lights were on, so at least his whole family wasn't in the hospital. For the first time, parked out on the street, he wondered whether she would have called him if Lauren was hurt bad. Or did his rights as a father not extend to being at her side if she were injured or sick? Ray wondered bitterly.

Sitting in his pickup, he rehearsed what he'd say. He tried it out loud. ''I did a dumb thing last night. I never meant anyone to be hurt. It's just that I love you and the girls, and not being here with you makes me crazy.''

Beth would be mad, he figured, but she'd get over it. What woman didn't like the idea of being so desirable she could drive a man to desperate acts? That was exactly what she'd done: cracked the whip until he jumped. She just maybe didn't expect him to jump so far, that was all.

''Yeah, okay.'' He slid his hands up and down on the steering wheel, palms sweating.

Were the girls up yet? He pictured Beth at the kitchen table in the fuzzy quilted flannel robe he'd given her for Christmas a couple of years ago. It was the exact blue of her eyes. She'd looked so pretty in that robe, especially in the morning when her hair was slipping out of the braid she usually confined it in at night. Her mouth would be soft, her eyelids heavy. She was more feminine then than later in the day, when she had starched herself and firmed her mouth until she'd become Ms. Businesswoman. The early-morning Beth was the woman he'd married, the woman he thought she still was inside.

Ray muttered a profanity. "What are you waiting for?" he asked himself.

Maybe he didn't have to say, "I did something dumb." Maybe he could tell her a neighbor had called and said he should know something bad had happened at his house last night. "Why didn't you call me?" he could demand. "Didn't you think I'd be worried about my own daughters?" He could just see what she would say.

The sight of her front door opening had him stiffening. Was she coming out for the newspaper? Or had she seen his pickup?

But it wasn't his wife who stepped out on the porch. Shock spread in Ray's breast like a paper towel blotting an ink stain. Sheriff Jack Murray was slipping out of Beth's house, his clothes and hair rumpled like those of a man who hadn't come prepared to spend the night but who undeniably had.

Thick and black, the shock became rage.

That slut. Her own daughters down the hall, and she was taking a man into her bed. Not just any man, but the cop who had tried to throw his weight around with Ray.

It looked like she wanted a man in her life again. But she hadn't chosen the one she'd promised to cherish and obey till death do them part. Hell, no! Now she wanted that bastard of a cop who thought Ray Sommers would tug on his forelock and say, "Yes, suh," every time he *suggested* how Ray could handle his own family.

Snarling, Ray watched the county sheriff take a quick look around as though to be sure no neighbors saw him sneaking out of the divorcée's house. His gaze didn't even pause at the pickup truck in front of the neighbor's house two doors down.

Then he walked away. Did she know how stupid it was to sleep with a man who sneaked in and out of her house? Ray thought viciously. The son of a bitch would dump her, once he got what he wanted.

Yeah, well, she'd get what she deserved, too.

To think he'd meant to apologize. Ray turned the key, the engine roared to life, and he squealed the tires pulling away from the curb.

Nothing he'd done or said had mattered to her at all. If Lauren had been hurt last night, it *was* Beth's fault.

She wanted war, and that's what she'd get.

"No, THE SHERIFF has gone home," Beth told Stephanie. "But he did spend the night, just like he promised he would." She flipped a pancake. "Please get the syrup out of the fridge and yell for Lauren. Breakfast is ready."

"How come he didn't stay for breakfast?" Lauren asked a few minutes later, as they all sat at the kitchen table.

"He had to go home and change clothes for work." She suspected that, even more, he was avoiding the inevitable awkwardness of sharing the breakfast table. He might have hoped to leave before neighbors started backing out of their driveways to go to work, too. There would be gossip, even in this day and age, if people knew he'd spent the night.

"I could stay home with Lauren if you don't think she should go to school," Stephanie suggested, her expression noble.

"Thank you for the offer," Beth said dryly, "but I think Lauren will do fine at school. And you, if I remember right, have a math test today."

"Yeah, but I could make it up," Steph said hopefully.

Her traitorous sister, appearing from the kitchen, said, "I *want* to go to school. It's boring at home. Besides, everybody will pay attention to me today, once they hear what happened. I'll be a *heroine*." She savored the word as well as the idea.

"You didn't *do* anything," Steph mumbled. "Mom had to slap you 'cause all you did was scream."

"You screamed, too! You even said!"

Beth sighed. "Enough. Eat. You're both going to be late if you don't get moving."

She had never wished more that she could just stay home. If she worked for someone else, like most people did, she could have called and explained, then gone back upstairs and succumbed to the exhaustion that still weighed her down as if it were humidity in the air.

But, no, Beth thought wryly. She'd been determined to be the boss, which meant she had to reap the bad with the good. Her only help today was a new employee fresh out of high school who was cheerful and willing and who could work the cash register, but who still didn't know the stock. She certainly couldn't meet with the office furniture rep coming by at ten.

BETH SUPPOSED she appeared much as usual. Jennifer, the young employee, chattered about her date the night before and her new roommate who had brought a big-screen TV with her that she apparently liked to watch into the wee hours. Jennifer's voice sounded slightly muffled to Beth, who still heard drumbeats thumping hollowly in her ears.

She decided not to carry the new line of office furniture, which was too high-priced for her clientele. Business was slow, a fact for which she was— just this once—grateful. She pretended to be busy in her small glass-enclosed office. Really, she brooded.

Had Ray thrown the rock and the fireworks last night? The police officers had promised to call her; why hadn't they? Ray would know she'd named him. What would he say the next time she saw him?

Beth wished she'd been able to suggest to the girls this morning that they not tell their friends about the incident. In a town this size, soon everyone would know and be gossiping. Just so the girls believed it *was* a prank, and didn't know that their mother suspected their father.

For some reason, it was easier to worry about Ray and what he might do next than it was to think about Jack, who had once again come rushing to her side the moment he knew she needed him.

She liked him. More than liked him. He made her feel like a teenager in love for the first time, giddy and anxious at the same time. Last night, if she hadn't been so tired… Beth blushed, remembering the hard feel of his body, the hand that had rested beneath her breast, brushing the plump underside, the way his tongue stroked hers.

He would want more soon. Not because he'd think she owed him, but because he was a man. Dating was different when you were all grown-up than it had been back in high school, when she and Ray had started going together. How patient would Jack be with her?

How patient did she want him to be?

What if she slept with him and her kids found out, or they heard gossip at school? She had to worry about the example she set. Would they read into her behavior a justification for sleeping with boyfriends when they were sixteen?

Did she really, truly, *want* to take a man's hand and draw him up the stairs to her bed? Beth wondered in confusion.

The day after Ray moved his clothes out, Beth had gone to the bedroom in a fury of energy and torn the old spread from the bed and the blinds from the window. That very afternoon she had moved the furniture and begun scraping paper from the wall.

What had been an impulse had become grim determination. She wanted no reminders of Ray.

Every subsequent choice, Beth realized now, had involved a near-physical wrench between who she had been and who she would be. When she was Mrs. Ray Sommers, everything always had to be the way he wanted it. Shopping, Beth would wistfully put back the sheets or towels or place mats or dishes or even paper napkins *she* liked. Ray hated yellow, she would think. Or he wouldn't like the pattern. They couldn't have it if he thought it was sissy or flimsy or a dust catcher. Over the years, she had come to make every choice only after an internal check: would Ray like this?

It had seemed essential to eradicate him from her bedroom to make a point to herself: her life was now her own. No man had a right to question her taste. This room, at least, was entirely hers.

So how could she, so quickly, be tempted to invite any man at all into her bedroom and her life?

And most especially, a man like Jack Murray?

Beyond her cubicle, Beth heard Jennifer's voice and winced.

"Gee, I don't know. I guess I could find out," she said doubtfully.

The customer murmured something; a moment later, Beth heard the front door close.

She should have gotten up and gone out to see what Jennifer didn't know, but she just flat-out didn't feel like it.

Beth lifted her cup, sipped and made a face at the cold coffee. Getting a fresh cup seemed like too much effort.

Flipping the pages of a catalog without interest, she reverted to her brooding.

Jack had lulled some of her fears. But a scene like last night's reawakened every one of them. She'd seen his expression when he saw the living room. He hadn't been shocked by the destruction the way she was. Angry on her behalf, but not aghast. How could he be? she admitted. He'd seen worse. Which was what scared her. She didn't even want to think about what he *had* seen.

But she knew. She read the newspaper. Jack was worried for her because he had seen firsthand what angry ex-husbands sometimes did to women. Murder and rape and multiple-fatality car accidents were part of his *job*. His very existence made a lie of the tales she and Ray had told themselves and each other when they moved to Elk Springs.

This was a safe community. The kids could walk to school. The pace was slower. Neighbors cared. Heck, probably nobody even locked their doors, they'd declared. Crime just wasn't an issue, they thought, because they wanted it to be true.

Now she knew that no place was safe, that no one was immune. But she sensed that she could recover her illusions if life went back to normal and she could again believe the people she knew were good.

In Jack's world, people were not all good. Too many were selfish, venal, remorseless or vicious. The good guys in his world were cops who slammed people against walls to cuff them.

What would *he* say about her porcelain dolls and floral wallpaper and lacy pillows? She saw him again, standing in her bedroom door looking around. He didn't *belong*.

And why was she even wondering these things? It seemed so *soon* to feel these confusing desires and fears and tugs toward and away from Jack. She hardly knew him.

Yet he had slept on her couch last night so that she and the girls would feel safe. Because of him, she had not lain awake listening for the shatter of glass, the creak of a footstep, the whisper of someone pushing through shrubbery.

Ray had formed her fears about men.

Jack protected her from Ray.

It was a simple equation. In more primitive times, that would have been reason enough to let Jack Murray claim her as his woman.

But she'd learned already that a man could be lover and enemy both. She had adored Ray, once upon a time. That he had chosen her seemed a miracle, when she was seventeen. How could she know that someday she would dread him coming home? Or that he was capable of terrorizing her and his own daughters?

Mightn't Jack Murray have the same potential for anger and violence? Ray had been tender in the early days, too. He had always been gentle with the girls. Now he felt wronged. What would happen when *Jack* lost his temper?

Was she crazy to hang around to find out?

If she had to be tempted by a man, why not that nice pharmacist who'd suggested dinner sometime?

''Ms. Sommers?'' Jennifer called. ''The copy machine says it's jammed, and I'm not sure how to open it.''

Beth rubbed her aching temples and wearily rose to her feet. Coming out of her tiny office, she smiled at the customer waiting for copies.

''The latches are right here,'' she said patiently.

DESPITE THE IBUPROFEN she'd taken earlier, Beth still had a headache that evening. She'd succumbed to temptation and had a pizza delivered for dinner, which pleased the girls. Usually they had to help clean the kitchen, but tonight she said, ''There's not much of a mess. You two go do your homework.''

''Okay.'' Lauren scrambled up.

''Can I call Roslyn?'' asked Steph, heading for the phone. ''She wanted help with the math.''

''Sure.'' Beth piled dirty plates. ''Just use the phone upstairs, okay?''

The girls raced up the stairs, their feet thundering. Beth carried the dirty dishes to the sink and bent to unload the dishwasher.

A knock on the kitchen door rattled the glass pane. Heartbeat leaping, Beth whirled.

Framed in the glass was Ray's face. When he saw that he had her attention, he gestured peremptorily.

Why was he here? And why at the back door?

How could she not let him in?

She unlocked the dead bolt and opened the door. ''What do you want, Ray?'' If she didn't sound friendly, she didn't care.

''To talk. Come on,'' he said impatiently. ''Let me in.''

"Have you been standing out there watching us?"

He was clean-shaven, but the smell of beer wafted on his breath and his eyes were bloodshot. "I waited a minute until Steph and Lauren left. So what? This is between you and me."

"All right." She backed up and let him pass, hating to have him even that close. Pretending a calm she didn't feel, Beth went back to putting dishes away in cupboards. "What is it you think we need to talk about?"

Ray leaned against the cabinet and crossed his arms. "Are you seeing that sheriff?"

She didn't look at him. "If you're asking whether I'm dating him, I don't think that's your concern."

"Not my concern?" He gave an incredulous laugh. "Damn it, Beth, I love you! I figured you needed some time to figure out we belonged together, and that was okay. Everybody gets their head screwed on wrong sometimes. I mean, we shouldn't have moved over here or bought that business. With you always working, we were bound to have problems. But, okay. You've had time. So, what? Now you're sleeping with some other guy?"

Old habits die hard. Without thinking, she shot back, "What would make you think I'm sleeping with him?"

His expression became crafty. "Let's just say, personal observation."

She breathed hard. "You're watching me. Stop!"

Ray straightened and leaned toward her, his anger as rank as the beer fumes. "All I want to know is, are you sleeping with this guy?"

"It's none of your business, but no!" After a moment fraught with tension, the two staring at each other, she was the one to break eye contact. Turning back to the cupboard, she carefully took a glass from where she'd set it with the bowls and moved it to where it belonged. Just as carefully, she stripped all emotion from her voice. "Ray, we are divorced. Not because I worked long hours, but because you didn't like who I've become and I'm not so sure I like who you've become, either. You can't tell me you enjoyed fighting all the time."

"We don't have to fight." His tone became wheedling and he reached across the open dishwasher and grabbed her hand. "Remember the good times, Beth? We were happy. Back before…"

When he stopped, Beth finished for him. "Before I dreamed up all that nonsense about going to college and getting a job? Before I discovered what I wanted to do with my life?"

"So sell the store and get a job." He was begging now. "Something you can leave behind at five o'clock. I know we could be happy again. *You* know we could. Think about the girls. This has been hard on them."

His shifting mood alarmed her as much as his anger had. How drunk was he? She yanked her hand from his and backed up a step. "You've made it harder than it had to be. What's all this been about, Ray? Keeping them late and challenging me constantly?"

His voice rose. "They're my kids, too."

"So it's okay to scare them?"

Was it her imagination, or did his expression become wary?

"Whaddaya mean, scare them?"

Hands on her hips, she said flatly, "You know exactly what I mean. Ringing the doorbell, phoning at all hours and then not saying anything. I'm not the one who was scared, Ray. It was Stephanie and Lauren. Your daughters."

His jaw worked. "Why can't you need me?"

Oh, she was getting mad now. "I was supposed to come running to you because I was being stalked? Is that it?"

"Stalked?" He made a dismissive sound. "Blow it up into some big deal, why don't you."

"Oh, and what about last night?" She slammed the dishwasher door shut to vent some of her fury. Her voice was rising, but she couldn't seem to help herself. "That wasn't a big deal? Do you know how close Lauren came to being badly hurt?"

"It was just a warning!" he shouted.

She sucked in a breath and stared at this stocky, strong man she had once loved. "You admit it," she whispered. "You threw a rock and a cherry bomb through our front window."

"I was getting desperate." He cleared his throat. "Desperate for you, I mean. Damn it, Beth. Missing you has made me crazy! A man does stupid things sometimes when he's in love." He grabbed at her clumsily.

Beth shoved with all her might and he staggered back. "Don't you ever touch me again," she said with loathing.

He stared at her in bafflement. "I didn't mean to

hurt anybody. Especially not sweet Lauren.'' His voice slurred on his daughter's name. ''You know she's the apple of my eye. I wouldn't hurt her.''

''You almost did.'' Beth went to the back door and opened it. ''Now get out.''

She saw the moment comprehension entered his eyes. ''I'm not done saying what I got to say. You're just mad. Okay. I screwed up big time. But what do you want me to do? Crawl on my belly?''

''Leave. That's what I want you to do. I'm done listening.'' Her hand was locked in a death grip on the knob.

''I'm not going anywhere!'' he shouted. He looked twice as wide suddenly, a looming frightening presence in her small kitchen. He was crazy.

Scared for the first time, she waited white-faced. ''Please go. The girls are going to hear you.''

''I don't give a good goddamn! Let 'em hear!'' He shouted at the ceiling, ''Steph and Lauren, are you listening? You want us to be a family, don't you? Come tell Mom. Come say, 'I want my daddy home.''' He slammed a fist against a cupboard door and snarled at Beth, ''The truth is, sweetheart, they're going to wonder, just like I do, whether Mom didn't kick Dad out because she's got an itch in her pants for some other man.'' He made an ugly sound. ''Next time you try threatening me with losing visitation, think how that'll play to the judge. He'll want to hear all about who is creeping out of here in the morning.''

In a harsh whisper, Beth said, ''For your information, Jack Murray spent the night on the couch so that we could sleep soundly after *you*—Lauren and Stephanie's devoted father—nearly killed your own child.''

He loomed over her, bloodshot eyes glittering with rage. "You think I'll go quietly, you're wrong! If this is my fault, it's only because I let you have your way too often. A woman who doesn't want to be a wife isn't...isn't any kind of woman at all! What are you teaching my girls? You're no kind of mother. You shouldn't have them.''

Shaking now, she repeated, "Get out! Before I call the police!''

His face darkened. "Don't threaten me, bitch!''

Standing up to him was the hardest thing she'd ever done, but she didn't waver. "Now.''

He lashed out so fast she didn't see it coming. His hand cracked across her cheekbone and she fell back against the stove. His hand lifted once more, and she tried to regain her footing, get her hands up to shield her face.

In a blur someone else was there. Ray was bodily lifted and flung cursing back against the cabinets.

In a voice she'd never heard before, Jack Murray said, "What kind of scum hurts a woman?''

On a stream of obscenities, Ray fought back. Beth cringed in the corner of the kitchen and watched the sheriff slam her ex-husband against the refrigerator so hard blood poured from his nose, splattering the white surface and dripping to the floor. In a moment, Jack had wrestled him to the floor. A knee shoved in the small of his back, Jack cuffed him, yanking Ray's arms back until he screamed with pain.

Both men were cursing, sweating, straining. To her horrified eyes, their rage and blood-engorged faces looked alike. She was nothing to them now; their battle was too primal for her to matter.

Vision blurry, hand pressed to her mouth, she looked across the big man grinding Ray's face against the floor and into her daughter's shocked eyes.

Stephanie looked at the men and then back at her mother. ''Mommy?''

''You have the right to remain silent.'' Voice brutal in its matter-of-factness, Jack wrenched Stephanie's father to his feet and shoved him up against the bloody refrigerator. ''You have the right to an attorney.''

Oh God, oh God, oh God. Beth didn't hear the rest. Back pressed to the counter, she inched by, staying as far from the two men as she could get. Only when safely past did she fly to her daughter and snatch Stephanie into her arms, turning her away from the horrific sight of Ray with swollen eye and blood-smeared face.

And from the sight of their noble protector, so casually hurting and humiliating a drunk man who had lost his family.

''I called him,'' Stephanie mumbled against her shoulder. ''I got scared and called Jack.''

''It's all right,'' Beth whispered. ''It's all right.''

But it wasn't, and they both knew it.

CHAPTER NINE

ADRENALINE HAD roared through his body from the moment he heard the girl's voice on the phone. She sounded unbearably young.

"Mr. Murray...I mean, Sheriff..." She quavered to a stop. Swallowed. "This is...this is Stephanie Sommers. My...my dad is here, and he's yelling at Mom, and Lauren and me, we're scared."

"I'm on my way," he promised her, and hit the street at a run. Two blocks took him no more than a minute. He didn't give a damn that one neighbor had to slam on his brakes backing out of a driveway, or that another who was mowing turned to stare.

Outside Beth's place, Jack listened for raised voices. Nothing. Had the bastard already knocked her out? Fresh fear had him taking the steps two at a time.

Before he could knock, the front door swung open. Stephanie had been waiting for him. Face pinched, she stood back and said in a low, frightened voice, "They're in the kitchen."

"You were smart to call," he told her with an approving nod.

Muffled by walls came a drunken bellow. "I don't give a good goddamn!"

The girl flinched. "He used to yell like that all

the time. Why does he get so mad?'' she asked in sad bewilderment.

"I don't know.'' Jack didn't like the tone of what he was hearing. "Sweetheart, why don't you go up to your bedroom? I'll talk to your father.''

He didn't wait to see if she obeyed. Stepping quietly, he passed the dining room just as Ray Sommers's snarl rattled pictures on the wall. "Don't threaten me, bitch!''

Jack entered the kitchen unseen. Sommers had his back turned. Beth stood with one hand on the open back door, facing Jack, but with her entire being focused on her ex-husband.

"*Now,*'' she ordered, her face pale but set, fear in her eyes but her chin held as defiantly as ever.

Jack had never admired her more. Her very determination made him hesitate. Would she thank him for interfering?

Sommers was clearly drunk; his broad stance didn't disguise a momentary weave. He might just go without ever having to know his daughter had been so scared of him, she'd called Jack.

Things happened so damned fast, Jack was still flat-footed. With lightning speed, Sommers backhanded Beth, sending her staggering back against the stove. Jack moved then, with the despairing knowledge that he was too late to keep her from being hurt. As he grabbed the son of a bitch and flung him away from Beth, all Jack could think was, *I shouldn't have hesitated. Damn it, I shouldn't have hesitated!*

Out of the corner of his eye he saw her face, swelling, turning purple. Sick anger gave him the strength to easily counter her drunken ex-husband's blind punches. Blood splattered when Sommers's nose met the refrigerator. Let the bastard learn what it felt like. He wrestled Ray Sommers to the floor and yanked handcuffs from his back pocket.

He started reading him his rights without thinking. Halfway through Jack stopped, realizing this wasn't his arrest. He looked up to see that Beth had scooted past and she and her gutsy daughter now stood clutching each other and staring with equal horror.

"Call the Elk Springs P.D.," Jack said from between gritted teeth. "This is their turf."

Sommers tried to flip himself over, grunting obscenities.

Jack applied his knee. "You don't want your daughter hearing that kind of language."

Ray Sommers lifted his head awkwardly and saw Stephanie with her mother. On a groan, he let his forehead drop with a clunk onto the hard floor.

Jack met Beth's eyes. "Take her out of here," he ordered, with a nod toward the door.

She gave him a last look so full of shock and something painfully like hate, he could tell she was still as focused on her ex-husband as ever. Gratitude was going to be slow coming.

He heard her make the call. Sommers had quit fighting. When Jack looked down, he saw tears track the blood on the man's cheeks.

"What have I done?" Ray Sommers asked hoarsely. "Oh, my God, what have I done?"

Jack could almost feel sorry for him. Almost, but no cigar.

"You've blown it, you bastard," he said. "That's

what you've done. Say goodbye to your nice family.''

He hauled Beth's ex to his feet and planted him in a kitchen chair. Sommers slumped, head hanging, and wept. He hadn't said another word when the Elk Springs P.D. came, raised eyebrows at Jack's presence, went through the formalities and hauled Ray Sommers away.

Jack went looking for Beth and found her sitting on the living room couch, staring straight ahead at her boarded-over front window.

In profile, her face had a purity that awakened an ache under his breastbone. Somehow, even as an adult, she'd maintained an innocence that stirred a sense of chivalry in him. She and her daughter weren't so different, both doing what they had to do but not understanding why anyone could want to hurt them.

But she heard his footstep and turned her head, revealing her right cheek, swollen and already purple. Her eye would be black tomorrow; she saw him only through a slit in the puffy flesh and through her one good eye.

''Is he gone?''

''Yeah. We need to get you to Emergency.''

She shook her head and then flinched. ''No. I'm okay. I'll get an ice pack.''

''Beth…'' He sat on the couch beside her.

''No.'' Sounding completely inflexible, she looked back implacably, nothing in her stiff posture suggesting she wanted to be held. ''I'm not leaving the girls, and I'm not making them sit in a hospital waiting room for two hours. There's nothing wrong with me that ice and a few hours won't cure.''

''Where are they?''

''Upstairs. I made them go so they wouldn't see their own father being shoved out in handcuffs.''

A frown began gathering on Jack's brow. ''You sound like you'd rather he strolled out and drove himself away.''

For the first time, her gaze fell from his. ''No, I... I don't know what I want. I just don't understand why it came to this.''

''Because he's obsessed with you and determined that you be the obedient little woman.''

''I never wanted to see him beaten up or bleeding.'' Her voice was almost inaudible.

Beaten up? Maybe he was a little slow, but not until now had Jack realized that he, not her son of a bitch of an ex-husband, was being cast as the bad guy. The stereotypical brutal cop, apparently.

''What in hell does that mean?'' he asked evenly.

Even her damaged eye sparked. ''It means you enjoyed throwing him around! It means that for a minute there I was scared of you, too! It means—'' Her voice cracked.

Jack shot to his feet. ''He'd just hit the woman I'm falling in love with. How was I supposed to handle him? Ask him politely to leave? The way you did?''

She hugged herself, her unwavering gaze plainly despising. ''The woman you're falling in love with. You sound like *him*.'' She couldn't say his name; even ''him'' tasted bitter, Jack could see. ''I know you mean well, but you're just like him. You were as furious as he was, as ready to hurt someone. I want no part of it, Jack. Thank you for coming tonight—but please leave now.''

God. She was kicking him out. She didn't want him because he'd defended her the way he should have defended Meg all those years ago.

Furious and afraid at the same time, he stalked toward the front door, then swung back to face her. Unclenching his jaw, he said harshly, ''Tonight I handled your ex-husband exactly the way I would have any violent man who wouldn't back off and who resisted arrest. He was drunk and blind to sense.''

Her mouth worked. ''I saw your face.''

''And I saw yours.'' His voice was pure gravel, scraping skin raw. ''You don't think you were angry? You don't think you could lash back, if someone hurt one of your daughters? If you'd walked in to see that son of a bitch backhanding Stephanie? 'Please leave?''' He followed up a savage mimicry with a scathing, ''You know what, sweetheart? You *wanted* me to protect you from your ex-husband. What do you say? Was that all that attracted you to me in the first place? Well, maybe tonight you'd better think it over—how did you think I *would* protect you? Or did you get exactly what you asked for?''

He felt a primitive satisfaction in slamming her front door behind him. Night had descended, a deep purple-black. The anger Beth had feared in him kept Jack warm halfway home before it wore off. He stopped suddenly and gripped the pickets of a neighbor's fence, his own head bowed as he struggled for ragged breaths.

Beth Sommers had plenty of reason to fear any manifestation of male violence. He'd known that all along. He could have been more understanding.

He let out an oath that would have widened her eyes. How could she not see the difference between him and Ray Sommers? Her ex was on the thin edge, drunk and in a rage; he wouldn't have been satisfied with giving her a black eye. In his view, she threatened his masculinity. Her very resistance goaded him. Until he was willing to admit his own problem, he was a dangerous man. He'd have hurt Beth badly tonight if he hadn't been stopped.

Jack lifted his head and stared across Mrs. Finley's dark yard to her golden, lace-curtained window beyond which, mercifully, no shadows shifted.

I did what I had to do, he told himself, but his self-righteousness crumbled under a sickening thought: *On that long-ago day, did Ed Patton say the same, after he beat the crap out of his daughter's boyfriend?* Patton had been defending Meg, hadn't he? Did he justify a moment of remorse the same way?

Had Ed Patton conducted his whole career as a brutal law enforcement officer under the same unshakable belief that he was doing what he had to do?

The very possibility made Jack feel sick. He'd worked under Police Chief Ed Patton's tutelage. He had been determined to be a man who would never crawl again, never beg, never fail a woman the way he had Meg. Who better to learn from, he had thought, than the man who had been able to humiliate him so easily?

Somewhere along the way he'd known how warped that thinking was. Too far along the way, maybe. There'd been a time he was a cop too much like the man he now recognized as a monster. He had been too ready to use his fists or his weapons, too ready not to understand the shame in a man's eyes, too blinkered to see the whole picture.

But he'd have sworn he didn't wear those blinkers anymore, that he was a good cop and a decent man. Stumbling home, he asked himself: Had there been another way to stop Ray Sommers? Or had he, Jack Murray the man, not the cop, been itching to hurt him?

He spent half the night staring at the dark ceiling and rerunning the scene over and over, a director in the editing room wondering how it would play to audiences. How else could he have reacted? What if the woman wasn't Beth, the man not Ray Sommers? What if he'd walked in on two strangers, like he had that first time when Sommers was shattering clay pots against her front door?

He examined his own emotions as well as he could remember them. Had he *enjoyed* the rush of adrenaline, the way some cops did?

God help him, how would Ed Patton have handled it?

Groaning, he grabbed the pillow and buried his face in it. Okay, how about Renee or Meg Patton? he asked himself. They were good cops both, but possessing a woman's touch he'd once seen as weakness.

But no matter how many times he played it, Jack couldn't come up with an alternative for him. He'd walked in too late; he'd let himself be a step behind, in part because he was trying too hard to respect Beth's ability to deal with her ex-husband on her own. There was no way he could have let Ray Sommers's fist connect with Beth's face again.

And the bastard had fought. Jack had had to manhandle him. He hadn't intended him to smash his nose against the refrigerator. It hadn't bothered him. *Okay, admit it,* he told himself, fingers clenching the pillow, *you did feel a moment of blood lust, of satisfaction Meg or Renee wouldn't have shared.* But he hadn't tried to draw blood. He had wrestled Sommers to the ground as efficiently as he could, given that the other man was fighting him with all his strength. He'd cuffed him neatly, held him down in the regulation way.

Jack saw again the hostility and contempt in Beth's eyes, and a groan shuddered from deep in his chest. He was in love with a woman who detested him because he was who he was, because he'd done no more than what she asked of him.

His teenage girlfriend had despised him because he couldn't fight back. Beth despised him as much because he had.

He had never expected again to feel the anguish he had the day Johnny Murray lost his girl and his self-respect. Meg was gone forever, but he'd spent a lifetime fighting to be able to look at himself in the mirror. Jack Murray hoped like hell he wasn't wrong to stare squarely at himself tomorrow morning.

RAY SOMMERS AWAKENED in a jail cell for the second time in his life. Somebody was using a maul to split open his head as if it were a round of knotty hemlock. In a nightmarish sequence, he rolled over and puked his guts out into a basin waiting for him.

Only then, with a foul taste in his mouth and agony crashing through his skull, did he remember why he was here.

Stephanie. His pretty, gentle daughter. Behind closed eyelids, he saw her stare as if he were the psycho stepping out of her closet in a slasher movie.

Ray let out a hoarse cry. She was right. God help him, she was right. He wasn't her daddy anymore. How long had it been since he'd thought about what she needed or wanted?

His belly empty, his mouth full of cotton, he lay back on the bunk with his forearm blocking the painful light from his eyes. The sledge kept whamming down, driving that sharp-pointed maul into his skull. The steady throb was like a deep-toned bass, background music to his black thoughts and the visions that came as quick as he could banish them.

Him sitting at the wheel of the pickup last night, downing beers. Not getting drunk; not him. But, wincing, Ray saw the pile of empties on the passenger-side floor. Must've guzzled eight twelve-ouncers. He who'd never drank more than a six-pack a week, not in his married days.

Next he was standing outside the kitchen door peering in, a damned Peeping Tom, not so much hungry for the sight of Beth's face or his children's as he was angry because they were in there and he was outside.

The shouting... He could hear himself, although it was hazy what he'd said or she'd said. *I love you and want you back,* was what he meant to say. Maybe he had, maybe he hadn't.

Most of all, he kept seeing her face. She didn't love him, that was plain. She looked at him with such contempt and sometimes fear. Ray wasn't sure which was worse.

Again he groaned, his face twisting as he fought to hold back tears.

He was a lowlife who deserved both. He'd hit her. Hit his own wife. His *ex*-wife. No matter how much rage washed through him, he'd never done such a thing before. Never even thought about it.

That expression on her face had been more than he could stand. Without Beth his life was nothing. Empty. And there she was, staring at him as if he were a kindergarten teacher caught slapping the five-year-olds. He had almost heard the crack as his self-control snapped. He hurt so bad, he wanted her to hurt that bad, too. He wanted her sorry. He wanted...

Sweating now, Ray curled into a fetal position on his side. Mother of God, what would he have done to her if that cop hadn't come? Would he have kept hitting and hitting until the red haze covering his vision cleared?

Was it in him to kill a woman?

He whispered a hoarse prayer, though he wasn't a praying man.

He didn't deserve Beth. Never mind his girls. He didn't deserve to live. Whatever the law did to him wasn't enough.

And Stephanie had seen him. She must have been the one who'd called the sheriff. She'd seen her own dad spitting blood, facedown on the floor in handcuffs. She knew who had hit her mother.

He hadn't just lost Beth for good last night, Ray thought in despair. He had lost at least Stephanie. Who could blame her if she never wanted to set eyes on him again?

The hot, humiliating tears came then, wrenched out of him by racking sobs.

"Not my little girls," he cried into cupped hands. "Don't let me lose my little girls, too."

BETH STAYED UP into the small hours comforting Stephanie and Lauren, explaining again and again what grief and alcohol could do to a decent man. She had to reassure Stephanie that she had done the right thing to call Jack even though her own heart was breaking and she would have given almost anything for him not to have come.

She knew what a fool she was even to give the time of day to such an idiotic thought. If Jack hadn't come, Ray would have hurt her even worse. He might have killed her. It happened. Jack had saved her.

How could she *blame* him for riding to her rescue?

"Do you hurt really bad, Mommy?" Lauren's small hand touched her mother's injured cheek with incredible delicacy.

"No, no!" She smiled, although that *did* hurt. "It looks worse than it feels."

The girls lay on each side of her on the bed, both

nestled so close she knew they were afraid to be separated from her.

Throat closing, she wondered how could she blame Jack when he had saved not just her, but her daughters, from worse?

"Dad is really in jail?" Stephanie asked gruffly.

"Yep, and probably feeling pretty crummy by now. I could tell he was drunk."

"Will they let him out tomorrow?"

Both girls were very still, waiting for her answer. She gave them each a squeeze. "I don't know. But you don't need to worry. He's going to be ashamed of himself and in plenty of hot water. We're just going to have to wait and see what happens."

"Will he make us keep going with him for weekends?" Stephanie asked, eyes pleading.

"Not for a while. Not until he works out his problems." *If he ever does,* remained unspoken. "But I hope you can eventually. I know he loves you."

At least, she'd *thought* he loved them. How could she be sure now? But some lies had to be told.

Eventually the girls fell asleep. Pressed between them, treasuring their closeness but also feeling trapped by their need, Beth had more than enough time to brood.

She heard Jack's scathing voice. *How did you think I would protect you?*

Looking back, Beth despised herself. He was right; she had craved, so desperately, the security she felt with him. Had she *wanted* that sense of security to be an illusion? How could she be angry because he'd proved it wasn't?

She told herself for the hundredth time that she *was* grateful he had come, that she didn't blame him for anything he had done. It was only that she didn't want to be involved with a man capable of that kind of violence. She hated the rage that had risen from both men like the smell of sweat, the bared teeth, the guttural obscenities as they struggled.

From now on, she would *know*. Her mind's eye would see the snarl beneath the smile, and she would be afraid of what he could be. Jack had been kind to her thus far, but she couldn't live with the possibilities.

No—if she were ever to have another serious relationship, it had to be with a gentle man.

One who would have been incapable of wrestling her crazed ex-husband into submission, a small voice whispered in her head. *Who might not even have come when Stephanie called.* Was that really what she wanted?

Her daughters found Jack a comfort; obviously, Stephanie had trusted him more than she did her own father.

Eyes feeling grainy, Beth stared into the darkness. She couldn't date Jack just to keep him around like a security blanket for her children.

Or for herself, she added hastily, in the fear that he was right in his accusation. Perhaps the very facet of him that she now feared was what had attracted her initially, when she needed him.

But they had no future unless she could trust him. And she could never completely relax around a man so readily capable of violence. She would always wonder when it might be unleashed on her.

Beth slept finally, and was surprised not to awaken until hot bands of sunlight passing between window blinds laid golden bars across the bed. Ten-thirty, she saw, turning groggy eyes on the clock. Stephanie stirred beside her, while Lauren murmured and burrowed into her pillow.

"Hey, sleepyheads," she teased. "Rise and shine."

She hadn't set the alarm. *Write notes for both girls excusing their late arrivals,* Beth added to her mental list for the morning routine. Better than sending them to school tired and fearful.

Beth didn't hear from either man that day. Would probably never hear from Jack again, she admitted to herself, not after the things she'd said to him. She would have to call and thank him again, soften what had sounded like criticism. She hated to think he didn't understand. She knew in her heart that the problem wasn't with him, it was with *her.*

Which didn't change the outcome.

The arresting officer from the Elk Springs P.D. did leave a message saying that Ray had gotten out on bail but was fully cooperating. What did *that* mean? she wondered bitterly, before erasing the message on the answering machine so the girls didn't hear it.

Ray phoned her at work the following day. She was alone in her office working on orders for a new line of greeting cards while a clerk covered the register. When she recognized his voice, Beth almost slammed down the phone.

"Don't!" he pleaded, as though he'd read her mind.

Breathing hard, she hesitated, holding the receiver away from her as if it embodied him.

"Beth, I'm sorry. I had to tell you once, I'm sorry."

She swallowed and replied with steel in her voice, "I won't accept this apology. I'm sure you understand."

"Yeah. I understand." He sounded…sober.

"Why, Ray? What did I ever do?"

"Nothing." Defeat came through in his voice. "I just couldn't deal with losing you. That's no excuse. I don't want you to think I'm making one. I'm just…" A rasping sound might have been a suppressed sob. "I just went crazy."

Tears rained down her cheeks, although she could not—would not—let him hear them. "Yes. You did. Not just last night, either. You've been crazy for a long time now."

He was silent for a long moment. "I've been drinking."

"I know that, too."

"I went to AA last night."

Surprise held her silent.

"If I can't make it on my own, I'll check in to a treatment place. But I think I can do it. I want to see Steph and Lauren again."

A hand closed over her heart. "Is that a demand?"

"No, I…" He noisily cleared his throat. "I have to earn the right. I know that. I'm…asking. Hoping."

She said nothing. Was this complete humility a ploy? How was she ever to believe him again?

"Say something." His plea was ragged. "I love Steph and Lauren. I never meant…"

"To hurt them? But you did." How hard she sounded!

Suddenly he was crying. "I didn't mean… When I saw her face…"

"Stephanie's?"

"She hates me, doesn't she? She should." He struggled with the sobs, mastered them. Voice gritty, her ex-husband said, "They're all I have to live for. Please give me the chance to make it up to them."

"With candy and late movies?"

Another silence. "You can't forgive anything I've done, can you?"

"Not yet," she said. "Maybe eventually."

"I want to be their father. That's all. I'm begging, Beth. Please. Give me a chance."

She was shocked to have to wonder whether she was enjoying his desperation. How much did she want him to crawl?

Heaven help her, was she really any better than Jack, who had given an ugly smile when Ray's blood splattered?

"Yes. Of course." She closed her eyes wearily. "You can talk to them. I'm not going to force them to visit you, not if they're afraid. But you can come see them this weekend, as long as you're sober."

He sucked in a breath. Voice low, Ray said, "Thank you, Beth. I'll come Saturday. One o'clock, if that's okay."

"One o'clock," she repeated, before adding, "I've supported you as a father all along, not for your sake but for theirs. I thought they needed you.

I'm not so sure anymore." It was one of the hardest things she'd ever had to say, but she had no choice. "Ray, I'm going to be plain here. This is your last chance. If you scare them again, I'll go to court and have your visitation rescinded. Don't think that I won't." She didn't wait for a response. Instead, Beth quietly hung up the telephone without saying goodbye.

I have to open the door to him, she had once told Jack. Now she knew the enemy for certain, yet still she had to invite him in. He was her children's father. How could she not?

CHAPTER TEN

CONSIDERING he hadn't known the woman all that long, he was sure as hell taking her rejection hard. Jack went through every stage of grief from denial to depression, A to Z.

During denial he called Beth several times, leaving messages on her answering machine that went unanswered. She'd have awakened the next day and realized she was wrong about him, he convinced himself. That distant thank-you speech she left on *his* answering machine was meant to be conciliatory.

Yeah? Then why didn't she return his calls?

Because she didn't want to talk to him, Jack finally had to admit. If he hadn't finished himself off in her eyes by slamming her husband's face against her refrigerator and leaving his blood for her to clean up, he had done the deed by cloaking himself in outrage and accusing her of hypocrisy.

What the hell else had he expected? She was scared to death of her creep of an ex-husband, who'd just hurt her. Then the two men had fought across her kitchen; she'd seen the father of her children slammed to the floor and cuffed; she'd had to comfort her daughter who'd seen the same. And what does her knight errant do? Jack mocked himself. Dry her tears? Accept her hysterics?

Nah. He'd lashed back with words damn near as vicious as her husband's heavy hand.

Now he wanted her to call with soft apologies. If anybody owed those, it was him.

But that message, the one in which he groveled, didn't win a response, either.

Somewhere in there he hit the stage of grief called anger. Beth *had* used him, he decided. Or maybe she was getting back together with the bastard. Women did that all the time. Call the cops, scream, "He's hitting me! Please come. I'm so afraid!" Then refuse to file charges, and next thing you knew they were a happy couple again.

Only, from what he heard she wasn't backing down, and Ray Sommers wasn't fighting the charges. Wally Stevens, the arresting officer, said when he returned Jack's call, "The guy's going to AA every day, I hear. Ms. Sommers says she's agreed to let him talk to the children this weekend, with no other concessions on her part. Hell, maybe this was a one-time thing."

"One-time? He's been stalking her!"

"Booze muddies a man's thinking."

"You're starting to sound like all those pathetic women who plead with their men to come home." Jack realized his lips were drawn back from his teeth. Why was his temper stirring at the mildest of suggestions that Ray Sommers might have some redeeming qualities? For Lauren and Stephanie Sommers's sakes, he should hope so.

"I'm waiting to make a judgment," the ESPD detective said, not rising to meet Jack's irritation.

"I don't like the guy," he growled in explanation.

"You have good reason."

But not necessarily the ones he should have, Jack thought in disgust once he'd hung up. There he went again, rummaging in his soul as if it were a junk drawer on his tool bench. As he drew out bits and pieces, he could feel and see the rust, crumbly and red as dried blood. His fingers stuck to gluey, un-identified globs covered not with hair and dirt from being in the bottom of the drawer, but rather with petty or cruel things he'd done or said, with mem-ories of pleasure taken in the way a man quailed at a nightstick or business end of a revolver.

Sitting right there in his government-decorated of-fice, starkly lit by fluorescent panels, his desk as untidy as his secretary would let it become, Jack was suddenly somewhere else. Some*body* else.

He was Johnny Murray, teenage jock, cocky as hell because he'd aced a physics final that morning and because the prettiest girl in school was his. Not only his, but so hungry for him she'd talked him into sneaking off campus at lunchtime to go to her house, empty with Daddy at work. Which meant she wanted him bad, right?

Johnny was so damned horny, he kept grabbing her breasts and nibbling on her neck right there in her living room.

Of course, she wanted to be persuaded. She was worried about her father coming home for lunch.

"In the middle of the day?" He put all the force of his charm into his grin. "You said yourself he never does."

"Yes, but…" She closed her eyes when he peeled her shirt over her head. "We should…at least…go up to my bedroom.'' On a gasp, she let her head fall back and he nipped the silky flesh. ''In case…'' she whispered.

''In case what?'' He sucked on her breast and thought he might explode.

''In case…''

''Your dad's not coming home,'' he said with absolute confidence. Her musky scent rose as he peeled off her panties.

Oh, she was sweet and hot. He couldn't wait. Her fingers were fumbling now with the buttons on his fly. The little butterfly touches, tap, tap, tap, were sweet torture. Jack ran his hands up and down her smooth thighs, squeezing her buttocks.

He was on his knees, his jeans around his ankles, stroking her and ready to ram home, when some sound jarred him from the mood.

''Oh, my God!'' Meg screamed. ''Johnny!''

He fell backward onto his butt and tried to stagger to his feet as he yanked his jeans up. A frantic glance showed her father standing in the living room doorway. Even when he was being polite, Police Chief Ed Patton was intimidating. Today, his face purple with rage and his hand resting on the butt of his gun, he was scary.

Hands shaking, Johnny half turned away and tried to get his fly buttoned over a woody. He was swearing silently, stupid with shock. What would her father do? He wouldn't *shoot* Jack, would he?

''Get dressed,'' Chief Patton said, in this dead, cold voice.

Meg's face was bleached of color; she stared up

at her father as if he were a cobra rearing above her, ready to strike.

"Get dressed!" Patton bellowed. "I won't have a whore sitting here naked in my living room!"

Though terrified, Johnny was impelled to protest. "Sir, I..." He was humiliated when his voice cracked. "It's not her fault," he tried to say. "I..."

Her father crossed the room swiftly. Johnny didn't even see his fist coming. Just...*crack.* He fell across the coffee table, blood splattering and blinding him.

Meg was screaming; he could hear her. A grenade seemed to explode against his chest. Agony blossomed. He tried to lift his cheek from the solid wood top of the coffee table to tell Meg he was all right and to quiet her screaming. Through the haze of pain and blood, he saw her father clobber her before swinging back around.

"Get up," he ordered. His boot lashed out again, sending Johnny tumbling back off the table.

On his hands and knees, he retched.

"Get up. Face me like a man."

Somehow, Johnny shoved himself to his feet and staggered upright. He tried to wipe the blood from his face.

The most merciless eyes he'd ever seen drilled him. "How do you feel about my daughter?"

"I..." The pain was unbearable, shrinking his world to a desire to escape this room. "I don't know."

"Are you ever going to touch her again?"

He would have said anything. "No, sir."

"Call her?" Patton snapped.

Johnny shook his head. He was going to pass out.

He knew it. The floor wanted to rush upward. Bile gathered in his throat.

"See her?"

One eye was swollen shut. He closed the other so that he couldn't see her staring, staring, from where she still sat on the couch.

"No," he whispered.

Ed Patton's fist slammed into his face, just below the swollen eye. The pain was so intense Johnny thought he was dying as he crashed to the floor again. This time the scream was Johnny's, as high-pitched as a girl's.

"What if she calls you?" that hard, cruel voice asked.

He couldn't get to his feet. Johnny began crawling toward the door.

The booted foot smashed into his ribs again. "What if she calls you?"

His guts heaving, Johnny cried, "I'll hang up."

One more kick. "Then get the hell out of here!"

Somehow he did get up. Reeling, almost falling, he made it to the door, staggered out. Clinging to the rail, he got down the porch steps and threw himself into his beater.

Instinct more than vision got the key into the ignition; he slammed his foot onto the accelerator and rocketed back into the street without looking to see if another car was coming.

Get away. Get away. Get away.

He didn't think about her. Didn't think about anything but his own miserable, sniveling hide.

He got away, all right, and left her to face…what?

All Johnny could find out, when he secretly called her house two days later, was that Meg was gone.

A sixteen-year-old girl had had to face the devil alone, because he'd abandoned her. Something terrible had happened to her. Maybe she was even dead.

Because he'd let her old man beat the crap out of him. Hadn't even fought back. No, he'd just tucked his tail between his legs and run as fast as he could without even thinking about her.

What did that make him?

Unfortunately, Johnny Murray looked at his swollen face in the mirror the next day and knew....

"Sheriff?" asked a voice from the doorway.

Jack swung around so fast, he bashed his foot on the desk. "What?" he snapped.

The young sergeant inched backward until not much more than his nose showed around the door frame. "Uh...uh, telephone call. Sir. Chief Patton. Sir."

"Yeah. Okay."

At the quiet click of the door, Jack planted his elbows on his desk, buried his face in his hands and knotted his fingers in his short dark hair. *Damn.* Double damn.

What in hell was wrong with him, tumbling back in the past so far he lost sight of the present?

He wasn't that sniveling kid anymore. Twenty years of history had passed under the bridge. He wasn't just a cop, but *sheriff* of the whole of Butte County. He'd taken Ed Patton's job as chief of the Elk Springs P.D. and done it better than that bastard ever could, and then he'd one upped him by being elected sheriff of the larger law enforcement agency.

He had no reason—goddamn it, *no reason*—still to sweat when he remembered Johnny Murray. Johnny Murray, jock, 3.75 GPA high school student, who thought the world came easy, was dead and buried. He's dug his own grave, said the requiems and been born again.

Jack Murray ran from no man.

Instead, he splattered other men's blood with his fist. He saw it, thick sullen droplets running and smearing on the shiny white door of the refrigerator, right below a cartoonish schoolgirl drawing of a home surrounded by comically bright trees and flowers.

Jack gave his hair a painful yank and lifted his head.

Not his fist! He hadn't punched Ray Sommers. Hadn't meant to hurt him. *He was not Ed Patton reincarnated.*

Yeah? he mocked himself, a cruel edge to his reflections. Didn't seem as if he'd quite convinced himself, any more than he was confident bone-deep that Johnny Murray had stayed buried. Hell of a man he was: not sure whether he was a brute who enjoyed hurting other people or a gutless wonder who would still save his own skin even if it meant throwing a woman to the wolves.

The red light on his telephone flashed rhythmically. Renee Patton. Could be worse. Might be Meg calling to find out if he'd talked to their son recently. The son she would have told him about that day, if

Johnny Murray hadn't crawled away and left her to her fate.

He shook his head again like a wounded animal and finally made a guttural sound, stabbing the blinking light and picking up the receiver. He'd summoned other voices from his past—why not add one, right here on the telephone?

"Murray here."

"Hi, this is Renee. Am I interrupting something?"

A bath in self-pity.

"Nah. What can I do for you?"

"We had a jewelry store robbery last night. Not as crude as you'd expect. This had the feel of a pro. I wonder if you've heard of others."

He sharpened to attention. "Yeah, yeah. Let me think."

It took him a minute, but he remembered a similar heist in a jewelry store in Juanita, a small resort town that fed on the ski area, and another he'd heard about in Bend.

Renee made thoughtful sounds and took notes. He gave her what names and numbers he could and asked her to keep him informed.

Then, on impulse, he said, "Can I ask you something?"

"Sure." She sounded surprised. "What's up?"

He was already sorry he'd opened his mouth. How did he say, *Are you a better cop than I am?*

"I handled a domestic disturbance call the other day."

"You did?" Surprise had edged into astonishment. The sheriff of a large county handled politicians, not drunken husbands.

"A neighbor. The little girl called me because she was scared."

"Uh-huh."

He rubbed his chest where his esophagus was burning. "Afterward, the woman was angry at me. She claimed her ex and I were two of a kind. But, damn it, I handled him the only way I knew how!" He let out a breath that harrumphed. More evenly, Jack continued, "I don't like to think I'm too much like your father. You and I have worked together for a long time. So tell me—do I use force too readily? Do I look like I *enjoy* hurting somebody?"

"No." Renee Patton didn't even hesitate. "I won't lie to you, Jack. There was a time when I wasn't so sure. Not that you were like him. You never were. To him everything was black and white. Somebody did wrong, Chief Patton smashed him like a bug. People thought he was hard on crime. Victims groups hailed him. But they were all wrong. He did what he did because he enjoyed every minute of it. Do you remember that poor bastard who was going to torch his girlfriend's house? The one who lit himself on fire and died in agony while my father laughed?" Her shudder came through the telephone connection. "That was Ed Patton. You are not and never were anything like him."

"But?" He waited for what she hadn't said.

"You wore blinkers. The victims were the only ones whose humanity you saw. On a domestic disturbance call, *her* pain, her fear, blinded you to the pain and shame in *his* eyes. I was never sure why that was.''

With sudden clarity, he knew. *He* had been the victim.

''You've changed, Jack. You've...softened. I mean that in the best way.''

Still he sat silent.

''Tell me what happened. Since I'm being brutally honest, I'll tell you if I'd have done anything differently.''

He sounded as emotional as a kid standing up in front of a class giving a report on Ethiopia or Belize. The hardest part was admitting to his initial hesitation.

When he was done, Renee said, ''What's giving you pause about this? What *could* you have done differently?'' She sounded genuinely puzzled.

''Talked him into walking away, maybe.''

''You think he was going to stroll out with you?''

''No.'' Ray Sommers had been incapable of rational decision at that point.

''What if he'd hit her one more time? What if he'd really hurt her?''

''What are you saying?'' Jack asked. ''That you would have jumped the bastard, too?''

''I'd have done exactly what you did, except I might have pulled my gun. If he was as crazed as you describe and he'd ignored me, I might even have had to shoot him. That woman complaining doesn't know what she's talking about,'' Renee said flatly. ''Go in peace, Sheriff.''

Feeling lighter than he had in days, Jack let out

a rumble of laughter. "Consigning me to down under already?"

"Wouldn't think of it. Somebody might decide I should run for your job. God forbid," she added piously. "The mayor is bad enough. The county council is all yours."

They talked politics briefly more as a decompression than because they had anything to say, then exchanged goodbyes.

Jack hung up with a steady hand and a hopeful heart. Before he could have second thoughts, he called Beth's house again.

To her answering machine, he said, "I want you to think, Beth. I stopped Ray the only way I could. Whatever you may think, I didn't want to hurt him. I didn't want your daughter to see him cuffed on the floor, either. I do my job. I don't figure humiliating a man is part of it. I understand why the scene upset you so much, and I shouldn't have said the things I did. I, uh, miss you, Beth." He took a breath. "I'm a cop. I can't change that. But I'm more than that. I thought we were getting to know each other. Will you think about the man you do know? And call me?"

He hung up feeling dissatisfied, wishing he were more eloquent. But he'd said what he had to say. If she didn't respond this time…

Jack pressed the heel of his hand to quell his heartburn. If she didn't call him back, he didn't know what he'd do. He hadn't loved often in his life. Why she was the one, he didn't know. But he very much feared she was. Forty was creeping up on him.

Beth Sommers, he guessed, was his last chance at the kind of happiness all three Patton sisters had found. And that chance seemed to be waving a regretful goodbye.

BETH FIDGETED in the kitchen. From the living room she heard the soft murmur of voices, the pauses, some painfully long. She'd agreed to let Ray talk to the girls alone, but she didn't have to like it.

The temptation to eavesdrop was almost irresistible. She would have liked to think nobility kept her from invading the privacy of her children and their father. But, no. Beth knew better. She was staying clear of the living room half out of fear of being caught hovering outside the door, and half… She gave a soundless sigh and resumed pacing. The other half—admit it—was that she didn't want to hear Ray abuse himself. The only way he'd ever win his daughters' trust again was by being completely honest now, by admitting to flaws he would have bitterly denied to her even a week ago.

He had so much to confess. First up was looking Lauren in the eye and telling her that *he* had thrown the cherry bomb that terrified and almost deafened her. He had to admit to having frightened them with those phone calls and ringing doorbells. To having lied to them, used them. To his alcoholism, and rage.

Strangely, she didn't want to hear what would be a pathetic confession. His children were the ones who had to forgive. She would rather cling to memories of Ray as a decent, strong man.

And to her anger.

She opened a cupboard and stared into it without

any memory of why she'd gone to it. Did she want a cup of tea? She was too restless. She needed something to *do*.

Pacing the length of the kitchen again, she happened to glance at the answering machine that hung on the wall. No new messages; one old.

The one she'd saved several days ago, listened to at least once every evening after the girls had gone to bed.

I, uh, miss you. Closing her eyes, she heard the soft rumble of Jack's voice. That small hesitation, almost a throat-clearing, got to her; more than anything, it revealed how hard it was for a man like him to admit even so much about his emotions.

Resting her forehead against the cool painted wood of the kitchen cupboard, Beth whispered, ''I miss you, too.''

Was it as simple as he made it sound? She couldn't deny there was more to him than the badge he wore or the gun he carried. The flash of anger and violence was no more Jack Murray than the tears she'd shed that night were Beth Sommers. They were a part, not the whole.

So what had her running scared?

He might be like Ray.

But Ray wasn't a cop. He was a truck driver. Any man could be controlling, whatever his outward guise. A profession did not define character.

Jack's expression when he'd fought with Ray had scared her. But what did she expect? A few of Ray's wild swings must have connected to Jack's chin or the belly. He *had* seen Ray clobber her. Ray was drunk, his language obscene. What was Jack supposed to do, say politely, "Sir, please extend your hands so that I may cuff them?"

She'd been a fool, Beth thought unhappily. Understanding that, unfortunately, didn't dispel her fear.

Her pacing had taken her almost into the hall, where she paused, straining to hear. A small giggle made her blink and then smile reluctantly. Her children were generous. They needed their father and wanted desperately to be able to forgive him.

The voices resumed, still too hushed for her to hear. After a moment, she went back into the kitchen and returned to her reverie.

It had been so hard to get her college degree despite Ray's disapproval, to work toward a job that would give her some self-esteem, to stand up to him during those endless fights in their last year of marriage. It had taken every bit of courage she had to ask him to leave.

She could not face living with an angry man again.

Who asked you to live with Jack? her commonsense side inquired.

But she wasn't a casual woman. She couldn't see dating a man if there was no possibility at all of the relationship going somewhere. Fun wasn't enough for her.

She might be misreading Jack. After all, he had to be in his mid-thirties, and he'd never married. So maybe he wasn't interested in anything beyond a flirtation or a short affair. Maybe that was all that ever interested him. But...well, he *seemed* serious. The glint in his eyes was very, very serious.

That, she guessed, was what scared her most. She didn't know if she ever wanted to give her life into any man's keeping.

But she did miss him. Oh, she did! And she knew the girls did as well. He had been so kind, so protective, so easy to talk to. And there were those kisses.

What if she never had a chance again to feel the way she did with him? She wasn't quite ready—but fate didn't always wait until a convenient moment to knock. Was she really going to be a coward now, huddling inside and not answering that knock on the door?

It could get awfully lonely in here, Beth admitted. The girls were growing up. Right now they needed her full-time, but Stephanie was nearly a teenager and Lauren not that far behind.

She should think about her own life, too. And how big a risk was it, really, to see Jack again? The first time he yelled at her, she'd say goodbye. She'd done it once, she could do it again.

Her hand had been creeping toward the telephone even before she had reasoned her way to a conclusion.

She dialed his number from memory, which embarrassed her considering how few excuses she'd had to call him.

The mechanical form of his voice said, "Murray here. Leave a message if you want me to call."

"Jack, this is Beth." She sounded breathless. She kept stealing glances toward the hall so that she'd know if Ray or the girls approached. "I wonder if you're free this evening. I thought perhaps you'd like to come over for dessert. We could talk after the girls go to bed.''

The phone rattled into its cradle, her hand was shaking so much by the time she hung up. In disgust she balled her hands into fists. For Pete's sake, all she'd done was ask a man for a date.

A man who scared her.

"Mommy?" Lauren called. "Where are you? Daddy went home!"

She hadn't even heard the front door. Beth hurried to the living room. "I'm right here. He left already?"

"He said to say goodbye." Stephanie, perhaps symbolically, sat in the armchair a little removed from her sister and from where her dad had sat on the couch.

"Oh." Beth hesitated. "How did it go?"

Stephanie shrugged, almost sullenly. Lauren said, "Okay."

Did she probe?

Darn right! She wasn't being nosy; she was giving her girls a chance to talk about something important to them.

"Do you want to tell me what he said?" she asked, perching on the arm of Stephanie's chair. More symbolism.

"It was a bunch of excuses," her oldest daughter mumbled.

Lauren gave her sister a chastening look. "He said he was sorry. He said he'd been drinking too much beer, and he missed you and us and he got confused and mad and did dumb things. But he promised he won't do them again."

"He *said* he's quit drinking." Stephanie hunched her shoulders.

Beth was careful not to touch her daughter. "That's what he told me, too. I think he can. It will make a big difference in his personality. Alcohol makes him angrier and less in control. You know, he wasn't always like this. Quitting drinking will help."

Stephanie looked up, eyes miserable. "Do I *have* to go to his house?"

"No." This time, she'd go to court and fight him tooth and nail to protect Steph's right to choose. "But," Beth continued, "I hope you'll want to." She smiled at the surprise on her daughter's face. "He really does love you, you know. He was a good father, and I hope he can be again. There might come a time when he doesn't deserve to be given another chance, but I don't think that time has come yet."

Stephanie opened her mouth, but Beth held up a hand. "No, I'm not done. I hope you do give him another chance, for your sake, but I'm not going to make you. The decision is yours, and I'll back you up whichever way you go." Her glance took in Lauren, curled in a small ball at the end of the couch. "Both of you. It's okay if one of you wants to see him and the other doesn't. Whichever way you want to go," she repeated.

Stephanie's stiff posture relaxed, but her tone was scathing. "*She's* ready to say, 'Oh, gee, it's okay, Daddy.' *She* didn't see him."

Now Beth did lay a hand on Steph's thin shoulder. "Lauren's younger. It's maybe easier for her."

"Daddy's nice!" Lauren protested, a cloud gathering on her brow. "*You* liked it when he took us to that movie and bought all that candy and stuff!"

"Until I found out he did it just so he could make Mom mad. It's not like he cared whether *we* had fun!"

"Don't yell!" Her sister clapped her hands over her ears.

Stephanie sucked in a breath as if to scream back, but with a loud harrumph she sagged lower on the chair. "She's such a baby."

"She's your best friend and ally," Beth pointed out. "She's always been closer to her dad."

It *was* easier for Lauren, always had been. Her sunny nature didn't allow her to poke beneath the surface, to hunt suspiciously for dark motives. She wouldn't recognize them if she found them.

From the time she was a baby, Stephanie had always had a way of gazing searchingly into someone's eyes, a pucker gathering her brow.

"Damn it," Ray used to complain, "she looks like she thinks I'm lying to her no matter what I say."

Sensitive, easily wounded, Stephanie would not forgive her father easily. Perhaps, she never would entirely. He must have left here today realizing that.

For the first time, Beth felt deeply, genuinely sorry for Ray. Today he must have discovered what he'd lost. Would he surrender to drink again? Or would he be man enough to fight for his daughters' love?

"So, how'd you leave it with him?" Beth asked.

Stephanie's head was bowed. "He'll call."

"And maybe see if we want to go to a movie or something next weekend," Lauren contributed in a small voice. "If you say it's okay."

"We'll see." Beth squeezed Stephanie's shoulder. "Remember," she said softly, "it's your choice. Okay?"

Her almost-teenager nodded.

Beth smiled at them both. "How about if you guys help me peel some apples? I invited Jack over for dessert, so I guess I'd better have something to offer him."

Steph's head shot up. "Really? You asked him?"

"Yep."

"But you said... You weren't sure..."

"Sometimes," she said especially for this daughter, "we have to take chances. We'd be awfully lonely if we waited to be sure. I decided I missed him. So...we'll see what happens, okay?"

"Yes!" Stephanie surged to her feet. "*We* get some pie, right?"

"Maybe." Beth caught Lauren in a hug when her youngest flung herself off the couch at her. "If you peel."

"Jack's cool," Stephanie threw over her shoulder on the way to the kitchen. "Right, Lauren?"

Looking perplexed by her sister's enthusiasm, Lauren said, "Yeah. I guess."

Steph disappeared. Beth held her youngest back. "Do you not like Jack?"

"He's nice." Lauren shrugged. "I just don't know why *she* likes him so much."

Because he'd come to the rescue.

"Well, I have to admit, I like him, too," Beth

said lightly. "But you know what? You can reserve judgment. Let me know what you think later, okay? Today, or a week from now, or six months. No hurry."

"You're not getting married or something?"

"Just dessert," Beth promised. "You'll be the first to know if I get more serious than that."

"Oh. Okay." Lauren's face cleared. "Well, I like apple pie. So I guess I'll peel, too."

"Then let's do it."

CHAPTER ELEVEN

HE'D RATHER HAVE SEEN her by herself, but a man had to take what he could get. Jack ate apple pie and chatted with Beth's children as if he wouldn't rather grab her shoulders, give her a shake and demand, ''Are we going somewhere with this or aren't we?''

He was sipping coffee and eyeing a second piece of pie when her oldest said a little too loudly, ''Mom says I don't have to visit my dad anymore if I don't want.''

Beth met his eyes in silent appeal.

Jack lifted his brows at the girl. ''Don't you want to?''

She looked at him as if he were crazy. ''You arrested him!''

Actually, in the end he wasn't the one to make the collar; he was out of his jurisdiction here in Elk Springs. But she wasn't being literal, of course.

''Have you talked to him?''

She rolled her eyes. ''He says he's sorry.'' She made the very concept ludicrous.

''You know,'' Jack said thoughtfully, ''I've never had much sympathy for men who abuse their wives or children.''

Stephanie shot a glance at her mother in which he read both triumph and pain.

"On the other hand, people go through bad patches in their lives. I know I have. No, I never hit the bottle like your dad did, but because of something that happened to me, I spent my early years as a police officer trying too hard to show how tough I was. I could be a real jerk. I think back to incidents I wish I'd handled very differently. I can only hope I didn't ruin somebody's life. It's not the same thing your dad has gone through, but I can sure understand how he might feel now that he's waking up, shaking his head and wondering what in... tarnation he did to you and to himself."

Beth's smile was so warm and grateful, Jack basked in it.

Stephanie, in contrast, studied him as if he were a slab of meat with a tint of green. "You think it's *okay* that he hit Mom and...and threw that firework in the front window and kept hanging up when he called just to scare us?" she asked incredulously.

"Okay? No."

The son of a bitch deserved for his daughter never to speak to him again, in Jack's estimation. But whose loss would it be if she didn't? All Ray Sommers's? Jack wasn't sure.

"You have every reason to be plenty ticked at your father. More than that. Wary. I'm guessing that trusting him won't come easy. It shouldn't. That doesn't mean that someday you can't trust him again."

"You sound just like Mom!" the girl complained.

"Maybe," Beth said, "we adults are more optimistic than kids are. Or maybe we know how important the people who love you are."

"Or maybe we've fouled up often enough ourselves, we're more accepting of other people's mistakes," Jack suggested.

The kid's rolled eyes said, *Grown-ups!*

At last the two girls reluctantly headed upstairs for baths and to get ready for bed. Beth made a production out of clearing the table and offering more coffee, all the while chatting about nothing as if this were the merest of social occasions.

"Beth," he finally got in while she drew breath. "Can we talk?"

She paused with the coffeepot held before her like a shield. Her gaze met his cautiously. "Well, of course. Shall we go in the living room?"

"What's wrong with right here?"

"Let me take this back to the kitchen...."

"Why don't you just set it down?"

For another moment she hesitated, but apparently couldn't think of a good argument to his suggestions. She placed the coffeepot carefully down, then sat as primly as a first-grader on her first day of school.

"I should have called you sooner."

"I don't want apologies," Jack said roughly. "I'm the one who wasn't very understanding. I'm sorry you had to see what you did."

"You came the minute Stephanie called." Beth's eyes were huge and blue, her smile painful. "That makes you a hero in her eyes."

"Only hers?" he asked softly.

"Mine, too. Of course." She compressed her lips.

"I...hope you got my phone message. I really am grateful. I was terrified. Ray just seemed to go insane." She bowed her head, her neck long and graceful with a bundle of dark hair loose on her nape. "He might have really hurt me."

"He did hurt you." Renewed anger stirred in Jack, although whether at Ray Sommers or at her he couldn't have said. "Did I lose my temper? Yeah, probably. Did I act on it? No. I handled the entire incident appropriately as a police officer, even though I'd have liked to flatten his nose. Am I just like him because I wanted to protect you, because part of me *would* have liked to hurt him? I guess that's something you have to decide."

She met his eyes with disarming directness. "What you said that night...about how I'd have reacted if he had hurt one of the girls..." She let out a long breath. "You were right. When he kept them so late those times, and I imagined him kidnapping them... I was so enraged, so afraid, I could have killed him. I *wanted* something bad to happen to him."

Jack moved his chair, scraping it across the floor so that he could reach her hand to grasp it in his. "Feeling that way is normal."

Now her gaze clung desperately to his. "Until the past couple of years, I didn't know it was possible to feel so angry! I don't like it."

She might have been a little girl wailing about how the world was unfair.

"Sweetheart," he said, "feelings don't count as much as actions. You were angry. Okay. You didn't cut the brake line on your ex's pickup truck. Instead, you've dealt with him fairly and bent over backward to help his relationship with the girls. *That's* what counts. Not the fact that you were steamed.''

Beth gave a small, broken laugh. ''I sound ridiculous, don't I?'' Her hand turned to meet his, palm to palm.

''No. You sound like a nice woman pushed out of her comfort zone.''

''I don't like to think I'm so unable to cope with anything difficult.'' She made a face. ''If I'm honest, I have to admit that I haven't coped well. It took me too long to leave Ray. Even the little stuff... I endured those stupid phone calls for weeks before I got Caller ID! I don't know why I dragged my feet. Because of what I might discover? Or because I was afraid he'd find another way to torment us that would be worse? I really, truly don't know.''

''He was your husband. Once upon a time, you loved him.'' Jack found himself wishing for one fierce moment that she hadn't, that she had some other excuse for having married the jerk, bearing his children. He wanted her to love him and only him, her heart given without reservations, with no scars of past loves.

Impossible. Neither of them was twenty years old. He bore scars himself, deeper, more disfiguring ones than she could guess. Total, instinctive faith was beyond either of them now.

''I think,'' Beth said meditatively, ''I haven't really loved Ray in a very long time. Isn't that sad? I never admitted that to myself until the end. We moved to Elk Springs so full of hope. On my part, at least, it was hope that he would get excited about my owning the store and maybe become more supportive, that with a fresh start he'd see *me* differently." She gave a faint sigh. "I doubt a new setting ever changes anyone deep down."

"Probably not," Jack agreed. "Any more than having a baby fixes a bad marriage."

Beth wrinkled her nose. "At least we had our children before our problems."

"Either way, your marriage is past tense now." He hoped. His doubts were reflected in his grim tone. "I'm asking that you not make assumptions about me based on what your ex-husband would have done."

"I will try." It sounded remarkably to him like a vow; her extraordinary eyes now gazed solemnly at him. "That's all I can do."

The pressure in his chest intensified. "You've changed your mind about me?"

"I have reminded myself that you're not on the streets busting crack houses and roughing up kids in gangs. You police a quiet town. I don't know what I was imagining, but it isn't Elk Springs or Butte County." She smiled. "Your deputies probably hand out more speeding tickets than anything, right?"

The rape-murder of a fourteen-year-old girl by a school vice-principal a couple of years ago passed through Jack's mind, as did the stabbing death last night at a tavern, the brutal beating of a teenage prostitute the day before, the dozen or more calls about breaking and entering handled every day, last week's arson resulting in the death of an elderly man known for giving a hard time to middle-school kids who cut across his lawn.

A quiet town? Sure. Relatively speaking. Elk Springs wasn't New York City or Miami. His beat was a rural one. But crime they had, big city problems joining the age-old ones of passion, greed and despair.

"We give a lot of traffic tickets," he agreed. "But I have detectives who handle major crime."

"You don't do real police work at all anymore, do you?" Beth asked.

"Not a hell of a lot," Jack said with some regret. "I'm an administrator and politician now. I provide the means for my officers to do their jobs. That translates to finding enough money so that they have adequate equipment and backup. I'm their advocate to the folks who write the paychecks, but in return I lean on my deputies if they're not busting their guts to serve this county. If tough decisions have to be made, I'm the lucky guy who makes 'em. If you mean, do I answer calls when a house has been broken into, no. Not anymore."

"I don't know why it scared me," she mused. "Your job, that is. If Ray were a police officer... But of course he isn't. I suppose *cop* just conjures up an image that scared me. It isn't really you."

Hadn't she listened to him earlier, when he worried aloud to her daughter about lives he might have ruined by not handling incidents as sensitively as he might have? What did she think he was talking about? Giving a speeding ticket to someone only clocking five miles above the limit instead of ten?

Okay. She didn't want to deal with what his job

meant, not right now. It suggested violence to her. It made her think guns, fists, nightsticks, raised voices and obscenities. Right now she wanted to picture him as a CEO in a suit who never did any dirty work. Preferably, never had. Jack could live with that.

Eventually she'd be ready to hear what he really did for a living. She'd be ready to hold him when he came home after seeing a child's brains spilled onto pavement, after he had to tell a mother and father their son was dead. She would listen when he talked about the politics of a murder investigation or the ruthless side of white collar crime. Beth Sommers was a woman who listened well and wouldn't expect him to be Mr. Macho all the time.

For now, he had no trouble with letting her cling to a few illusions. They'd gotten to know each other too quickly. She hadn't been happy needing a man she wasn't sure she even liked. Give her time, Jack figured.

He was too relieved that she was willing to keep seeing him to insist she rip the blinders from her eyes.

"I'll have to take you to a county council meeting with me some time," he said. "Let you watch me in action. Now, *there's* the old west. Forget the OK Corral."

Her chuckle was as sweet and rich as chocolate. She parted her lips to say something, then tilted her head to one side. "Oh, I can hear the girls. Let me go tuck them in."

He was waiting when she came back. Not sitting, like a good boy. Instead he prowled the dining room until she appeared. Beth hesitated in the doorway when she didn't see him sitting where she'd left him, giving him a second to study her.

Damn, she was pretty. He loved the delicacy of her features, the contrast of pale skin with dark wavy hair, the grace of her every move. She had an old-fashioned look that attracted him, suggesting a gentleness and femininity at odds with the new millennium. He could see how she would have appeared to be the perfect stay-home mother and wife to a man like Ray.

What Ray hadn't gotten was that the sexy and intriguing quality about Beth was the contrast between her pretty, gentle looks and the fact that she was a strong woman who had fought for an education and taught herself everything she had to know to run a business that employed half a dozen people. The gutsy, ambitious, smart side of her was where he'd seen a resemblance to Meg Patton.

"I'd like to kiss you," he said in a voice made gravelly by a surge of pure sexual hunger.

Her eyes widened as she turned her head and saw him. If her nod was nervous, he understood. Other kisses had been more spontaneous. This time, it felt more like a vow. *I will try.*

Stopping in front of her, Jack lifted her hands and laid them on his chest. "Are you scared?" he asked quietly.

Her vivid eyes flashed at him again. "Only of what you make me feel. It's…new to me. I…really want you to kiss me."

It's new to me.

New. Jack had to grit his teeth against the triumph

and desire that rose like a tide pulled by the moon. He, Jack, made her feel something unfamiliar. Maybe, just maybe, he'd been wrong and they could fall in love like a couple of twenty-year-olds. Hell, maybe two people in love didn't *see* wrinkles and scars.

"You scare me a little, too," he admitted, continuing awkwardly, "The first time I saw you I felt something I hardly recognized. I was standing there talking to Ray and knowing I had no business being attracted to you. Not just physically attracted, either. I felt this little click, like a key fitting into a lock. As if you were…right."

That wasn't very romantic or poetic, but the blue of her eyes deepened and she flushed a pale rose. Her hands crept up around his neck. "I think," she said, "for that, I have to kiss you."

"Sounds like a plan to me," he said huskily.

Their lips met, a shy brush as if he and she were young and unpracticed. He wrapped one hand around her nape and felt the heavy silk of her hair and the smooth delicacy of her skin. He kneaded gently until her head fell back and her eyes became slumbrous. Then he kissed her again, nibbling on her lower lip, persuading her to let his tongue slide along hers. Tenderness was a strong rein on the jolt of need that made him want to crush her mouth under his, lift her skirt and grip her buttocks, wrap her legs around him, take her right here on the dining room table with her children awake upstairs.

Or maybe no rein was strong enough. The kiss deepened; his mouth hardened. She made small gasps and leaned against him. One of her hands squeezed his shoulder, the other threaded through his hair and tugged when he tried to lift his mouth.

He heard his own groan and couldn't seem to prevent himself from flattening a hand on the small of her back and pulling her tight against the bulge she had to feel through his slacks and her jumper. She arched and rubbed her cheek against his rougher one.

"I wish…" she breathed as much as said.

Jack wished, too. That her children weren't home. That he was surer about how ready Beth was.

"Wish what?" If ever a man needed to clear his throat.

"Never mind." Pink as her cheeks were, she blushed more deeply yet.

"Our time will come," he promised, his gaze holding hers with clear intent. "We can be patient."

Her small wriggle almost undid him. "I don't *feel* patient," she complained.

Fingers biting into her arms, Jack eased her back. "No," he agreed, with a hint of grimness. "I don't feel very patient, either."

She laughed at him, her eyes sparkling. "Good."

Suddenly amused despite his acute frustration, Jack asked, "Are you flirting with me?"

"Yes." Beth's mouth formed an O of surprise. "Yes, I think I am. Well. That's something I haven't done in a long time. I didn't know I still knew how."

"I think—" he grinned at her "—you must have been damned good at it. Something comes easy, you don't forget."

"I never was that good at flirting." She made a

face. "My father wouldn't let me date until I was seventeen. He didn't like me even *looking* at boys. He grounded me once for a month because a friend and I went to the mall and he caught us hanging around with some boys from school."

"So naturally you married the first guy you seriously dated," Jack concluded.

"Yep." This smile, a little sad, didn't brighten her whole face the way the last one had. "If I'd had a chance to...to play, the way other girls did. And if I hadn't been in such a hurry to leave home..." She sighed.

"We can always second-guess ourselves, and our parents."

If I'd punched Ed Patton's lights out, Jack couldn't help thinking. *If Meg had trusted me with our son...*

But for the first time, the bitter regret was missing. One step forward and he could be kissing Beth Sommers again, feeling her delicate strength and shy passion. He wasn't so sure he wanted to be anywhere else in his life. Another road might have missed this moment, and he intensely wanted to be here.

If only her house were empty... Now, there was a regret he felt.

"Mmm." Beth touched his jaw with her hand. "I'd better say good-night. I know perfectly well Stephanie is lying up there wondering why you haven't gone and what we're doing down here."

"Do they like me?"

"Are you kidding? They rushed to peel all the apples for the pie because I said you were coming.

I assure you they don't rush to help in the kitchen very often.''

He heard an undertone she meant to hide from him. "But?"

"But." Beth lowered her voice as they reached the foot of the stairs. "Lauren is a little nervous about you, I think. Despite everything, she's still a big fan of her dad's. Maybe she's hoping we'll get back together. She asked tonight if you were coming just for dessert or forever. Now, Steph is in the mood to take to you just because she wants to reject her father. So…yeah, they like you, but their feelings are complicated."

Dessert or forever. The pie had been good, but forever sounded better to him. The realization made him edgy.

Be certain, he thought. *Make damn sure this is more than the thrill of being Sir Galahad.*

"Your feelings and mine aren't as basic as first grade arithmetic either," he pointed out. "One plus one doesn't equal two anymore."

"Or maybe it does," she said softly, her face tilted up, "and we just don't remember how to trust anything so simple."

In a rough voice, Jack said, "Trust, we can work on. If you're willing."

"I think," she spoke with wonder, "that I am. Or I wouldn't have called you today."

"Good." On the one, inadequate word, he kissed her hard and turned and blundered out before he was tempted to do more.

Patience had never been one of his virtues, which was maybe one reason he'd been a hard-ass cop and not a hostage negotiator. But for Beth, and for the possibility of a life that didn't feel empty, he could work on this, too.

Patience and trust. Now was when he felt the ache of old scars, and guessed as she quietly shut the door behind him that she did, too.

But he wanted her trust, he wanted her touch, he wanted her love. Since an emotional plastic surgeon wasn't available, he guessed this wouldn't come as easily as he'd like.

But, hell, what in life worth having did?

RAY SAT ON THE HARD wooden chair, facing the circle of a dozen men in the anger management class. One was a dentist; Ray knew, because Doug Renfrew had filled a cavity for him once. Generally the men didn't talk about professions and went by first names only. Others around the circle were blue collar like Ray. They had callused hands, poor grammar.

All had wives who had left them or were threatening to. Several, Ray gathered, were here under court order.

They were him. He was them.

Decent men, mostly, who couldn't control their anger. Who let it spill over until they hit their wives or children. A few resented being here; others were ashamed. Ray was one of the latter.

He still had moments when he blamed Beth. Why had she had to change? Why couldn't she have stayed the gentle, compliant girl he'd married? He wasn't such a bad husband; what was her excuse for kicking him out?

But lately he'd wondered: Did anybody stay the same? Had he been taking out anger about other things on her? It wasn't as if she hadn't been a loving wife and mother even when she did work. If he'd given her more credit...

"When I'm at work," one of the men said suddenly, "I get so pissed, but what can you do? Punch the boss? It just boils in me all day. Then I go home, and the woman hasn't even put dinner on. The kids are screaming and running in circles and their crap is all over the floor. What's she done all day?" He looked around, bafflement and remembered anger on his bluff face. "And then she gives me some lip, and I just lose it. She calls the cops, and it's my fault. Yeah, I shouldn't have hit her, but why can't she try?"

The counselor stubbed out his cigarette. "You ever asked her what she does all day?"

"Oh, she gives me this goddamned list, but it doesn't put food on the table or shut the kids up."

"What about work?" the dentist said. "What's happening that makes you so angry?"

They talked about work for a while. Most of these men were too old to walk out on a job they hated and start over. Ray had been thinking, though. All he'd ever wanted was to be a long-haul trucker, his own boss. But it seemed in recent years that there was more and more pressure to deliver loads in unreasonably short periods. He'd taken to popping uppers and swilling coffee until he had the jitters even when his eyelids weighed more than the load. Last week he'd woken up behind the wheel just before he clipped the rail. It scared him, and he'd pulled over for a nap. He was half an hour late getting to his destination, and he didn't get paid. Half an hour! The goddamn cheapskates didn't want to keep any inventory. It was okay if he risked his life bailing their asses out at the last minute. He was sick of it.

"Ray?" The counselor sounded as if this wasn't the first time he'd spoken Ray's name. "You haven't said much."

Voice loud and clipped, he said, "I get pissed at work, too. I used to come home wanting to hurt somebody. I'd go three, four days without sleep. I never did hit Beth—my wife. But we yelled a lot. We've been divorced a year, and I blamed her for the breakup. Now I'm thinking…maybe if I'd made some changes, we could have stuck together."

"What kind of changes?"

"I'm a long-haul trucker. I own my own rig. Maybe I'm getting too old for it. I don't know. I never wanted to work for anybody else. But the idea of coming home to my own bed every night looks better all the time. I could have a life like other people." He shrugged. "I'd make less money, but I could go to my kids' school plays. You know?"

The thought stuck with him. When he called the girls that evening, he asked Stephanie, "Would you like it if I was around more? Consolidated is hiring drivers. I'd be home every night."

"You mean…you'd want to see us every day?" She sounded doubtful—no, hell, admit it—appalled.

"No. You live with your mom. I was just thinking…well, that I could come to things at school. Or see you sometimes during the week instead of just over a weekend."

"Like, we could just have dinner with you instead of spending two days?"

"Sure. Maybe I could get you to those tae kwon do lessons you've been wanting to take."

"That'd be cool!"

This, the first spark of enthusiasm he had heard from her in a long time, decided him. He put off his next run and went by the Consolidated distribution center the following day. The pay wouldn't equal what he made now, but he guessed he'd be okay with it. He'd be making runs to Grants Pass and Ashland and over into Idaho. Nothing longer than a ten-hour day. Ray calculated that with what he could get selling his rig, he could buy himself a house.

Or maybe, if he could show Beth that he was making a sincere effort to change his life, he could win her back. It didn't have to be too late.

Galvanized by hope, Ray picked up the phone. He'd be spending Thanksgiving alone, but he had already made plans to take both girls to lunch and a movie on Saturday. Tonight they debated about which one, Lauren on the phone with him, Stephanie in the background. When they'd agreed on a movie, he said casually, "Can I talk to your mom for a minute?"

"Mo-om!" Lauren yelled. "Dad wants to talk to you!"

He winced away from the phone.

After a moment, Beth came on. "Hello?" she said cautiously.

"Jeez, I could have bellowed for you myself."

After a brief pause, she gave a reluctant chuckle.

"I should suggest she cover the mouthpiece before she blasts."

Pleased at the way he'd lightened her up already, Ray said, "The girls said they could go to lunch and a movie Saturday."

"Yes, that's fine, Ray. What movie are you going to see?"

"We compromised on Steve Martin's new comedy. They never want to see the same thing anymore."

"Stephanie is getting to be a teenager. Lauren resents it."

"Well, I do, too," Ray said easily. "Makes me feel old."

He'd earned another small laugh. "I know what you mean," Beth agreed.

"You haven't seen this movie, have you?" he asked, as though the thought had just occurred to him.

"Nope. Steve Martin is usually funny, though."

"You want to come?" he asked. "We could make it a family day."

Her voice cooled, became formal. "Thank you, Ray, but this is your time with the girls."

He gripped the phone harder. "You know," he said, "it might be good for Steph and Lauren to see that we can be friends. I wouldn't read anything else into it."

"But they might. They need to get used to the fact that we're not married. Lauren especially still has illusions. No, thank you, Ray," Beth said with complete finality, "but I've made other plans for Saturday."

Illusions. Which meant that what he'd been having were delusions.

"Yeah, okay," he managed to get out. "No problem."

A moment later he hung up the phone and slammed his fist into the wall.

He had all evening with a pack of ice and no beer to realize that Beth was gone for good. Saturday, while he had their daughters, she was going to be with Sheriff Jack Murray.

There wasn't a damn thing he could do about it except live with his mistakes and be glad that this time he'd only hurt himself, not someone he loved.

CHAPTER TWELVE

"THANK YOU," Beth said nervously, accepting the drink Jack handed her.

She sat at the tiled breakfast bar in his kitchen watching him stir-fry. When he had suggested lunch at his house, she'd known what he was really asking. What she feared was that her eyes had given away that knowledge when Ray picked up the girls. Ray had given her one searching look before turning away with despair on his face.

Beth didn't feel guilt so much as sadness. And, she had to confess, some fear. Ray seemed to be genuinely trying to get a grip on his own problems and mend fences with the girls, but she didn't trust him. Was he still convinced that, if he was a good boy, she'd take him back? What would happen when he found out she wouldn't?

"Penny for your thoughts."

Beth blinked and focused on the big, dark man with a white chef's apron over his T-shirt and jeans.

"Oh...Ray."

Jack's eyes narrowed for a second.

"I didn't tell him I was coming here today, but the girls probably did. It just...scares me still."

"You said he's doing well."

"Yes. Yes, he is. Even Stephanie is softening toward him. But...what if he's pretending?"

Jack frowned at her over the wok. Steam rising from it formed a veil between them. "Do you have some reason to believe he is?"

"No." She smiled wryly. "Paranoia."

"That, you have reason to suffer from."

"Thank you." Beth gave herself a shake. "Let's talk about something besides my ex-husband. The topic isn't recommended for a date."

"But I'll bet it's a common one."

"Probably. In fact, there's a...well, another businessman here in Elk Springs who has suggested dinner a couple of times. But every time we talk, he goes on and on about his ex. I have to admit, it's a little bit of a turnoff."

Jack gave a grunt of amusement. "I'll bet she's not throwing cherry bombs through his front window."

"No, she's whining because the child support isn't adequate, according to him. Of course, he's complaining to the wrong person." She had to smile. "Considering I'm on the other side of the scenario."

"Does Ray pay his?"

"If I beg. But maybe that will change. He actually handed me a check last week without comment." She sighed. "Enough Ray."

They talked about small things over lunch, the first time they'd been alone all week. Jack had come to her house Thursday, for Thanksgiving. Will was with his mom and family, and was spending Friday with his dad. So Jack had shared turkey and stuffing and pumpkin pies with Beth and the girls, sneaking one kiss outside on the cold porch before he went home.

Now conversation ranged through movies, books, local politics, childhoods, friends. Those revealing bits and pieces that individually counted not at all—who married a man because he loved *Lord of the Rings,* thus revealing a romantic streak?—but that in tandem mattered more than she'd realized when she was eighteen and getting married the first time. It hadn't occurred to her then, for example, that on Saturday nights she would see nothing but movies with gigantic explosions if she married Ray. Or that, if he wouldn't take her to "chick flicks" then, he probably never would.

Beth found herself babbling so that she didn't have time to think about what she was probably—surely—going to do here today. Ray was the only man she'd ever even seriously made out with. She had never dreamed that she would, in cold blood, decide to have sex with another man. But she had.

Or perhaps she hadn't made the decision in cold blood, because she couldn't think about Jack without her blood heating.

Now, as they ate and talked, she kept looking at his hands, big, tanned fingers square-tipped, and imagined them on her bare skin. Or her glance would sneak up to his strong neck and she would become fascinated with his throat or the way his jaw muscles knotted when he thought. Or his mouth...

"Keep looking at me like that," he said, "and this will be a very short lunch."

Blushing fiercely, Beth said, "Like what?"

His eyes had darkened, his voice roughened. "You're not going to lie to me and say you were meditating on whether you prefer toast or cereal for breakfast, now are you?"

Was *that* what they'd been talking about?

His mouth quirked. "Yep. You asked what I usually eat."

"Oh."

"Cereal. Bran with raisins."

"Oh," she said again, inanely. "I like toast. English muffins or cinnamon bread."

"But that's not what you were thinking about."

"No," she admitted, cheeks still warm. "It's not. I, um, like to look at you."

He made a sound in his throat. "I'm about to lunge across this table."

The chicken stir-fry with cashews was good, she thought. Beth peeked down to see that she'd eaten about half. She stole a look back up at Jack.

"Why don't you?" she asked, daringly.

He shoved back his chair, circled the table and snatched her out of hers. "Being festooned with food doesn't strike the right mood," he murmured.

"No," she agreed, her voice a thread because she was breathless. "I like you...this way."

"Beth." His jaw was tight, his tone suddenly grim. "You're sure you want to do this. I can wait."

She was terrified and positive all at the same time. "I know you can," she whispered. "But I feel as if we *have* been waiting. Even though I know it hasn't really been that long."

"I've wanted you since the day we met."

"I still don't understand why." She'd always despised people who begged for compliments, and now she had become one of them. But she really, truly, wished she understood why Jack Murray had seen anything special in her.

"You're beautiful," he said in that rich, deep voice she found so sexy. "You're brave and loving. When you smile—" his fingertip traced her lips "—really smile, you light up the world. You make me feel like a teenager in love."

"Oh!" Beth tilted her head back. "I feel that way, too. So young, when sometimes I feel so old."

"Life does that." His mouth followed his fingertip; hers trembled beneath his. Breath warm on her, he said huskily, "It does this, too."

She swayed and had to wrap her arms around his neck for support. "I'd forgotten," she said simply.

"Then let me remind you."

His mouth descended again, no longer tender but hungry. She drowned in that kiss and quit thinking or worrying. How could she think? His tongue stroked hers in erotic demand, his hands moved urgently on her hips and waist, pulling her tighter against him so that she felt every powerful inch of his body. Even his heartbeat vibrated with her own until she couldn't tell whether the rhythm she felt was his or hers.

He nipped her earlobe and steered her out of the kitchen. Somehow she went, although she was kissing his throat, tasting the salt of his skin, reveling in the groans she awakened.

At the foot of the stairs, Jack peeled her shirt over her head and lifted her up two steps so that he could nuzzle her cleavage.

She gasped and grabbed the newel for support. Jack unhooked her bra and, as it fell away, cupped her breasts in hands that were rough-textured and tender at the same time. He was saying things, sweet words as erotic as his touch. Made bold by the delight on his face, Beth reached out and tugged at his T-shirt.

"Don't like being the only one who's naked?" he asked huskily, as he cooperated in her clumsy effort to get it off.

"Fair's fair."

He was a beautiful man, rangy but powerful, his muscles developed enough to show that he worked at staying in shape. Not an ounce of fat softened a taut belly. Murmuring in pleasure, Beth flattened her hands on his chest, blurred by soft dark hairs. His skin rippled in response and he sucked in a ragged breath.

"Do you know how many nights I've lain in bed imagining your hands on me?"

"I've imagined this, too," she whispered, closing her eyes as he bent his dark head and kissed her breast. "Oooh. That feels…"

His tongue circled her nipple. "What?"

"Wonderful."

He swore suddenly and lifted her in his arms.

Giving a squeak, Beth wrapped her legs around his waist. "What?"

"We won't get up these stairs if we don't go now."

Over his shoulder she saw her bra hanging drunkenly from a banister post and both their shirts forming pools of color on the hardwood floor of the entry. She could only hope that Will didn't have an unexpected urge to surprise his father with a visit. And when she left, she'd have to creep down here just so that she could get dressed.

"My clothes…"

Jack's grin was feral. "I like you without them."

His skin was smooth and hot under her hands. Suddenly she didn't care about her bra or anything beyond the next few minutes. She'd worry about getting dressed later. After.

She was rewarded by another of those ragged sounds when she pressed small kisses to his throat. He kneaded her rear as he took the stairs and carried her down the hall. When she nibbled on his neck, he came to an abrupt stop and backed her against a door molding. When Beth lifted her face in inquiry, his mouth slammed down on hers. She didn't have time for breath, didn't need air, not when she had him.

Dimly she was aware that he shouldered open the door. She had a crazy, kaleidoscopic glimpse of cream-colored plaster walls and black-and-white photographs displayed starkly above a dark wood dresser. Beth refused to let go when Jack lowered her onto the bed. So he came with her, knee between her thighs.

"Let me…get your pants…off," he said, between deep, hungry kisses.

"Yours…first."

Who was this woman, groping for his belt buckle, bumping the erection beneath it?

Jack groaned. "Demanding, aren't you?"

Her breathy chuckle sounded wanton. "Yes."

Their pants were shed nearly simultaneously, Beth wriggling to free her hips from her own even as she tugged at his. Jack kissed her face and throat and breasts as she moaned and tangled her calves around his hair-roughened legs.

"You feel…so good," she marveled.

"Oh, yeah." The flash of a smile was wickedly sexy. "You've got it right. I'm feeling damned good."

She punched him lightly. His mouth claimed hers again and her head swam. His every touch was intoxicating, his gentleness in the midst of passion incredibly seductive. Although he loomed above her, his shoulders broad enough to command her world, he never tried to dominate her with strength or size. His mouth teased and tempted, his hands sent shivers of sensation through her skin. Warmth and urgency built until she was arching her hips upward and begging wordlessly for him to enter her. He fumbled in his bedside drawer and ripped open the package.

Even when he finally parted her thighs and pressed in, she felt his restraint in the tension of his shoulders and arms, saw it in his gritted teeth, heard it in the hoarse rasp of his breath.

"Ah, sweetheart," he said in an unrecognizable voice. "That's it, love. Let me in. Like that." A long groan as he buried himself and paused, shaking from the strain, seeming to wait for her.

Need was building in her, a glowing hot coil in her belly that was almost familiar but not quite. She'd never wanted like this, beyond self-consciousness, to the point where she could arch against him, clutch at his back and whisper, "Again. Please. Again."

"Yes!" he said exultantly, eyes revealing desire that did to her what his deft hands couldn't. He moved then, pulling back, then thrusting again, but always with that incredible control, never with blind sexual need. She moved and sighed and even whimpered with pleasure, while Jack groaned and filled her over and over again.

Her climax was a long, glorious slide into ecstasy, wave after slow wave that had her crying out with wonder. Still he moved, those deliberate slow thrusts drawing out her release until she thought she couldn't bear it. Only when she was done did she feel him jerk, hear her name said rawly, experience the ultimate feminine satisfaction of giving and receiving such intimate joy.

For a minute Jack collapsed onto her, but the moment she stirred he rolled to one side and drew her with him, his arms a tender haven.

"Are you all right?" he asked, his lips against the tiny hairs curling at her temple.

"Very." She sounded smug. And was, Beth realized with a smile that played with becoming a laugh. She had never felt so...contented.

"I may never move."

She loved having her ear against his bare shoulder so that she felt the vibration of his words. "Good," she told him. "I like you right where you are."

His chuckle was even better, a minor earthquake beneath her cheek. "Of course, eventually moving may be appealing." His hand traveled down the small of her back to the curve of her buttocks.

She squirmed happily. "I may want you to…eventually."

He nuzzled her hair. "But not yet."

"No," Beth agreed. "Not yet."

She toyed with the fine-textured hair on his chest, curling it around her finger, tugging gently, drawing whorls in it. "You worked so hard on lunch, and it went to waste."

"Nothing about today has been a waste." He began to knead her lower back.

Her hand stilled. "Mmm. Oh, that feels good."

"And I thought I was having trouble sleeping before this," he said meditatively. His lips moved against her forehead. "Now I'll know what I'm missing."

"You're not missing anything today."

In a sudden movement he flipped her onto her back and reared above her. New urgency deepened his voice. "I'll miss you the minute you're gone."

The thrill she felt was primitive, the satisfaction of a drive as deep as breathing: *Make him care, be sure he comes back so that he's there when you need him.* The thought startled and disquieted her, making her wonder anew whether she was truly falling in love with this man or only using him, but the perturbation was drowned in a kiss that was edgy with hunger.

She couldn't possibly want him again so soon; he couldn't be growing hard already. But she did; he was. And, oh, it was delicious to know her own power over him. For a woman who had had to fight for any power at all, a gift like this couldn't be wasted.

"But not yet," she said throatily, her head falling back as his mouth found her breast again. "You don't have to miss me yet."

JACK WAS ALMOST completely happy those next weeks. He'd have liked it better, of course, if he could have openly shared Beth's bed instead of skulking into it on those rare occasions when her children were away. In fact, he'd have liked to see more of her, period.

She had him over for dinner twice a week, at least, and they managed an official date at least once more, sometimes when the girls were with their father, sometimes by hiring a baby-sitter. But damn it, seeing Beth three times a week wasn't enough! He was hungry for her smiles, her kisses, her breathless laughter. Hungry to hear what she thought of local political races, a book he'd talked her into reading, the color purple. Anything. He was giddily in love as he couldn't ever remember being. He wanted to learn everything about Beth Sommers, and he was making a good start.

He understood the need for patience. Her kids needed to get to know him. They'd had a tough year. He needed to win them as well as Beth, if he was to become their stepfather.

Putting into words what he already knew—that he intended to marry Beth—gave him pause for only a second. He'd always been a man who knew his mind; he was an effective cop partly because he was decisive. He knew what he wanted, and he could wait. For her.

It wasn't her children, or even her caution, that

ate at him. It was something he couldn't at first put
a finger on, but finally identified. He wanted to know
everything about her. She *didn't* want to know everything about him.

A week passed, then another and another. They
Christmas-shopped together, listened to street car-
olers, admired the lights strung down Main Street,
complained about the increased traffic and crowds
now that the skiers had come to town. He and she
talked about a million and one things, trivial and not.
His job fell in the trivial part. He could tell funny
stories, talk about personalities, politics, frustrations.
But she didn't ask about the bad times, although
she'd heard him tell Stephanie that he thought he
might have damaged people's lives. If she'd said
something like that about herself, he'd have asked
what she was talking about. She didn't.

Plainly, she didn't want to hear about cops who
hurt someone or got hurt themselves. The blood and
despair and dark, painful mysteries that made up a
working detective's day were anathema to her. She
was determined that Jack be a kind of businessman,
government-style.

The longer he knew her, the more he wanted to
confess his mistakes, ask for her absolution. He
needed her to say, "You were young. You had reason to make the choices you did. But now you're
the kind of man you always meant to be. Don't
worry about who you used to be."

He couldn't say she didn't give him an opening.
Caution made him hold back. All he had to do was
remember the repugnance with which she'd looked
at him the night he cuffed her ex-husband. And her

words…hell, he'd never forget what she'd said: *You're just like him. You were as furious as he was, as ready to hurt someone.*

Sure he was. What kind of cop would he be if he *wasn't* ready to physically defend the citizens of this county?

But that wasn't the point. Maybe Beth even agreed that a cop needed to have the capacity to use force. That's exactly why she was wary about him, had been from the beginning. The qualities she wanted to see in a law enforcement officer weren't the same thing she could love and admire in a husband.

What he needed to prove to her was that his willingness to use force didn't equate to her husband's. Jack was not an angry man. He rarely lost his temper. He didn't enjoy dominating his fellow man—or woman.

But the only way he could think to prove it was to let time tell its tale. If he was unfailingly gentle, if he didn't rub her face in what his occupation implied about him, she'd learn to trust him. It came down, as always, to patience.

Trouble was, he didn't feel patient. He could have talked to her twenty hours a day. He'd never before had this craving to tell another person everything about his life, learn just as much about hers. The first thing he did when he got home every evening was call Beth. Sometimes they talked for an hour or more.

But she never asked about his secrets or regrets or mistakes. All he could do was take his cue from that.

Tonight he pushed the boundaries a little bit, because he was on the verge of having to discipline a deputy. Usually he didn't suffer from doubts. This time he had some.

Partly, that was because he'd known Gary Hansen for years. When Jack was still with the Elk Springs P.D., he'd worked with Gary on bringing an end to a sophisticated burglary ring that didn't respect jurisdictional boundaries. Gary had been a good cop, first a patrolman, then a detective in Investigations and finally Major Crimes. But the past year had seen a spiral downward. Clearly, he had a problem with booze. He was late to work. Once he had failed to respond to a crime in progress call only two blocks from where he was parked. Napping, he claimed, but another cop had reluctantly told Jack he smelled whiskey on Hansen's breath.

First Jack had demoted him. Tomorrow, he was calling him on the carpet again. Putting him at a desk job at the least, suspending him maybe.

"I don't know what's right," Jack said to Beth. They'd had dinner out, but had agreed afterward to have coffee at Jack's place. Coffee, and one of those rare intervals for kissing or even making love. Tiffany, the neighbor kid, was baby-sitting. Because it was Sunday, Beth would have to be home early. Maybe he should be taking advantage of their limited time to throw Beth over his shoulder and take her to his bed. But tonight, more than usual, he found he wanted her perspective on an issue.

Beth sat on one of the bar stools in his kitchen, her feet curled around the legs and her elbows on the tiled countertop. Tonight she wore drapey black pants made of some silky fabric with a fuzzy pale blue sweater that fit snuggly and looked sexy as hell. Her dark hair was fastened loosely with iridescent butterfly clips on each side, the curls tumbling over her shoulders and back. He kept wanting to pet the sweater—and then the silky vee of skin where it revealed the beginnings of cleavage.

"What do you mean, what's right?" she asked.

He dragged his mind back to Hansen's troubles. "Oh, hell, it's almost Christmas, for one thing. Mainly, though, this cop has had a lot of years on the force. I don't want to dump him. But how can I risk other officers when I know he's slacking?"

Her expression changed subtly. "Risk?"

"What if someone needs backup and he's the closest, but he's boozed up?" Forgetting her silky skin, Jack grimaced. "If he's actually boozing on the job, I can't let this slide. I can't have him out there on the street with impaired judgment."

"If he got in a car accident or something?" She didn't want to understand him. "That would be scary."

"What if he pulls his gun when he shouldn't? Or doesn't when he should?"

"But…police around here hardly ever have to use their guns."

"More often than you'd think." Make her see that life out there wasn't a rose garden, Jack thought. If she could accept that much, he might not seem such a brute to her. "Do you think you're the only one who's needed a cop lately? I can assure you, you're not."

Her chin came up. "I've looked at the crime report in the paper. It's pretty minor stuff."

"That's the Elk Springs P.D. crime stats. Not the county's."

"You don't have to convince me that you do something important." Her smile coaxed him to forget the nasty topic—or so he suspected. "You came to my rescue twice. You're my hero. And the girls'."

"Most of what we do isn't heroic," Jack said flatly. "Necessary, but not noble. Let's not make it prettier than it is."

"You sound as if you don't like your job." She tilted her head and studied him, perplexity crinkling her forehead.

"I don't like it when I have to fire a good man who has personal problems."

She pushed her stool back. "Now you know why I didn't like seeing you handcuff Ray."

"Your ex and a cop who is drinking a little too much aren't comparable."

"Aren't they?" she asked quietly.

"Forget it." He was starting to feel irritated. He didn't get her. She apparently still sympathized with Sommers, and she didn't want to hear about the stresses of being a cop and what it could do to a man.

"I think maybe we should," she agreed. "Actually, I should get home."

His frustration with the conversation instantly became sexual. "Don't go. Not yet."

She didn't smile. "Why?"

"I haven't kissed you." He reached out and gripped her shoulders. "I missed you yesterday."

Beth flowed off the stool into his arms. "I missed you, too."

"I called."

"I know. I heard your message."

"Come upstairs with me." He brushed his mouth over hers, nibbled at her plump lower lip.

"Mmm." Her head fell back and her dark lashes formed crescents against porcelain skin. "Are you sure?"

His insatiable need for her was partly physical and partly emotional. The sexual desire, he had no doubts about.

"Oh, yeah," he said, low in his throat. "I need you, Beth."

He'd spoken the magic words. She melted. This time, they made it up the stairs before shedding clothes. Otherwise, not much had changed since the first time they'd made love. They were incredibly compatible. His every touch seemed to please her. She didn't grab his hand and say, "No, not like that. Like this." He didn't move too fast or too slow for her.

The only time she froze at all was when he became too aggressive. If his tongue plundered her mouth too deeply or his hands squeezed too roughly, she would stiffen. He had to be careful, not let desire go to his head. He didn't dare do anything that would make her think of him as a beast; he didn't dare lose control. He was damned careful not to.

Her touches invariably held an innocent wonder that fueled his hunger. She wasn't clumsy, but her hands weren't practiced, either. She read his responses with unerring accuracy. If something didn't turn him on, she didn't do it again. Instead, she was learning what did push his buttons, and seemed to enjoy the way his muscles jerked in response or he groaned at a featherlight touch.

Every single time he penetrated her, he had the same feeling of having come home. The fit was perfect. Yeah, she was tight but not too small, and he liked the way she wrapped her legs around his waist. But it wasn't that. The sensation wasn't so much physical as... Oh, hell. He didn't even know. Just that she was right for him. That he wanted to make love to her every night for the rest of his life, even if he did have to hold something back, if sometimes it took every ounce of will he possessed not to hammer into her, not to have wild sex instead of gentle lovemaking. But here in bed, the price was worth the reward.

This part, he thought half an hour later, as he stroked her bare flank and felt her lips tickle his skin as she brushed tiny kisses over his chest, he could do.

He was less sure he could keep hiding the ignoble things he'd done, the history of violence, the shame that had been a companion for twenty years. For Beth, he was willing to try.

He just wished he didn't have to.

"THIS SUSPENSION is temporary." Jack felt like a grade-A SOB, kicking a man when he was down. And two weeks before Christmas. But what could he do? "You've got to get a handle on your problems. You know the department pays for alcohol treatment.''

Gary Hansen sat in the chair with his feet planted right together and his elbows at his side, shoulders back and crew-cut blond head held high. Not until now had he shown any real response.

A nerve twitched under one eye. ''I'm not an alcoholic.''

''Maybe not.'' Jack moved his shoulders to unkink taut muscles. ''But you've got booze on your breath and a bottle in your desk drawer. You've picked two fights with fellow officers, and you weren't there when another one needed you.''

Anger flared in Hansen's eyes. ''You've never pulled over for a catnap? It was the middle of the damned night! Nothing was happening. The wife and I had it out the day before and I didn't get any sleep.''

''You trying to tell me you weren't drinking?''

''Yeah, that's what I'm telling you.'' His outthrust chin was suddenly belligerent.

''I hear different.'' Jack held up a hand. ''I don't listen to gossip. I've been watching you for a while. Damn it, Hansen, look at yourself! You've got the shakes. Your eyes are bloodshot. Something is wrong. Maybe you're not an alcoholic. Maybe you're just anesthetizing yourself because something else is making you hurt like hell. I don't know. I can't know unless you tell me. But I also can't let you go out there operating at fifty percent or less. You know that.''

''It was Wentz, wasn't it?'' Damn near vibrating with anger, Hansen half stood, then sank back into the chair. "You know we've never gotten along. Why in hell would you listen to him?" He uttered a profanity. "The bastard doesn't drink! He doesn't think anyone else should."

Actually, it had been Ben Shea, Meg's brother-in-law, who had reluctantly come to Jack with rumors. What Hansen didn't get was that *he* was the issue here, not his accuser.

"Get help." Jack flattened his hands on his desk. "If you want your badge back, you'll talk to the psychologist and you'll go into Fairhaven. You can't tell me Janet won't support you if you give up the booze."

Hansen gave a bitter laugh. "Support me? That's a laugh."

Torn between dismay—Jack didn't like playing Ann Landers—and satisfaction because Gary Hansen was finally coming out with what had been eating at him, Jack made a noncommittal sound.

"She's talking about leaving me." Hansen's gray eyes burned. "She doesn't like the hours. She doesn't like the moods. No matter what's happened at work, I'm supposed to come home and play happy husband and daddy. Crap!" he exclaimed violently. "She knew I was a cop from the get-go. For better or worse, she promised. 'Better' is all she had in mind."

"Your drinking an issue at home?" Jack asked mildly.

The stocky thirty-year-old shot to his feet. "It has to be my fault?"

"I didn't say that. The divorce rate is high for police officers. You know the statistics. Living with a cop isn't easy. I've met your wife a few times. Seemed like a nice lady who loved you. I'm wondering what's changed.''

"Hell if I know.'' Hansen paced jerkily. "Okay. Things are tough at home. I've taken nips a few times from the bottle when I was seriously pissed. I'm not doing antidepressants or tranquilizers. I've had a drink or two. I won't do it on the job again.''

"That's not good enough.'' Jack didn't let his expression react to the blistering anger and despair he saw on the other man's face. "Talk to Bill Zuelhke. Maybe he can suggest a marriage counselor, if Janet is willing. But for now, I have to ask for your badge.''

Hansen stepped back, his face twisted. "Don't do this.''

"I have no choice.'' Jack rose slowly to his feet and waited, hurting inside but inflexible. The department was a family. Sometimes, if you cared about someone, you had to force him to get help.

Beth had made him think. *Was* Hansen any different from her husband? Should Jack be giving him a break because he'd been a good cop? Even on a desk job, he could do some damage.

She was right for another reason, too. Ray Sommers had cracked. Gary Hansen teetered on the edge. Out there, a cop had to be able to trust his fellow officers. Hansen wasn't dependable.

The deputy flung his badge and holstered weapon onto the desk. "Keep 'em,'' he said hoarsely. "I won't be wanting this one.''

He stalked out and slammed the door so hard the pane of glass shimmied. Jack had one glimpse of a rage-engorged face before Gary Hansen stormed out of the police station.

A tingle of alarm walked over Jack's skin, raising the hair on his arms. *This one.* He wouldn't have meant the badge. It had to be the revolver he was talking about.

Like most cops, he probably had an arsenal at home. God almighty. Was he thinking of swallowing a bullet?

Jack didn't want to think so, but he opened his intercom and asked his secretary to look up Janet Hansen's work phone number, if she had one. Maybe he should have talked to her before today's meeting, but it seemed a man should be able to confide his own troubles to his wife, not have his boss ratting on him.

But this…this she should know.

While Jack waited, his thoughts turned inexorably to Beth. He'd told the truth. Cops' marriages had a rate of failure twice the average. Their work hours were long and erratic; they had moods because of the horrors they saw, the waste of lives; and the threat of violent death was ever present for them.

If he couldn't talk about any of this with Beth, how could he imagine her becoming a cop's wife? His wife?

She had guts. She was independent. But he didn't dare let her see who he was, what he was. She might look at him again with horror and fear. He couldn't face that. Yet, without a clear-eyed beginning, did they have any hope?

He swore aloud, the single profane word echoing sharply in the silent office.

Be honest, he thought. Was she refusing to see him, or was he the one hiding from her? Had she ever really tried to cut him off when he started to tell her something? Was she really the fragile flower he treated her as?

So what was it? Did he want her to meet the real Jack Murray, or didn't he?

Face it. The real question might be, did he want her to dig deep enough to meet Johnny, the boy who'd crawled away and left Meg Patton to her fate?

Meg's love had died that day. Jack and she were friendly enough now, for Will's sake, but she had no reason to forgive him, and he knew deep inside that she didn't respect him as a man, even if she did as a cop and her boss. Nothing he ever did, ever became, could—or should—change how she felt.

The trouble was, he ached to be loved all the way through. *For better or worse.* He didn't give a damn about Meg Patton anymore. But he'd learned something from her. He needed a woman to love not just Jack Murray, sheriff, but Johnny Murray, the confused kid whose dreams had died as a sacrifice to his cowardice.

He wanted Beth to hear him, and to say, ''I love you anyway.''

Or maybe he was terrified she'd hear him and not be able to love the boy he'd been or the man he'd become. Maybe that was why he was tiptoeing around her.

Jack bowed his head and pinched the bridge of his nose. God. He should be hoping she could bear being a cop's wife, not fantasizing that she would have loved him twenty years ago when he was still a gutless little wonder.

Hell, he should just hope she ever said, "I love you." Forget the "anyway." The "no matter what."

A minute later, his secretary brought him the phone number. With her quietly closing the door behind her, he dialed Janet Hansen's work number even as he rehearsed the words to warn her that her husband was out of a job and potentially suicidal.

Maybe it was just as well he wasn't seeing Beth and her children tonight. He might be in one of those moods.

CHAPTER THIRTEEN

BETH FINGERED the thick, strong texture of a butter-yellow quilt that was old enough to have frayed in places. The bits of fabric were pieced to look like pinwheels, golden yellow and green muted by time to seafoam.

"Isn't this beautiful?" she asked Jack.

He came to her side in the antique store. "How much?"

"Um." She unfolded the quilt, looking for stains and the tiny tag that she found safety-pinned to the binding. "Ugh. Two hundred and fifty dollars."

"That's not bad for one in good shape."

"Those fabrics look 1930s to me. Stephanie would love it."

"You going to buy it?"

"Are you kidding?" She let the corner drop. "I've spent enough on Christmas."

"Then—" his dark eyes held hers "—I think I'll buy it. For…one of my upstairs bedrooms. Seems to me it might go just right."

Her heart did a tap dance. One of those upstairs bedrooms might be Stephanie's someday. He was buying it on promise. She was an incredibly lucky woman.

Antique shopping had been his suggestion. Both

had all their Christmas gifts purchased already. Since buying a turn-of-the century house, he had been slowly furnishing it, learning as he went. Keeping him company had sounded like fun.

When she asked what he was looking for, Jack had shrugged.

"Something that jumps out at me. And doesn't cost the earth. Most of the bedrooms are still empty."

They'd first visited a false-fronted building on the main street, sandwiched between the bookstore and a vegetarian restaurant.

A two-block stroll had given them time to admire the Christmas lights again. No snow had yet fallen in Elk Springs this winter, although the mountains were white and the streets clogged with cars and SUVs topped with ski racks. 'Twas the season.

Now Jack and she were at an old Carnegie-style building with lions guarding the granite steps. Both lions sported Santa hats and wooden elves sat on the steps.

"Used to be the police station," Jack had told her as they came in.

An antique mall had taken over the building when the Elk Springs Police Department moved to a modern brick public-safety building. What had been squad room and even jail held the offerings of individual antique shops. This particular shop in a corner room offered lace and vintage clothes, quilts and wonderful hats like those Beth's great-grandmother had worn. Hangers displayed World War II–era dresses; the quilts and afghans and matelassé coverlets were draped over racks. Hankies and delicate doilies spilled from baskets.

Jack looked around with a peculiarly bemused expression. "This was the police chief's office once upon a time. Ed Patton's."

"Meg's father?" She'd asked old-time Elk Springs residents about Meg Patton and heard plenty of stories about Chief Patton and his three daughters.

He grunted, and she saw the way his face darkened as though his memories were disturbing.

"You didn't like him."

"We got along." His tone was curt. "He was a bastard."

"Oh." She didn't quite know what to say. This wasn't the first time she'd been in this spot.

She'd been discovering how reluctant Jack seemed to be to talk about his past or the ugly parts of his job. She was terribly conscious sometimes of how one-sided their conversations could be. She brooded about her marriage, her upbringing by a strict father, her secret contempt for her mother. Jack was probably sick of hearing about her marriage to Ray, but he was polite enough, or curious enough, to ask her questions and get her going.

When he became the topic, however, she felt the invisible wall, as solid as if it had been built of brick. At first she thought indulgently how typical it was of a man that he didn't see any point in raking over the past. But within a few weeks, Beth realized something more was going on. He talked about his childhood and family readily. And Will—get Jack started about his son, and he would brag until the cows came home.

But whatever had happened to drive Meg away was another story. And he was strangely reticent about his years as a police officer.

Now she said only, "I wonder what your Chief Patton would think about his office now."

Jack gave a short, savage laugh. "He's probably scrabbling at the earth even as we speak, trying to get out so he can throw every piece of lace on a bonfire. He might have rested in peace if his office held antique guns and knives."

Beth had never heard Jack sound like that.

She should have probed, Beth thought unhappily, that evening after Jack dropped her at home and insisted on paying the baby-sitter. She was being a coward, not wanting to be forced to confront the violent nature of his job.

Once the antique store closed, he'd taken her to a French restaurant, where over dinner he'd mentioned in passing a murder investigation that was in the news nightly. She had wondered whether he had *seen* the body, pulled from the Deschutes River. How did he feel when he saw the horrific things people did to each other? Had he ever worked homicide? Did ghastly waxen faces haunt his dreams? After he'd had to touch a bloody corpse, did he go home and wash his hands over and over, like Lady Macbeth unable to get the blood out?

But she didn't ask. She wasn't even sure why. Because this was a date and that wasn't the kind of thing you talked about? Because she didn't want her macabre musings to take shape, so that she had to know what he had done and seen?

Or because she didn't know how he'd respond to her doubtless foolish questions?

The other night, for example, she had sensed his irritation when he was telling her about the deputy with a drinking problem. What popped out of her mouth, but that he'd be at risk for a car accident.

Of course that wasn't what Jack was worried about! She knew that county deputies carried guns and even used them sometimes. Just a few days ago, a brawl at a tavern on the outskirts of town had led to a shooting. County deputies had broken up the fight and arrested two men. Even around here, that kind of thing happened.

Who would know that better than she? Beth thought bitterly. Her ex-husband had stalked and then assaulted her. That wasn't the kind of thing that was supposed to happen to someone like her, or in a town like this, but it had. It did to other women, too.

She'd sounded stupid and...and naive. Which she wasn't. But she didn't like to think about Jack slamming suspects up against a wall, pulling his gun, maybe even shooting someone. She tried not to let herself wonder if he had ever killed anyone. Every time she opened her mouth to ask questions about what it was like to be a police officer, she had a flash of memory: his lips drawn back from his teeth in an expression of ferocity she had taken for a savage grin. The swearing, the grunts, the thud of bodies and fists connecting, the metallic click of the handcuffs closing on Ray's wrists...

She shuddered, remembering.

Beth had already slipped upstairs to be sure the

girls were in bed, kissing both although they already slept, faces untroubled, soft with dreams she hoped were of triumphs and wonder. She should be doing something useful: ironing, so she wouldn't have to in the morning, or unloading the dishwasher that Tiffany had loaded earlier. Maybe wrapping the gifts that were piling up in her closet.

Instead she sat in the dining room with a cup of herb tea, and remembered every touch and sensation of making love with Jack tonight. He was so tender, so invariably gentle and unselfish, what woman wouldn't glory in the recollections?

Sex had never been that great with Ray. It had hurt so awfully the first time Ray made her his, on the bench seat of his pickup truck. Afterward he'd kissed away her tears and told her how great it would be the next time.

It had been better. Not great, but better. But she had no real grounds for comparison. Her friends weren't the kind of girls who talked about things like that, even if they were doing them. She could hardly ask her mother what sex should be like. And she'd been so crazy about Ray, so excited that he wanted her, Beth had loved the fact that she could please him so utterly. She was thrilled when he lost control. The feel of him jerking in climax inside of her gave her purely feminine pleasure. He needed her. What more could she want?

Except that she had wanted something more, she just hadn't known what. Eventually, she did have orgasms sometimes. Ray wasn't an inconsiderate lover. She wasn't sure he ever noticed when she did or didn't climax, though. He was too engrossed in his own drive to satisfaction.

In the early years, they'd cuddled afterward and talked, but the talk became scanter and the time came when Ray would just roll over and fall asleep with insulting speed. Once in a while he'd mutter something like, ''You'd better have ironed my blue shirt,'' before the first snore rasped out.

Would that happen with Jack, too? Beth worried. Did the passage of years always erase the fascination with each other?

But he made love so differently, that gave her hope. He always saw *her*. No matter what, he didn't climax until she did. The iron control awed her. Sometimes, being a woman, she longed to shatter it. Not always—she loved the tender, patient way he aroused her and let her explore his body and what pleased him. But it would be nice to know that she could do it. That he wanted her enough to lose control.

But, just as she trembled on the verge of asking questions that she wasn't sure she wanted answers to, just as she never actually *asked* those questions, Beth never let herself be so wanton as to tempt him to treat her with less than gentle care. Maybe she was afraid she'd fail and look foolish.

Or, more likely, she was afraid of the result. She'd seen him just once when his control had snapped, and he'd scared her as much as Ray did. She didn't really believe Jack would hurt her, but what if he reminded her of Ray for a fleeting moment and she couldn't hide her fear?

She *hated* being afraid. Only recently had Beth

come to realize that her father had set her up to be a timid, subservient wife. Ralph Nowell had never hit either his wife or daughter; he rarely even raised his voice. But his will was law, and no one defied him. There had been so many things her friends could do that Beth wasn't allowed to join in. Her father hadn't trusted her, she had finally understood, even though she was a good student and obedient daughter. But if she was allowed out from under his thumb, she would surely go wild, he clearly believed.

To Beth, it had seemed natural when her husband wanted his way, when her opinion or desires were always secondary or even to be scoffed at. She should have stood up to Ray from the beginning, she knew now. Their marriage might have turned out differently. He wasn't that bad a man, only living patterns he'd learned from his parents in turn. They could have forged new ones, if Beth hadn't been conditioned to nod and agree although she rebelled inside.

Too late, she thought for the thousandth time. She couldn't go back. She'd remade herself, and she was raising her daughters to be strong women.

So why did she still quail inside at the very thought of raised masculine voices? Why did she have to squeeze her hands together to hide their trembling every time she had to say "no" to Ray?

Why was she so terrified not that Jack would become abusive but that she might someday be afraid of Jack?

Impatiently she went to the kitchen and dumped the cool remnants of the herb tea.

"Face it when it comes," she said aloud to herself. A quote teased at the edge of her mind. "The only thing we have to fear is fear itself." Roosevelt, she thought, had said that. It seemed apropos. That was her problem: she wasn't afraid of Jack, but she feared that she might become so.

Ridiculous. The day she'd gone back to college she had vowed to live boldly, to become the kind of strong woman she admired.

Right now, she seemed to be halfway there. It was time to travel the rest of the way.

She was starting up the stairs to get ready for bed when the phone rang. Once upon a time, a call at this time of night would have made her nervous. Somebody was sick; something was wrong.

Now, her heart leaped. *Jack,* she thought, a smile irresistibly tugging at her mouth. He often called to wish her good-night, even when he'd kissed her on the front porch only an hour before.

Instead of going upstairs, she hurried back down to the kitchen and answered the phone there.

She almost answered with an eager "Jack?" Caution—what if it were Ray?—made her say a more conventional "Hello?"

"Ms. Sommers?" The voice was male, familiar, but strained. "This is Will Patton. We met at my dad's house."

"Will! I thought it might be your dad calling."

Her smile had died and her heart had taken up a hard, fast tempo. *Somebody was sick; something was wrong.*

"No. I'm over at college. They just called me. I thought maybe you wouldn't know."

Lights danced in front of her eyes. "Know what?"

Suddenly the college student sounded like a little boy. "My dad. He's been taken hostage." He swallowed audibly. "No. Not taken. He volunteered, to save somebody else. It's…it's this cop Dad fired. He says he's going to shoot his wife and Dad, too."

"WE CAN'T LEAVE that kid in there." Jack stood behind the squad car and scowled over the roof at the brick-fronted ranch-style house, lit by brilliant floodlights. He'd gone to a barbecue once in that backyard, where two crab apple trees sheltered circular beds of pansies. Gary Hansen had worn a white apron over jeans and a polo shirt. He and his wife had flirted while he flipped burgers.

Jack shook his head in disbelief.

The lieutenant beside him loosed a blistering obscenity. "You're not actually thinking about doing it?" he asked incredulously.

With good reason. Standard department policy— universal police policy—was that you never traded a cop for a civilian in hostage situations.

"The bastard has a grudge against you!" Ben Shea exclaimed. "You're going to walk in there and let him shoot you?"

"I don't plan to let him shoot me." Jack thumped his fist on top of the car. "Damn! Gary's a cop. He's not going to shoot anybody."

Shea grunted. "You willing to bet your life on it?"

That was the question, wasn't it?

The entire street had been blocked with barricades, the neighboring houses evacuated. Cops crouched in the dark shadows behind police cars. Bundled against the cold night, neighbors crowded the street beyond the yellow tape, their avid faces illuminated by a street lamp. Christmas lights twinkled along eaves and on trees and shrubs up and down the street, lending a weird, ironic feel to the grim scene.

Sharpshooters were stationed on nearby rooftops. Jack had his doubts about how much good they could—or would—do. Who wanted to take down a fellow officer?

Gary Hansen had his wife and a teenage babysitter in there. He'd let the kids go. It was the older one who'd called 911 from a neighbor's house.

Jack had heard the tape, rerun a dozen times.

"Daddy says," she'd gulped on a sob, "that he wants to talk to the sheriff. Just the sheriff."

On the drive here, Jack had beaten himself up over misreading Gary Hansen's state of mind. Yeah, he was suicidal, all right. He just wanted to take some other people out with him.

Jack couldn't quit asking himself why the hell he hadn't considered this possibility. Beth had pointed out the parallels between Hansen and her ex. Two men whose lives were going awry; two men who were taking refuge in a bottle and in anger. Depressed men might want to kill themselves; angry ones wanted to hurt somebody else.

Jack had warned Janet Hansen, he reminded himself.

Warned? No. He'd gently expressed concern about her husband's state of mind. He'd remarked that Gary was depressed, asked if he had said anything to make her think he was suicidal. Suggested she lock up guns.

He had not said bluntly, "I think he's going to use one of those guns." It had never crossed his mind to come right out with "He's pretty angry at you. He might use one of them against you."

Gary Hansen was a cop. Jack had worn blinkers. Good cops didn't crack. They hit rough patches, they worked out their problems. At worst, they turned in their badges and found a new career.

They didn't threaten to kill a sixteen-year-old girl.

When Jack got here, he'd taken the phone from Shea and called Gary Hansen's number.

"You came." Hansen didn't sound surprised.

"I'm here. Let's talk."

"Oh, yeah. We can talk. But not over the phone. You've got to come in."

"You know I can't do that." Jack had stared at the blank facade of the house. The blinds and drapes were all pulled. In which room was the maverick cop holed up with his hostages?

"Policy." The former deputy's voice suddenly thickened with rage. "Well, screw policy! I've got things to say. I want to say them to your face."

"Let your wife and the girl go. Come out and we'll talk. So far, nothing bad has happened. Leave it that way. We'll get you help."

"I'll never wear a badge again after this."

Damn straight. "Probably not," Jack said evenly, "but you don't have to go to prison, either."

Hansen gave a short laugh. "You know, I don't think I want help."

The negotiator, listening in on another phone, started mouthing a calming spiel. Jack had barely begun it when Hansen interrupted.

"I'm going to die today. I have things to say first. If you disarm and walk in the front door, I'll let the baby-sitter go. Otherwise, I'll throw her body out. Your choice."

Straightening from behind the car, Jack exclaimed, "Damn it, Gary, she's a kid! You wouldn't…"

"She doesn't mean shit to me. I am a dead man. Dead men don't feel pity. Your choice. You have five minutes." Click.

Two minutes had passed. Jack didn't have to turn his head to see the teenage girl's parents. He heard the rhythmic sob of the mother, the choked mumble of the father comforting her.

"Get me a vest." Shrugging out of his suit jacket, he unbuckled his shoulder holster and began unbuttoning his white shirt.

Ben Shea shook his dark head. "You can't do this."

"I'm doing it," Jack said flatly. Funny. There hadn't even been a moment of decision. He took the bulletproof vest that was handed to him and put it on.

"I should punch you out and bundle you into that car."

Jack found himself grinning. "And lose your badge?"

"Better than explaining to my sister-in-law and occasional partner why the father of her son is dead with a bullet in his head," Shea said gloomily. He was married to Abby, the youngest of the three Patton sisters.

"She'll know why. I'm a bullheaded SOB."

The vest felt bulky and he doubted it would do any good anyway. Hansen would know he was wearing it. But, hey.

He and Ben Shea briefly discussed what might go down in there. How he could signal for help.

Jack tucked his shirt into his pants and buckled his belt, then pulled on his suit coat. Had to look good for the TV cameras, he thought ironically.

He glanced over his shoulder at the parents. Huddled together, neither was looking at him. They didn't know Gary Hansen had offered a trade.

In minutes, either their daughter would walk out free, or not. Jack wanted to have faith that the man he'd once known would keep his word.

"Wish me luck."

Lieutenant Shea held out his hand. They shook with the solemnity of two men who never expected to see each other again. Then Shea stepped back and Jack started across the street toward the house. Onlookers fell silent. Even the mother's sobs ceased.

Feeling like a circus performer, Jack had never been so conscious of the act of walking, the swing of each step. Blank windows stared at him, golden light filtering between slats of the blinds. Did Hansen see him coming? How certain was he that Jack would comply with his demand?

In the absolute silence, Jack heard his own heartbeat. Fast but steady. Adrenaline pumped, but he wasn't scared. He felt…exhilarated.

This moment, he thought with unnatural calm,

was a gift. How often in his life did a man have a chance to atone for past mistakes?

He had just been handed one.

As he reached the driveway, the garage door began to roll up with a faint hum. Automatic, triggered from inside. The interior light was on, the garage compulsively neat, cardboard boxes labeled in black marker side by side on shelves, tools hung on a Peg Board, two cars filling the space. Still nobody in sight.

Hansen might be sitting in one of the cars, Jack thought with one part of his mind. With the other part, he pictured first Beth and then Will with regret.

He couldn't have faced either if he had let the girl die when he could have saved her. At seventeen, he hadn't known the price exacted for thinking of himself first.

The moment he crossed the threshold of the garage, the door began its descent. He kept his hands at his side and walked forward, between the two cars. A sidelong scan of both told him they were empty.

A washer and dryer stood at the back, the dryer open with clothes spilling out into a bright red plastic basket. A purse sat atop it. Jack pictured Janet Hansen pulling into the garage, deciding to grab a load of laundry on her way into the house. Had the baby-sitter called to her? Or had her husband opened the door and pointed a gun at her?

A thump from the side had Jack swinging around, his pulse leaping. A cat. *Damn.* A cat. The orange tabby stared with wide, wary eyes from a perch atop the workbench.

Deliberately Jack rotated his shoulders and breathed a couple of times, slowly. He should have noticed the pet flap in the door. Careless. He should notice everything.

He climbed the two steps and opened the door. The cold barrel of a gun met his cheekbone, hard.

"Good of you to drop in," Hansen said.

They were in a short hall with a half bath to one side. Beyond her husband, Jack glimpsed Janet Hansen, sitting on the closed seat of the toilet, her face puffy with tears long dried, left eye swollen shut and turning purple. Kneeling beside her was a slight blond girl who, in the one lightning glance, didn't look sixteen. Thirteen or fourteen, maybe. Not much older than Stephanie. Janet's arm was around her and the girl was crying with quiet intensity. She didn't seem even to notice Jack's arrival. Gary Hansen half blocked the bathroom doorway, both hands gripping the revolver that ground into Jack's cheek.

Despite the pain, he said calmly, "Let her go. Let them both go."

"Janet's not going anywhere. She's not leaving me. I already told her that."

"The girl's not involved in this."

"Shari." Hansen didn't shift a millimeter, but he raised his voice. "Stand up."

The teenager froze, hiccuped. Despite what must be her own terror, Hansen's wife said quietly, "Shari. My husband is going to let you go now. Just do what he says."

With her help, the girl stumbled to her feet and faced the door. Drenched with tears, her eyes were wild with fear.

"Come on by me."

The girl ducked past. Those terrified eyes rolled upward to take in Jack's face before fastening on her captor.

"Janet. You, too."

She came with outward docility but a spark of rebellion and even hate in the one glance she cast her husband.

The woman and the girl walking in front, the gun bumping the back of Jack's head, they made an awkward convoy through the family room, kitchen and living room. They might conceivably be shadows seen through the blinds, no more. Even if they'd been spotlit, nobody could have gotten a shot. Hansen was careful to stay behind Jack.

"Stop," the former deputy said sharply. "Murray, walk her to the door. Yeah, like that."

Jack took the few steps forward, opened it, pushed the girl through. "Let Janet go. You and I can talk."

"No! Lock the goddamn door!"

The sixteen-year-old had stumbled down the front steps and begun to run toward the street. Jack shut the door and turned the dead bolt. He hoped if he died today she wouldn't carry it as a burden: *I should have been the one.* He wished there had been a way to let her know she'd done him a favor.

He turned to face the man he'd known for years. Thought he'd known.

"All right," Jack said. "Now what?"

"Now we go back the way we came."

During the procession through the house, Jack wondered if he could block Hansen long enough for Janet to flee out the back sliding door or into the garage. Could she activate the automatic opener from in there?

But instead of staying right on top of Jack, Hansen backed up a few steps. "Into the bathroom," he ordered. "Both of you. Look at me."

His wife retreated until she came up against the toilet; then she collapsed onto it. Jack shifted to stand between her and the stocky blond man with sharp, crazy eyes.

"Move over!" he snapped.

Lifting his hands, Jack obliged. "You did the right thing, letting the kid go," he said, voice as soothing as he could make it. "You're a cop at heart, Gary. You don't want anybody to get hurt."

"You took my badge, remember?" Hansen filled the doorway. "You and my dear wife between you have taken every single thing that mattered to me."

For the first time, his wife lifted her head and stared at him with open fury. "Your drinking did that."

"You thought I'd let you leave." His lips drew back from his teeth in a snarl as wild as a cornered coyote's. Those strangely glassy eyes turned to Jack. "And you. You're right. I'm a cop. What else did you think I could do? Sell shoes, maybe? Wash cars?"

"All you had to do was go into alcohol treatment and you could have had your badge back. You're a good cop, Gary."

"But not anymore." Despair slurred his words as if it were ninety proof. "You two took everything I had. I never did like losing. Made me a hell of an investigator. Nice irony, don't you think? Made me a good cop, and an ugly suicide. 'Cause, see, I'm not going to check out alone. Then you'd be winning and I'd be losing. This way... Well, hell. Maybe I don't win, but I don't lose, either. We'll call it a draw.''

"What about Jennifer?" Staring at her death, his wife fought back. "And Pete? Don't you love them at all?"

The gun swung her way. "I've already lost them, too, thanks to you, bitch!"

"They'll have nobody." It wasn't clear whether she was begging or stating a bleak fact.

"Gary, for God's sake," Jack said urgently, "think about what you're doing. Those kids love you. Get some help. It's not too late. Nothing bad has happened."

Knowing he was wasting his breath, Jack subtly shifted his weight and inched his right hand toward the .357 SIG tucked in the small of his back.

"But something bad is about to happen," Gary Hansen said with sudden eerie calm. "Right now."

The projector clicked to slow motion.

"Don't...do...it." Jack heard his own words, distorted by the very slowness, a record run on the wrong speed.

Jack saw in snapshots. The tendons standing out on the back of Gary's hands as he began to squeeze the trigger. The horror on his wife's face, mirrored strangely by the expression on Hansen's, as if he had suddenly seen what he was doing.

At the beginning of this microsecond that stretched bizarrely, Jack launched himself into the air. He was pulling his weapon as he flew, not at Gary Hansen but to intercept the bullet.

He was squeezing the trigger to kill when he was slammed in the chest. He crashed back onto Janet. Her "oomph" of pain was far away, tinny. The spreading agony in his chest was all-absorbing. They were tangled atop the toilet, Janet taking the worst of it.

Nonetheless, he lifted his head and the SIG at the same time. His ears ringing, he didn't know who had been shot.

Until he saw Gary Hansen lying on the bathroom floor, his face gone.

Janet Hansen screamed, kept screaming. The sound was a distant siren.

Jack tried to suck in air that wouldn't come and felt the darkness closing in.

CHAPTER FOURTEEN

STARING WITH burning eyes at the television set, Beth saw the grainy images of the front door opening, the teenager bursting out as if pushed, almost falling and clutching at the handrail, then stumbling down the stairs and beginning to run. When no one else emerged, when the door shut again, a sob tore from Beth's throat.

What if he died? How could he do something so insane? The TV station kept showing reruns of the Butte County sheriff himself walking unarmed across the street, his stride deliberate. In a hushed voice, the commentator said, "We're told that Gary Hansen, the deputy who resigned after being suspended from his job only days ago, has offered to trade the teenage baby-sitter for Sheriff Jack Murray. Unbelievably, Sheriff Murray seems to be accepting the deal."

The girl came out fairly quickly. Two SWAT team members in bulletproof vests rushed forward and enfolded her between them, escorting her behind the police cars where the TV cameras intruded on her sobbing reunion with her parents.

The minutes ticked by. Beth clutched the cordless phone so tightly in her fingers that the plastic creaked. The reporter murmured comments from time to time; the camera panned from the house to the huddles of cops, to the black-clothed SWAT team sharpshooters barely visible on rooftops.

When a muffled crack, crack sounded, Beth jerked. The reporter's voice rose in excitement. Police swarmed toward the house.

"It's unclear what has happened inside, but shots were certainly fired," the reporter declared.

Frozen with terror, Beth stared at the television and waited some more. Police crashed through the front door. What seemed an eternity later, some emerged. Between them was a dark-haired woman, one side of her face grotesquely swollen in the stark white of the floodlight. But she was walking, her head turning, turning, as she searched for something.

She was close enough to the TV cameras that her sob was audible when she saw her children. The two, a boy and a girl, ducked under the police tape and ran to her. She collapsed to her knees with her arms around them.

Tears ran down Beth's face.

"Oh, Jack, oh, Jack," she whispered.

"Thanks to the courage of Sheriff Jack Murray, both women survived tonight's terrible ordeal," intoned the reporter. "But where is he? Did he sacrifice his life for a woman we're told he barely knew and a teenage girl he'd never met?"

Suddenly more cops appeared in the broken doorway of the house. Beth's ragged breath caught in her throat. Oh, God. Oh, God. Was that Jack?

He walked out, the suit jacket missing, his white shirt partially buttoned and with the tails loose over his slacks. But he was walking, and he lifted a hand in acknowledgment of the cheers that rose from the crowd and police officers alike.

"Word comes now that Deputy Gary Hansen is dead, shot to death. At this point, we don't know whether he was killed by the sheriff, by his wife or by his own hand. The police are likely to be slow in revealing details."

Jack went straight to a squad car and climbed in the back. Immediately, it made its way through the parting crowd and disappeared down the street.

Beth turned off the television, laid her forehead on her knees and cried in profound relief. She'd known she was falling in love. She hadn't known the terror of loving a man who could walk into danger like that.

She could only love him more because of it.

AFTER THEY'D RELEASED him from the hospital and he'd filed a report, Jack drove straight to Beth's house. Maybe she had no idea what had happened. If not, the doorbell would wake her. All he knew was that he needed to see her and take her in his arms. All Jack had thought about since he saw Gary Hansen dead on the bathroom floor was that now he'd have a chance to hold Beth again. Somehow, against the odds, he had survived.

He hurt like hell. A huge bruise spread like a purple fungus on his chest. Without the bulletproof vest, he would have been dead.

Jack parked in front of Beth's house. Although other houses along the street were dark, tiny golden lights still shone along the eaves of her old house. Gazing at them, he didn't move for a moment. He was stiffening, feeling twinges of muscle soreness in odd places. Being slammed backward, falling over the toilet, cracking his head against the wall, sliding down into the narrow place between, had left reminders he'd be conscious of for days. Getting out of the damned 4×4 made him feel like an old man.

When he turned toward her house, the front door burst open and Beth flew out. She came down the porch steps so fast, he hurried forward to catch her if she fell.

She didn't, but she flung herself into his arms as if he were making a lifesaving catch. "Oh, my God," she cried. "You are alive. You scared me so badly."

Her tears soaked through his shirt. Jack realized with distant astonishment that dampness leaked from his eyes, too. Cheek against her hair, he hugged her and she hugged him and they rocked from foot to foot, murmuring everything and nothing. Two o'clock in the morning, and she had been waiting for him, expecting him, needing to see him as badly as he had needed to see her.

"I love you," he said finally.

She tilted her head back and glared at him. "Oh, how could you do it?"

A slow grin grew on his face. For the first time since he was seventeen years old, Jack didn't have to doubt himself.

"How could I not?" he asked simply, and didn't have to answer his own question: *Because you're a coward.*

"You saved their lives." Beth's gentle hands framed his face; her thumbs moved at the corners of his mouth. Her suddenly tender gaze searched his face.

The exhilaration, the adrenaline, drained away so fast his knees wanted to buckle. Jack swayed, his voice hoarse. "I had to kill a man tonight. A man I considered a friend."

"I know." Her arms accepted him into her embrace again as if it was the most natural thing in the world. "Oh, Jack. I'm so sorry you had to do that."

She half supported him as they went into her house. Inside, she insisted he phone Will while she made him a cup of herb tea sweetened with honey.

The first thing his son said was "Are you crazy, Dad?"

His laugh edged into hysteria. "Not yet. This was just…one of those things."

"Oh, yeah. One of those things every guy's dad has to do in a day's work."

He had to say this once to his son. "Your life, your mom's and mine would have been different if twenty years ago I'd had the guts to think of someone else ahead of myself."

"Is that why you walked in there tonight?" Will's voice rose and cracked, as if he were fifteen years old again. "To prove something to Mom or me?"

"To prove something to myself."

"You could have died!"

Jack squeezed his eyes shut. "I think he would have killed that girl. How could I have lived with that?"

His boy's voice softened. "You couldn't have. I just want you to know…. Um. You scared the crap out of me tonight, but… Jeez. I was proud of you. Really proud that you're my father.''

Now Jack did weep, unashamedly. He'd lived his whole life for those words. He'd needed to know that his son could be proud of him.

Beth gently took the phone from him, said a few quiet words to Will and held Jack while he cried.

''Was he a good friend?'' she asked eventually.

''More a colleague.'' He sounded choked. There he was, blowing his nose like a little kid after a bout of tears. ''Someone I respected.''

''Do you want to tell me what happened?''

He told her about those shocking slow-motion seconds when he'd seen Hansen's finger tightening on the trigger, when he had chosen to take the bullet himself and shoot this man he had known for years.

''Then you couldn't have done anything else,'' Beth concluded for him, clear eyes holding his. ''Whatever went wrong in his life is a tragedy, but if you hadn't killed him, he would have killed himself. *And* several other innocent people. Including—'' her voice became fierce ''—you.''

''I kept thinking about you.'' He cupped her face in his hands and drank in the sight of it.

Her mouth trembled. ''When I heard…''

He kissed her, just a taste, a moment of comfort for both of them.

''When I heard,'' she continued, voice thready, ''I thought, what if I never see him again? And then I thought, what if I'd already told him I never want to see him again, because of what he does? And *this* is what you do. Why didn't I understand sooner?''

He closed his eyes and entered for a moment the

dark shame he kept inside, a room he kept closed off but always knew was there. "I'm not a hero."

"Yes." Beth smiled through tears. "You were already mine. Now the whole world is going to see you that way."

Jack groaned and she laughed. "All those TV interviews?"

All those expectations. God help him, how that would have scared him ten years ago or ten days ago. Now, he felt…lighter. Maybe he could live up to the expectations. He had it in him to do so.

He wasn't a coward.

He kissed Beth with greater passion and need that wasn't just comfort, but affirmation. "I love you," he said huskily as his mouth moved damply down her neck, feeling the vibration in her throat as she made those soft helpless sounds.

"I should go," he said, when he realized his hands were under her shirt, cupping her breasts through her bra. "Your kids are home."

"Sound…asleep." Her eyes were huge pools of blue, her cheeks tinged with pink. "Come upstairs with me. I can lock my bedroom door."

"You're sure?" He sat up, away from her, giving her space to make a decision. "I want you, but I can wait." He didn't tell her how unbearable was the thought of his own empty house.

"I think—" she drew him to his feet "—I really need you to stay tonight. I need to know you're okay."

Always before, they had gone to bed at his house. Tonight felt very different, and not just because of everything that had happened to him. Beth turned out lights on the way, and he waited in the doorways of the two girls' bedrooms as Beth slipped in and kissed their foreheads, then carefully pulled their doors to a precise six inches ajar. A stained-glass night-light in the hall cast a pale rainbow to guide a child to the bathroom.

This, Jack thought, was what it would be like to go to bed with Beth every night, to live with her, to be married. His need for her tonight wasn't altogether sexual. Perhaps some nights they wouldn't make love; they might just hold each other, or one would already be asleep when the other came to bed. Having believed that he would never see her again, he knew that what he wanted most was to be with her, to awaken in the night to her soft breathing, her warmth beside him, to watch her wriggle into panty hose in the morning and make the girls' school lunches, to know they'd have time to talk over dinner.

When she quietly closed her bedroom door behind them and he heard the snick of the lock, Jack almost asked, *Will you marry me?*

But this didn't seem the time for the formality of those words.

Or perhaps he needed first to cleanse himself of the memory of the husband and wife who had started with love and vows, but ended in hate and bitterness. *You thought I'd let you leave.* A man willing to kill the mother of his children, leave them with nobody, rather than face his own flaws or the end of his marriage.

No, Jack preferred not to taint his marriage proposal with the gray smudge of Janet and Gary Hansen's tragedy.

Tonight, it was enough to know that Beth had wanted him to come to her as soon as he could. That she had *expected* him to come, waited up for him. That she was violating her own rules because she, too, needed to be together.

It was enough to gather her into his arms, feel her melt bonelessly against him, see the natural way she tilted her face up for his kiss.

His mellow awareness that they had years ahead of them went out the door. Urgency slammed into him as hard as the damned bullet in the chest. He devoured that sweetly offered mouth. Lifting her, he cradled his erection between her thighs and rocked against her. If she protested as he carried her to the bed, he didn't hear past the roaring of his own blood in his ears.

He stripped her, yanking at her clothes until they gave way, heedless of buttons or hooks. He suckled hard at her breasts and then bent to kiss her more intimately, beyond thinking about whether he'd shock her. She moaned and panted, her hands tugging ineffectually at his shirt.

Jack tore it off, too, buttons popping. The white undershirt went flying. He was pulling his belt off when Beth gasped.

"Jack! Your chest. You didn't tell me you were hurt!"

He glanced down at the spreading bruise. "Right now, that's not what hurts."

Her horrified gaze lowered to the rock-hard swell

beneath his zipper, and the pink in her cheeks deepened. "You're sure? We don't have to…"

"Yes." He didn't sound like anyone he knew, his voice a growl. "I have to. If you're going to stop me, do it now."

Eyes holding his, she answered wordlessly by deliberately unzipping his pants. She made it sweet torment, a fingertip trailing on his bare flesh.

With a growl he bore her back onto the bed and kissed her with mindless need. He had to bury himself in her and know he was alive and she was his. Nothing else mattered.

He didn't even get his damned pants off, although he did, with shaking hands, get a condom from his wallet and put it on. Then he drove into her with no tenderness, no restraint. With a mewling sound she lifted her hips and wrapped her legs around his waist, clutching at his bare back with desperate hands as he thrust again and again. One part of his mind was appalled at himself. What if he was scaring her? Disgusting her? But this bloody night had ripped from him any pretense of finesse or gentlemanly consideration.

She felt so good, so tight and hot. She twisted and fought to get closer. Her teeth closed on his neck, the sharp pain somehow part of the intense pleasure. *She's mine,* he thought in primal satisfaction.

He muffled her scream when her body convulsed, just as her openmouthed kiss muted his guttural cry. In complete exhaustion, Jack collapsed on top of her, unconscious for a moment of his weight or her need to breathe.

Awareness crept back and with a grunt he rolled

to one side, taking her with him. Arms and legs slack, she came, hair tangled across her face, hiding it from him.

Still breathing as roughly as if he'd run a four-hundred-meter sprint, Jack started to worry. Was she crying behind that curtain of hair? Apprehension knotting in his gut, he braced himself to brush it tenderly back.

Her mouth looked swollen, her blue eyes heavy-lidded. Thank God, no tears dampened her cheeks.

"I'm sorry," he said raggedly.

Beth lifted her head, although it wobbled. "Sorry?"

"I wasn't very gentle."

Her mouth curved in a mysterious smile. "No."

"Did I hurt you?"

"No." Her fingertips feathered delicately over his neck. "I, um, seem to have hurt you."

"Me?"

"I think I bit you."

"Ah." Laughter rumbled in his chest, surprising him. "I noticed. It felt sexy as hell."

"Oh." Beth blushed and buried her face against his shoulder. "I've never done anything like that."

"I've never been quite so out of control before."

That caused her to lift her head again and smile with unmistakable satisfaction. "I'm glad."

"You didn't mind?" He was dumbfounded. Hell, maybe when he'd cracked his head against the wall he had suffered a concussion.

"Mind? It's been bothering me that you were so...so restrained. As though I didn't excite you all that much."

This time his laugh wasn't quite so amused. "I've been trying to be considerate. Do you know how hard it's been sometimes to go slow, to be gentle, to wait until I was sure you were ready?"

"It was very sweet of you. But..." Her brow crinkled as she plainly hunted for a tactful way to tell him what he already knew: he was an idiot. "But secretly every woman wants to know her man is too desperate for her to keep his cool. You see?"

"I didn't want to remind you of Ray," Jack said bluntly.

She stared unblinking for an agonizingly long moment. "He wasn't, um...I mean, he didn't..."

"Rape you? I wasn't suggesting that. Just that you were afraid we were both violent men. I figured..."

"You'd prove you weren't. I get it." Beth gave a tentative smile. "I like it when you're gentle. I liked tonight, too. I guess you could tell."

He kissed her, savoring the sweet taste of her lips and the instant way they softened and formed to his. "I could tell," he said, then nipped at her lower lip.

"Oh, Jack." She hugged him suddenly, almost convulsively. "I've never been so scared in my life."

"Not even..." He bit back the question. Too late.

"Not even then. Did you know the TV cameras were filming you when you walked across the street and that garage door just glided up? They showed it over and over. The house seemed to swallow you. And then when the girl came out and you didn't..." She shuddered.

"It's over. I won't say I'm sorry I did what I did."

"No." Another hard hug. "I wouldn't ask that."

Tiredness came over him like a comforter settling its soft weight over them. Words slurring, Jack asked, "Should I leave?"

"No." Soft kisses brushed his unshaved cheek. "Just sleep. Stay in bed until the girls have left for school, if you don't mind. I'll get them off."

"...don't mind."

He couldn't keep his eyes open. Beth withdrew from his embrace for a moment and he heard the click of the lamp being switched off. Jack lasted only until Beth settled back against his side with her head on his shoulder as if she never slept anyplace else.

Then he dropped off.

The night was as dreamless and dense as hours under anesthesia. Beth could have been up and down ten times during the night for all he knew.

Small sounds intruded: a thump on the stairs, the hum of the furnace, a giggle, the slam of the front door and rumble of a school bus. He came awake in increments until he was fully conscious and knew where he was.

Alone in Beth's bed. He'd have liked it better if she were in it with him. Eight-thirty. If Stephanie and Lauren were on that school bus, they were gone. Jack rolled toward the edge of the bed and a grenade exploded in his chest. He let out a strangled groan and made it up to a sitting position. Yesterday's aches had matured into active pain. He looked ruefully down at his chest, not a pretty sight. Who knew there were so many shades of purple? Experience told him that a week or two from now, he'd be sporting an equal array of murky yellows.

Gambling that the girls really were gone, Jack took a very long, very hot shower that loosened a few kinks. With a sense of distaste, he put on yesterday's rumpled white shirt, missing buttons, and the jeans he'd changed into at the station after realizing Gary Hansen's blood had splattered his trouser legs. Then he headed downstairs.

The old house was very quiet. His bare feet made no sound on the wooden treads of the stairs or in the short hall that led to the kitchen. He took a moment, standing in the doorway, to appreciate the sight of Beth in a fuzzy bathrobe, her dark curls loose around her face, bare of makeup. Just the sight of her stirred something in him.

What would she say if he asked her to marry him, right now?

Steam curled out of a mug on the kitchen table. In profile to the kitchen doorway, Beth still hadn't noticed him. She was apparently reading the front page of the morning newspaper that lay flat on the table in front of her.

He must have moved, or made a sound, because she jerked and her head shot up. The look on her face closed a fist around his heart.

Repugnance. She stared at him as if he were a monster.

Jack took a couple of steps closer and saw the headline.

Questions Asked about Deputy's Death. And the subheading: Accusers Remind Investigators Sheriff

Murray Has a History of Questionable Use of Violence.

The woman who had received him last night with warmth and generosity, but who had *not* said, "I love you," had bought the newspaper's doubts hook, line and sinker.

HER SHOCK WAS ALMOST the equal to yesterday's as she watched the man she loved stroll across the street as casually as if he were going into Safeway instead of to trade his life for a teenager's.

Questionable Use of Violence. What were they talking about?

The reporter reminded readers of the debate during Jack Murray's campaign for Butte County sheriff about his record as a police officer and then chief with the Elk Springs Police Department. Numb, she scanned the stories the reporter resurrected: previous hostage situations when deaths had resulted, including one when a board of inquiry had not recommended firing him but had expressed reservations about his refusal to negotiate; a previous shooting, when he had been cleared by the ensuing investigation, but that had aroused questions; allegations of police brutality after a schizophrenic had apparently been "roughed up" during an arrest. Jack Murray had always been cleared, *but...*

She had thought him so noble. She'd held him under the assumption that he was traumatized by having had to shoot a man. And now she found out he'd done it before. He had refused to negotiate, when doing so might have saved lives. He had "roughed up" a suspect.

Oh, God. Oh, God.

All her fears rushed back, a viciously eddying tidal wave of doubts.

Jack's explanation replayed in her ears. *Did I lose my temper? Yeah, probably. Did I act on it? No. I handled the entire incident appropriately as a police officer.*

She had bought every word. The frightening, rough scene had been all Ray's fault. Jack had only been defending himself, trying to restrain Ray.

Now she saw again the snarl that might have been a grin transforming Jack's face until she didn't recognize him. Didn't *want* to recognize him.

And she heard something else he'd said, that night to Stephanie.

I spent my early years as a police officer trying too hard to show how tough I was. I could be a real jerk. I think back to incidents I wish I'd handled very differently. I can only hope I didn't ruin somebody's life.

Funny that she could remember what he'd said so clearly. At the time she hadn't *let* herself be curious about what he meant. About what "incidents" he wished he'd handled differently. What a euphemism! she thought in anguish. An "incident" had been a drunken man killing his children because the police officer outside took the hard line and wouldn't let him cool down.

Had she heard some of these stories? Beth asked herself. Some must have been repeated during the campaign when he ran for sheriff. Perhaps they had lurked in her subconscious. Could that be why she'd felt so uneasy about Jack from the beginning?

Oh, God. How could she have fallen in love with this man?

She kept reading the headlines and articles, over and over again, until they chanted like a circle of faceless accusers. *Investigators Reminded... Questionable Use of Violence... Questions Asked... Violated policy...*

Could he have gone in there, she asked herself with horror, because he *intended* to kill Gary Hansen?

A sound came from the doorway. Beth's heart skipped a beat and she jerked as if she'd thought herself alone in the house. She turned her head, knowing her tumult must show in her eyes, wishing desperately that he hadn't spent the night, that he wasn't here, that she had time to *think.*

He filled the doorway, wearing last night's jeans and wrinkled white shirt, with the buttons torn off. The monstrous bruise on his chest jarred her.

He threw himself in front of a bullet to save someone else. Remember that, her conscience whispered.

No time to think about that, either. Because the moment Jack saw her face, his expression closed as completely as if steel shutters had slid into place.

"I should have expected that," he said, nodding toward the newspaper that lay in front of her. "Scandal is more interesting than..."

"Heroism?" she finished, with unintended bitterness.

Muscles knotted in his jaw. "Facts, I was going to say." He strolled toward the table, pulled out a chair. "You shouldn't believe everything you read."

Beth closed her eyes for a second. "Why didn't

you tell me?'' she asked. ''You let me prattle
about...about traffic stops and shoplifting as if they
were the only crimes you'd ever seen! You've never
once talked about shooting someone, or being investigated for brutality, or letting children die because you wouldn't negotiate.'' Her voice was rising; she stared at him fiercely. ''Is this all lies?''

He ran a hand over his face and for a moment his
cool, expressionless facade fell, letting her see anguish to equal her own. He sat heavily. ''No. It's
not all lies. I told your daughter once that I've done
things I regretted. I wasn't so much telling her as
you. I wanted you to ask me, but you never did.''

''So it's *my* fault?'' she asked incredulously.

''No. I didn't mean to imply that. But answer me
this—If I'd told you about everything in there—''
he waved at the newspaper ''—would you have
agreed to date me?''

The answer he'd asked for showed on her face.

He grimaced. ''So I was damned if I did, and
damned if I didn't.''

''If...if you had explained, if I hadn't had to dis-
cover who you are on the pages of the newspaper,
I might have given you the benefit of the doubt.''
Was that true?

''Yeah. Sure.''

''You've shot someone before.'' That had hit her
especially hard. He had gone in there last night
knowing what he might need to do, knowing what
it felt like. And she had never guessed that he had
blood on his hands.

He swore suddenly and shoved his chair back
from the table, although then he didn't rise. ''I'm a

cop! I'd just watched my partner be gunned down. The son of a bitch swung around to shoot me and I got him first! I should apologize for that?''

''There was an investigation....''

Now he did rise to his feet, towering over her as he flattened hands on the table and leaned forward. Between gritted teeth, he said, ''There is *always* an investigation. Not even police officers can shoot citizens with impunity. There'll be one this time, too. What do you think all that crap is about?''

''Crap?''

He was in a rage. ''There were investigations every time. I have been exonerated every time. Violence is everywhere. You've never wanted to see that. You thought you lived in some kind of damned paradise, but you don't. People get murdered in Butte County, too. Throats get slit and children get raped. My job is to see that they don't, and when I fail at that part, I try to catch the scum who did it. Does that lower me to their level? Who the hell knows?''

''You didn't shoot Ray.'' Now, where had that come from?

''I didn't have to.''

''But you looked like you wanted to.'' A corrosive poison, this fear rose from deep within her, and she wished the moment the words were out that she hadn't spoken them. Hadn't thought them.

He looked as if she'd punched him. His eyes were dark, his stare stunned. ''Do you really think I'd kill a man for no other reason than my own temper?'' A muscle spasmed under his eye and he shook his head as though to clear it. "You think that's why I shot Gary Hansen?"

Shocked, she pressed a hand to her mouth. "No! Oh, no! I never thought…"

But she was too late.

Jack shoved the chair hard and walked out. She'd barely stumbled to her feet and started after him when the front door slammed hard enough to rattle the side panes.

He was gone. This time, she knew with terrible clarity, for good. Because, once again, she hadn't listened, had only reacted out of long-held fears.

Beth crumpled back into her chair and laid her forehead on her crossed arms. Her tears soaked the newspaper.

CHAPTER FIFTEEN

"MURRAY HERE. Leave a message if you want me to call."

She'd heard the same terse, canned response a dozen times. Beth moaned in despair and then hung up the telephone quickly, hoping the machine hadn't recorded her misery. Legs wrapped around the legs of the kitchen stool, she buried her face in her hands.

Where was Jack? Had he gone to work today or had he spent the day being grilled by—who did this kind of thing?—internal investigators? The FBI? Tonight, was he sitting in his huge old house listening to the phone ring and choosing to ignore both it and her earlier messages? Would his anger cool so he could forgive her? Or had she driven him away once and for all with her constant distrust—the distrust he had done nothing to earn?

"What's wrong, Mommy?" Her younger daughter's voice came from behind her.

Beth whipped her head up and tried to summon a smile. "I'm just tired, honey."

The sound of the television still came from the living room. Stephanie had probably turned on some program too teenage for her younger sister.

"You don't look tired." Lauren eyed her shrewdly. "You look sad."

Beth's first instinct was to lie. But how could she expect honesty from her children if she didn't give it in return?

"I suppose I am," she said with difficulty. "I did something stupid, and Jack's angry with me."

A frown gathered on Lauren's high, curved brow. "What did you do?"

Beth put it as simply as she could. "I didn't trust him when I should have."

"Why didn't you?" the eight-year-old asked in clear surprise.

There was the question. Why hadn't she?

Beth knew the answer: Because the newspaper article had echoed her fears as if it had been a personal letter. *Dear Beth, you were right all along.*

She had reacted to her own deep-rooted fear that all men turned angry eventually. She had reacted to her father, to Ray. Not to Jack at all.

"I haven't known him that long," she explained to her daughter, who came into the kitchen and leaned against her. The warm, sturdy body pressed so close brought a sting of tears to Beth's eyes and she wrapped an arm around Lauren. "When you're dating a man and thinking…thinking that you might want to marry him someday, you worry. Divorce isn't fun or easy, and it shouldn't be. When you marry, you intend it to be forever. But what if you don't know him as well as you think you do? What if he's hiding something from you?"

"Do you think Mr. Murray is?"

"I think now there are things he didn't tell me, because he knew they would worry me. I wish he had. Or I wish I'd asked."

Lauren didn't say anything for a long while. "You know Saturday, when Daddy took us for ice cream, even though it was so-o cold?"

Puzzled by the apparent non sequitur, Beth nodded.

"I asked if he still thought we'd be all together again someday. He said no. That we were still a family, but we'd never all live together again." She tilted her head back, eyes inquiring. "Does Daddy know that you're thinking about marrying Mr. Murray?"

"No...yes. I don't know," Beth said honestly. "What he knows is that he and I won't remarry, that we're happier living separately."

"Oh." Lauren burrowed her face against her mom and mumbled something.

Beth kissed the silky top of her head. "I couldn't hear you, honey."

"I said—" the words were barely louder "—that I think I might like it if you did marry Mr. Murray. He's nice."

Blunt knife to the heart. Her daughter knew without hesitating what Beth should have known.

"Yes," she whispered, tears seeping from beneath eyelids she'd squeezed shut. "Yes. He is."

JACK STARED at the frantically blinking red light on the answering machine. Twelve—no, he recounted, fourteen new messages. On a sound of disgust, he swung away. He wasn't in the mood for any of them.

He was, however, going to return Mark Dunford's call. The journalist who'd written this morning's splendid, front-page piece wanted the sheriff's comments. Jack had stewed all day over that one. The bastard had a nerve.

Well, it so happened that Jack did have a few *comments* to make. He'd waited this long in hopes he could make them more temperate than they would have been at ten o'clock this morning when his secretary had handed him the little pink message slip with Dunford's name on it, when his own rage and pain had felt like a heart attack.

Jack dialed the SOB's home number and waited while a woman went to get her husband.

"This is Mark Dunford," the other man said.

"Sheriff Murray."

"Ah. Thank you for returning my call. Our readers—the citizens who elected you—will be curious about any progress in the investigation of yesterday's tragedy. And particularly, of course, in your side of the story."

"Story?" The burning pain spread in his chest again. Harshly, he said, "What happened yesterday was the horrific end of a troubled man's life. It was the beginning of growing up without a father for two children, of struggling to survive as a single mother for his wife. I shot a man I liked and respected. Story? I understand what you do for a living, Dunford. Just remind yourself occasionally that you're writing about real people."

"Sheriff Murray, I became a journalist so that I could personalize news events, remind everyday folks that behind the headlines real people are suffering. If you took offense…"

"Yeah." Jack stalked through his house with no

goal, just needing to stay in motion. "I did. I've cooperated with you in the past. I've encouraged everyone in my department to do so, when it was possible without jeopardizing an investigation. Frankly, my interest in future cooperation dwindled this morning when I and every citizen of this county read that pack of innuendos about my career."

"I wrote nothing but fact—"

Ruthlessly, Jack overrode him. "And left out the parts that wouldn't have supported your thesis. You know damn well that in every case you cited, I was cleared without question. You know, too, that any cop who uses a weapon is automatically investigated. So why imply that a board of inquiry is looking into what happened not because that's routine, but because I'm a loose cannon? Tell me, did I shoot Gary Hansen because I was in a bad mood and felt like killing someone? Or maybe just because I didn't want to bother with that negotiation crap?"

"Sheriff…"

"You have my comments," Jack said coldly, and hung up.

He returned to the kitchen and slammed the phone back in its cradle. That was a phone call he probably shouldn't have made. It hadn't been politic. Maybe tomorrow he'd give a flying damn.

The red light on the answering machine kept winking at him, and he chose to ignore it some more. Right this minute, he didn't want to hear from anyone. Not even Beth.

He'd fantasized half the day that she would be on his doorstep when he got home, begging his forgiveness, swearing her undying faith in him. He wasn't young and foolish enough to believe his own fairy tale. Jack wasn't even sure he wanted to hear about her undying faith at this particular moment. Maybe he was feeling too cynical.

Maybe she'd hurt him too badly.

The doorbell rang and his heart squeezed in an extra beat of hope or despair, he wasn't sure. *Ignore it,* he told himself. Whoever was on his doorstep would go away. All he wanted was his solitude. If ever a man needed to lick his wounds…

It rang again, insistently.

"All right, damn it," he muttered. From the front room he could just catch a glimpse of the porch. A blond woman with a kid beside her stood with hand outstretched to ring the doorbell again.

Jack grunted in surprise and faint amusement. Meg Patton. Of course, she wouldn't go away and leave him in peace. On the job, she treated him with some deference. Out of uniform, that evaporated.

Cold air rushed in when he opened the door. Her nose and cheeks were gaudy red to match her hat and her breath was a puff of steam.

"Hi," she announced, looking him over with bright eyes.

Beside her, Evan McNeil, almost three years old, stared solemnly, his cheeks as red as Mom's and a lot rounder. He didn't see his half brother's father often enough to feel comfortable with him.

"I suppose this is where I say 'Come in,'" Jack said wryly.

"Yep." Meg stepped across the threshold with no appearance of shyness. Once inside, the door shut, she began unswathing layers of winter clothing, her own with one hand and her son's with the other.

"Planning to stay awhile?" This time Jack sounded downright disagreeable.

"I'm hot," Meg said simply.

For a woman her age—his age—who had a kid in college, she looked damned good—slim, leggy, tough. She was as pretty as she'd been in high school.

And he just wished she'd go away. He wished she was another woman.

He led the way into the kitchen and poured Evan a glass of apple juice. Meg turned down his offer of coffee. Hip against the counter, Jack crossed his arms and waited.

"I talked to Will tonight," Meg said, craning her neck to keep an eye on Evan, who was wandering into the dining room.

Jack grunted.

As direct as always, her blue eyes connected with his. "He says you traded yourself for the Hansen baby-sitter because of me. Because of that scene with my father."

The kid had a big mouth.

"I did it because I thought Hansen was serious about killing her. I didn't see a choice."

"Policy…"

Jack said the same, profane thing about policy he had the night before.

Meg made a face. "Yeah, okay."

"I couldn't take the chance he meant it."

"All right. But tell me the truth, Jack. Did you do it partly because of that day? In…atonement?"

Funny she should choose the very word he had. They knew each other too well. Came of sharing a child.

He rubbed the back of his neck and said with sudden weariness, "Maybe. Yeah. You know I've always felt guilty. I let you down, Meg. I guess I've always wondered whether I would again, if I had it to do over."

She studied him with the unnerving, unblinking scrutiny of a child who hasn't yet learned that you aren't supposed to stare. "And do you know now?" Meg asked.

"Now I know," he agreed.

"Well." Meg smiled, an irritating beam of sunshine. "It's about time."

"What the hell's that supposed to mean?" he asked grumpily.

"I've told you a thousand times. You were a boy. How could you have stood up to Chief Ed Patton?"

"I wanted to think I was a man."

"Those teenage years are tough," she said. "Darn it, where did Evan go?"

The boy was sitting at Jack's dining room table, drumming his heels against the cherry legs of the chair. His plastic cup of juice sat in front of him, about chin level.

The adults retired to the kitchen and left the kid to reign over the table. There wasn't anything he could get into in there, Jack figured.

"I hear you're dating someone," Meg said, changing tack in her disconcerting way.

"Beth Sommers." She'd know that much already,

thanks to Will's loose lips. "She owns the stationery store."

"I browsed in there the other day just to get a look at her."

His turn to stare.

She shrugged blithely. "I figure I have a proprietary interest. You *are* Will's father."

"Beth read the newspaper this morning and ditched me."

"What?" Outrage added syllables to the single word.

Now he was the one with the big mouth. "Oh, hell. That's not true. I walked out, not her. I needed her to be furious at the garbage they said about me. Instead, she believed every word and I could see in her eyes that she was sure she'd never really known me."

Meg cocked her head to one side. "Why?"

"Why what?" he asked, irritated.

"Why did she believe it?"

Jack swore and scrubbed a hand over his face. "Because her ex-husband was abusive, and I suspect her father was, too. Because I knew she was afraid of men and therefore tiptoed around the subject of my job. Hell, I made it sound like ticketing jaywalkers is my principal duty outside of playing politics. Thanks to Mark Dunford, she now knows better."

"Did you…well, *talk* to her?" Meg sounded unusually tentative.

"No. I already told you. I walked out in a huff." He gave a twisted smile. "But I will. Soon."

"Tonight?"

He made a rough sound. "You know what today was like. I talked myself hoarse. I had to explain every second, every thought that crossed my mind, every goddamned word Gary said. And then I had to start all over again. To cap off my day, I went to see Janet Hansen."

"Oh, dear," Meg said inadequately.

"She thinks it's her fault, that somehow she could have prevented his tumble into alcoholism and depression. I talked some more, with her nodding and not buying a word. Oh, yeah. It was a hell of a day. No, Meg, I'm not going to justify myself to a single other person."

"Even the woman you love?" she asked softly.

"Even her." He heard his own flat tone and wished she'd go home. Meg Patton, he realized, had slowly become a friend, even a good friend, in the years since she'd come back to Elk Springs with the fourteen-year-old son he hadn't known he had. He appreciated the fact that she'd visited tonight. But it was not her understanding, support and love he wanted.

And Beth's was not forthcoming. Nor was he going to beg for it, not tonight.

"Okay. I'll let you brood in peace." Meg hopped off the stool again and went to fetch her son. He held coats for them, watched as they tugged Polartec hats over their heads, wound mufflers around their necks, and squeezed hands into mittens. *Hurry,* he asked silently.

Meg stood on tiptoe and kissed his cheek. "It'll work out, Jack."

"Thanks." He opened the door for her and her

son. Not until they'd started down the steps did he see the woman standing on the sidewalk in front of his house. A few dry white flakes drifted from a dark sky. She looked incredibly lonely out there, wearing a bright blue parka but with her head bare.

"Beth?"

She still hadn't moved, still stood there, when Meg and the boy reached her. The two women exchanged a few words, Meg buckled her son into her 4×4, waved and got in herself. Jack gripped the door and waited, watching Beth come slowly up the walk. As she neared, he could see her face in the porch light, eyes huge in a face pinched from the cold—or apprehension.

Still one step down, Beth stopped. "Would you rather I went away?"

"No." He sounded hoarse. "You'd better come in before you freeze."

She didn't move. "Was that Meg?"

"Yeah." Jack felt...dissociated. He didn't care about Meg. Although he was mildly curious about one thing. "What did she say?"

"Good for you." One moment Beth was hesitating ten feet away, and the next she hurried past him as if plunging into the lion's den.

In a dream, Jack turned and shut the door. "That's it? 'Good for you?'"

"Does she know who I am?"

"Yep. Will told her all about you. Apparently she's been in your store."

"Oh." Beth shivered in his foyer, plucking at the fingers of her gloves without making any real effort to take them off. Her nose was as bright as Rudolph's, but her cheeks were bluish-white.

"Damn it, you are freezing," Jack said harshly. "How long were you standing out there?"

Another shiver racked her. "I wasn't sure you'd want to see me."

He wanted desperately to take her in his arms. Caution held him back.

"Why would you think that?"

"I left messages."

"I haven't heard them yet. Come on." He reached for her zipper. "Let's get you out of that coat. A cup of coffee will make you feel better."

She was clumsy getting her gloves off; he helped her out of her parka, trying not to touch her, however badly he wanted to. He had to put a hand on her back and propel her toward the kitchen. Jack poured a second cup of coffee. Her hands shook when she tried to lift the mug he put into them.

"I'm sorry. I didn't mean to get frostbite lurking outside." Her smile was a pathetic excuse for the real thing.

"You were afraid to come knock on the door?"

Her eyes met his at last. "It's hard, when you've hurt someone, to know if 'I'm sorry' is good enough. If it's not…"

He was afraid to hope. "The board of inquiry won't come to a conclusion for a few days." He still sounded harsh. Unfriendly.

"I don't care." She briefly closed her eyes. "Jack, even if you won't forgive me, I need you to know how sorry I am. I said things…" She looked at him again with naked honesty. "You are a brave, kind man. How could I question your integrity? You wouldn't have shot Gary Hansen or anyone else unless you had to. I know that.''

On a painful rush of relief, he took the mug from her unresisting hand and set it carefully on the counter, then wrapped his arms around her. "This morning was partly my fault. I was...hiding from you. I haven't always been brave or kind. I didn't want you to know that.''

"I don't believe you," she mumbled against his shoulder.

Jack breathed in the essence of her silky mass of dark hair. "Believe it.''

Beth pulled back then. "Tell me," she said. "But first, I need you to know that I love you. No matter what.''

A sound came from his throat. It was an animal sound, half groan, half sob, that shocked him. "Say that again," he said raggedly.

"I love you," she whispered.

He snatched her back into his arms and kissed her with raw need. Her cold mouth warmed and softened, accepting his savage hunger and then responding with a certain fierce need of her own. Jack was lost in her, the softness of her skin and tangle of hair, her gasps, her remarkable blue eyes. He had her backed up against the cabinet, his hips rocking against her, his hands gripping her buttocks.

"I want you. Now.''

"Yes.'' She yanked at his belt buckle. "Now.''

They were both rasping for breath; his hands shook as he shucked as many of her clothes as he had the patience to remove. Her hands shook as she helped with his. He kept kissing her, his tongue plunging, his teeth grinding against her full, soft lips. Somehow he held on to his self-control just long enough to put on a condom.

"Ooh!" she cried when he lifted her and thrust in one movement.

He should have waited, Jack thought in agony. She was slick but too tight. He must be hurting her. But he couldn't stop. He was blind with a need to claim her.

"I'm…sorry," he groaned.

She bit his neck, teeth sharp. "If anybody's sorry…"

He thrust again, hard, deep, fast. Ecstasy. "Hurting you…"

"No." The face she lifted to his was transformed, radiant. "Never."

He swore and staggered, then backed her up to the smooth door of the refrigerator. She laughed and held on, her legs clasping around his waist.

As he buried himself in her again, as deep as the fears he was determined to rout, she whispered, "I love you. I love you."

Her body convulsed. His convulsed, all to the mantra, "I love you."

He was saying it, too, he realized, as he carefully went to his knees and followed her down onto the hand-loomed cotton kitchen runner.

She also had tears on her cheeks, he discovered, as he feathered kisses from her neck toward her mouth.

"I did hurt you," he said raggedly.

"No." Her mouth met his. "I'm crying from happiness."

"Don't let yourself be too happy. There are things I have to tell you. Before I ask you to marry me."

"Yes!" Now she smothered his face with kisses. "I will marry you. No matter what."

He tried to pull back. "Listen to me first."

With sudden solemnity, Beth touched his cheek and gazed up at him, eyes so blue he felt himself falling in.

"All right. Talk. But I warn you, I intend to marry you. If you mean it."

"Oh, yeah. I mean it." Dread edged out his euphoria. She hadn't met Johnny Murray yet, or the hard man he'd tried to become. The outside air had somehow stolen into the room, chilling his bare skin. "I can't talk like this. Let's get dressed."

Beth kept sneaking peeks at him as they silently put their clothes back on. She finger-combed her hair and then nodded gravely when he suggested going into the living room.

There, Jack kept his distance, half-sitting on the arm of a chair facing Beth on one end of the couch.

"My name wasn't Jack when I grew up," he began. "It was Johnny. Johnny Murray was a..." He stopped and briefly squeezed his eyes shut. "God. I have to quit pretending. *I* was a feckless, cocky kid, a jock who could have been better if I'd been willing to work out harder, a student body president, Meg Patton's boyfriend. I thought someday I might become a biologist or a doctor or..." He grimaced. "I wasn't all that serious about the future. Which may be one reason I was careless using condoms."

Beth only waited.

He told her the story, then, as he had never told another soul. His humiliation, selfishness, terror. He spared Johnny Murray nothing. *Himself* nothing. He described the kid who decided to change his name and become a man, but thought the only way to do that was become like the man who had humiliated him. The rookie who saw his partner killed. The young cop who came home to Elk Springs, despising and fearing the police chief but trying to please him. Jack talked of sometimes subjugating his own sense of right or wrong to impress Meg Patton's father, the one man who had seen him crawl. The one man who could, he believed, give him back his sense of self-worth.

Jack told of the growing conflict between mentor and young cop, of his own attempts to become a better man. He talked until the grit in his voice seemed to scrape his throat raw. His terrible conflict when he met Will and found out that Meg had been pregnant that day shaped his story. As did his pride in his son.

Beth's blue eyes shimmered with tears that ran over. She made no move to dry them, only listened.

Jack admitted to the shame he had tried to kill, to escape, to ignore. "In my gut, I've always believed I was a coward," he finished. "My biggest mistakes were made trying to prove to the world that I wasn't."

Voice fierce, Beth demanded, "Did you even hesitate last night? When he threatened to kill that girl?"

"No." Jack's chest expanded with a huge breath.

The easiest breath he'd drawn since he was sixteen. The constricting knot of guilt and shame was gone.

"I doubt you were ever a coward." With the back of her hand, Beth wiped her cheeks. "You were a kid. Imagine Will at that age. What would he have done?"

"Not what I did." He raked his fingers through his hair. "Will has more strength of character than I did. At the very least, he would have come to his mother or me."

"It's not your fault that you didn't feel you could go to your parents," she said quietly.

"They're good people."

"But?"

"My father was ashamed of me because somebody had beaten me up. Why hadn't I given worse? he wanted to know."

"So you didn't tell him who did it?"

"How could I?" Jack rubbed his hands on his thighs. "They'd have had to know Meg's father walked in and caught me with my pants down around my ankles."

"Oh, Jack." She jumped up and came to him, sliding her arms around his neck. "Did you really think any of that would change my mind about you?"

He framed her face with his hands and drank in the sight of her eyes, still shimmering, the delicate line of her cheeks, streaked with tears, the salty droplet clinging to her lip. "Yes." He had to force the word out. "Yes, I did."

"I occasionally do dumb things," she said tremulously, "but not usually the same ones twice. I know you, Sheriff Murray. Last night, Gary Hansen's wife and that teenager were lucky to have you. Just as I've been lucky. Johnny Murray, Jack Murray...I'll call you whatever you want. I love you.''

Gritting his teeth against the tumult of emotion, he leaned his cheek against her hair, wrapped his arms around Beth and held her so tightly it must have hurt. She didn't offer even a squeak of protest. Instead, she squeezed back.

When he thought he could control his expression, he eased back reluctantly. She was crying anew. Gripping her hands, Jack dropped to one knee.

''I've never done this before, but I hear kneeling is standard.''

Beth gave a helpless laugh, then bit her lip.

Jack said straight out, ''I don't want an answer tonight. You need to think, and talk to Stephanie and Lauren. But let me ask. Beth Sommers, will you marry me?''

''You can ask only if I can answer.''

''I want you to be ready.'' Romantic posture or not, he sounded grim. ''Don't say yes if you don't mean it.''

''Oh, I mean it.'' This smile was a caress not spoiled a whit by her having to sniff. ''Even Lauren has agreed. Sheriff Murray is nice, she's decided.''

''Stephanie?''

''I think Stephanie is half in love with you herself. She's quite sure you're everything heroic and manly. Having you as a stepfather would be very cool, in her opinion. Besides, she likes your house.''

The first reluctant smile grew into a grin and then

an exuberant laugh. "All right, then. I surrender. Will you marry me?"

"Just try to get out of it."

He surged to his feet and bent his head, but her fingers stopped his mouth and her anxious eyes searched his.

"Are *you* sure?" she asked.

"This is my first proposal. Doesn't that tell you this isn't something I do lightly?"

Darned if tears didn't start falling again. "Why am I crying?" she wailed. "Oh, shoot. I have to blow my nose. What woman has to blow her nose in the middle of her marriage proposal?"

"Probably anonymous thousands." He tasted her tears and laughed. "Okay. Hold on. I'll get you a tissue."

He brought a handful. She firmly blew a nose that became even redder. Balling up the tissue, Beth said, "You haven't changed your mind?"

Jack shook his head.

"You know I put in long hours at the store."

"They're probably nothing to the hours *I* put in."

"You don't have to…well, exactly be a father. The girls do have one. But some effort in that direction would be welcome."

"My pleasure."

"Um… How would you feel about having a baby? Together?"

He had a flash of seeing her pregnant, of him holding a newborn with a puckered, red face, of both of them swinging a laughing dark-haired toddler between them. The images took his breath away. He hadn't even known this was something he wanted so badly.

"You'd think about it?"

"Think about it?" She kissed him. "I want your baby, Sheriff Murray."

Somehow his hands were under her turtleneck. "There's no time like the present to get started, Ms. Sommers."

"No," she agreed breathlessly. "We aren't getting any younger."

Their kiss was tender, achingly slow, passion momentarily held in check but simmering in readiness. He ended it just for the pleasure of looking at her, of playing his thumbs over her swollen lips.

Then it hit him. "Where are the girls?"

"The girls?" She looked as dazed as he felt. "Oh. You mean, my… Um, Stephanie and Lauren."

"Right. Them."

"Tiffany is with them. I do have to go home, but not yet. You can walk me. Later."

"Later," he echoed.

And he did, in the cold night on sidewalks powdered with snow, Christmas only days away. Jack liked the idea that their child might already have been conceived, on this day begun in despair and ended in joy.

Romance is just one click away!

online book **serials**

➤ *Exclusive* to our web site, get caught up in both the daily and weekly online installments of new romance stories.

➤ Try the Writing Round Robin. Contribute a chapter to a story created by our members. Plus, winners will get prizes.

romantic **travel**

➤ Want to know where the best place to kiss in New York City is, or which restaurant in Los Angeles is the most romantic? Check out our Romantic Hot Spots for the scoop.

➤ Share your travel tips and stories with us on the romantic travel message boards.

romantic reading **library**

➤ Relax as you read our collection of Romantic Poetry.

➤ Take a peek at the Top 10 Most Romantic Lines!

Visit us online at

www.eHarlequin.com

on Women.com Networks

Coming in June from

MAITLAND MATERNITY

When two sets
of twins are born at
Maitland Maternity Hospital on
the same day, unforgettable surprises
are sure to follow. Don't miss the fun, the
romance, the joy...as two special couples find
love just outside the delivery room door.

Watch for:
SURPRISE! SURPRISE!
by Tina Leonard
On sale June 2000.

I DO! I DO!
by Jacqueline Diamond
On sale July 2000.

And there will be many more Maitland Maternity
stories when a special twelve-book continuity series
launches in August 2000.

Don't miss any of these stories by wonderful
authors such as Marie Ferrarella, Jule McBride,
Muriel Jensen and Judy Christenberry.

Available at your favorite retail outlet.

HARLEQUIN®
Makes any time special ™

Visit us at www.eHarlequin.com.

HARLEQUIN®
SUPERROMANCE®

*Pregnant and alone—
these stories follow women
from the heartache of
betrayal to finding true love
and starting a family.*

THE FOURTH CHILD by **C.J. Carmichael.**
When Claire's marriage is in trouble, she tries to
save it—although she's not sure she can forgive her
husband's betrayal.
On sale May 2000.

AND BABY MAKES SIX by **Linda Markowiak.**
Jenny suddenly finds herself jobless and pregnant by
a man who doesn't want their child.
On sale June 2000.

MOM'S THE WORD by **Roz Denny Fox.**
After her feckless husband steals her inheritance and
leaves town with another woman, Hayley discovers she's
pregnant.
On sale July 2000.

Available wherever Harlequin books are sold.

HARLEQUIN®
Makes any time special ™